PRAISE FOR ONE NIGHT ONLY

'Kept me up all night'
R. E. Devon

'Filled with unrelenting tension that makes you want
to check your windows and doors are locked before
you dare to sleep'
Reviewers Board

'The true definition of a page turner. This had me
racing through the pages, unable to turn the lights
off once I'd put it down'
Dark Path Reviews

'A complex tale of unrequited love and the dangers
of obsession. This is a modern day Romeo and
Juliette, with all the ingredients of a dark fairytale'
Thrill Seekers

PRAISE FOR LOUISE MULLINS

'Layered with twists and turns that keep you
guessing until the very end'
Jump

'A tense full throttle ride, with more twists and turns
than a roller-coaster'
Thrill seekers

'Gets under your skin and doesn't let go even after
you've turned the final page'
Jump

'This will make you want to stay up late into the
night. Only when you put it down you won't be able
to sleep'
Karen Rogers

'A talented author who clearly understands the
psychology of her characters'
Dark Path Reviews

'Stayed with me long after I finished reading it'
Amazon #1 Reviewer

ONE NIGHT ONLY

LOUISE MULLINS

Published in Great Britain in 2016 by Dark Path Ltd, an imprint of Dockside publishing.

This paperback edition published in 2016.

Dark Path Ltd, Bristol, UK.

ISBN-13: 978-1523966455
ISBN-10: 1523966459

Printed and bound by CreateSpace
www.createspace.com

In the Bristol Crown Court

Case number: 1024065

Party: Claire Donoghue   Claimant

WITNESS STATEMENT

1. I, Claire Donoghue of 112 Sycamore Drive, Filton, Bristol, am the claimant in this case. The facts in this statement come from my personal knowledge [or as the case may be].

2. I understand that I am to give evidence by live link under the S51 Criminal Justice Act 2003 due to the severity of the charges I bring against the defendant to which I have suffered.

3. On the 11th November 2014 I was meeting Mr Ewan Carter for sex at his home address in Redland Park. Though I understand that it is an illegal offence I have chosen to remain honest and frank over my intentions during my visit to his house for the resolution of this case.

When I got to his house in Redland we spoke briefly whilst I put my coat on the hook, and then I followed him through the hall and into the large living room where there were hundreds of books. He left me to peruse them whilst he continued with the preparation for dinner.

When he returned to the room I drank one small glass of wine whilst he spoke about his mother, his job as a builder, and his intentions of one day getting married and having a family.

I knew some of this through the many telephone conversations we exchanged. We had spoken several times on the phone before agreeing to meet and I enjoyed his company.

After a short conversation he began to display some strange behaviour. He appeared agitated and distressed by something. When I asked him what was the matter he stood up from his seat and rushed towards the kitchen. I assumed he'd left something in the oven for too long or had forgotten something but then I heard voices.

I was slightly nervous when I heard a woman's voice and so I went out into the kitchen to see what was going on. That's when I saw her. Elise Fitzgerald. She'd been reported missing two months before.

I thought that he was lying when he told me that she wanted money from him to make a fresh start. I was angry and confused so I waited for her to leave before asking Ewan what was going on. He then kept asking me if I'd like a tour of the house. I wondered if he was mentally unstable so declined his offer to tour the house and told him that I wanted to leave . . .

BEFORE

HIM

I knew she was considering her next move as thoughtfully as anyone would who'd been held in a basement for fourteen days. Surviving on cheese sandwiches and diet coke. Unable to sleep. Unable to think of anything else other than how to escape from the internal walls that confined her. She was hungry and tired. And all the better for me, she was willing. A willing participant.

'What do you want me to do?' she says, in her cryptic way.

Her eyes glaze over as though just a fortnight in captivity had ripped away several tiny pieces of her outer confidence.

'I want you to want to be here. Nobody else matters. Just tell me that you won't do that again. Tell me you'll behave.'

'You're fucking crazy. You need to be locked up,' she says.

The irony is that this is exactly what I'm trying to explain to her. Some people need locking up for their own good. To stop them from destroying their own and others lives. But I doubt she sees that this way includes her own shelter.

'It was you that forced me into this. I didn't plan on leaving you alone all day. You brought this on yourself. If you'd have agreed I wouldn't have had to resort to this,' I say, as I reach down and tug on the handcuffs supporting her ankles to the bed.

I watch as she shudders from the grazes on her broken skin. I've left imprints on her that will take weeks to fade.

'If you let me go I won't hurt you. I promise. I'll just leave. You'll never have to see me again. I just don't want to be tied to this fucking bed any longer,' she says, tugging once more on the handcuffs that hold her wrists.

That's exactly what I expected her to say. Doesn't she remember why she's here?

The sound of the metal scraping against the wrought iron bedstead sends a shiver down my spine. Though I don't react I can see in her eyes how much she enjoys fighting against everything I say.

I ignore her last comment, hoping not to break into another argument over whether I was right or wrong to tie her to the bed.

'I did this for you. Can't you see that?'

She turns her head, twisting away from me to avoid my heavy stare.

I know she dislikes looking into my eyes.

It must be something to do with that friend of hers. The one with the auburn hair and the fake smile. I think she was attracted to him once. Before he left her, taking with him any ounce of self-respect or esteem she once owned. Just as everyone else seems to have done, considering nobody is looking for her.

All she has is me now.

'I can't let you do that.'

'Do what?' she says as though she has already

forgotten what it was she'd said only a few moments ago.

'I can't let you go. You know that. I'm going to see this out whatever you say. It will be easier on you if you try to remain calm. Accept that this is how it's going to be if you continue to attack me.

'How the fuck am I going to explain this to everyone? My family. I've lost everything because of you. My job. My flat . . .'

Her words become incomprehensible as she lowers her head, staring vacantly at the floor to the side of the bed where the key to all four sets of handcuffs rests above the box where I forced her to discard her clothes.

'Everything is gone,' she says, through her tears.

It's true. That fat, irritating landlord needed no convincing to dump her stuff in storage and charge her for it even though she's been missing for two weeks, and she was only a week behind on the rent. How did he expect she'd be able to pay for that on top of the £240 rent she owed?

It isn't worth that much money anyway. I've seen her flat. It looks as though a group of students had a party in it and gave up trying to fix the mess. Only it's been like that for months. Since her boyfriend left her.

Joe.

How original a name it is.

I bend down and take the key from where it's been lying all this time. Deliberately kept where she can see it if she turns her head, but far away enough that she knows even a miracle wouldn't enable her to grab them and undo the handcuffs; the ties that bind her to me.

I snatch the keys up in my hand and stand a few moments waiting for her to continue.

'Just let me go,' she says.

Her eyes fill once more with ready to shed tears.

I haven't yet broken her spirit enough for her to see

that if she'd just do as she's told she could have some of the freedom back. The freedom I can see that she desperately craves, now that it's been taken away from her.

'I won't do that. Not until you promise to behave.'

'I will,' she says, locking eyes with me for perhaps the first time since she came here.

'I'll be good. I promise,' she says, hopeful that this will placate me.

'Very well. When you start eating the meals I provide for you, I'll consider giving you some more leeway.'

'What the fuck is that supposed to mean?' she says, darting an evil look my way.

'When you prove to me that you can be trusted not to attack me, I'll take the handcuffs away. So you can have more room to move around.'

I turn to leave, but before I step another foot forward spittle lands on my left shoulder.

'Are we going to have a repeat performance of yesterday?'

She visibly shudders from this comment. Knowing only too well what I can do. She both acknowledges the power I have over her in yet can't seem to stop herself from pushing the boundaries I've placed between us; she's both afraid and exhilarated in this position.

Is this what she wanted all along? Somebody to love her. Care for her. Be kind enough to offer her another way to live. A second chance? Yet equally, somebody not to be messed with?

'I won't tolerate that. There's no need for you to treat me like some evil freak who snatched you away from your wonderful life.'

'Can't you see that's exactly what you are and what you have done?' she says, aghast.

Doesn't she see how far from a wonderful life she had been living until now?

'Is that how you see this? Do you truly believe your own words?'

'I don't know what to believe any more. I don't know who you are or what you want. I don't even think I know who I am any more. Just tell me what it is you want that I'm so far not giving you? We can work this out. There's no need for this,' she says, wrestling with the cuff on her right arm. The one she professed had been hurting and swollen this morning when I came to loosen them.

She forces a smile and twists her head to better inspect me. I wonder what she sees when she looks me over like that.

Her teeth are losing their white glow. The whitening toothpaste she used really must work. There is a definite tenderness to her lips now. I can see that the inside cut has caused the upper half of her lips on one side to extend slightly above the lower half. She shouldn't have bitten me. There's no telling what bacteria she's carrying. That's why I did it. I had too. Can't she see that? I can see as she swallows and winces at the memory of Corsodyl forced down her throat. The taste still there, hours later that she probably doesn't.

'Please, don't leave me here like this,' she says.

A plea is one thing, begging quite another.

'I'll see you later.'

I turn back to the closed door of the basement.

I can hear her behind me shuffling about, trying to get comfortable. The sound of the water repellant sheets which cover the mattress beneath her crinkle, leaving me with no doubt over what it is she's trying to do.

I won't turn and look. I'm actually amazed though at how easily she is able to piss herself though perhaps it isn't that at all. She's grown used to waking up in sodden sheets hasn't she. That's why I removed her urine soaked clothes. The ones that are still strewn inside the metal box, probably moulding away as each day passes. I wasn't about to throw them into the bin outside in case the police began to search them. I was also kind enough to allow her the privacy to pee whenever she wished, washing her afterwards, and not daring to touch her skin with my bare fingertips. Though I wanted to, I wouldn't. This has nothing to do with sex. If it had, she wouldn't be so mouthy after I'd laid claim to her. I think she knows that. I think she knows that if I wanted her I could have her, at any time.

I'm not sure at this stage what it is that causes me to slip. I've walked the floor of this basement several times today and not once have I come across a leaking water pipe or a bottle of spilt coke.

When I fall it's awkward. My right foot goes out at an angle and my left finds itself tucked behind me. I know it's broken. I know I won't be able to move. At least not until the pain in the back of my head dulls a little and my sight clears enough. Until then I'm forced to lie here, on the cold concrete floor with the faint sounds of the frantic woman who has no intention of being quiet that I am forced from unconsciousness. But it doesn't come. I'm floating through space. Blackness enfolds me. Darkness like nothing I've ever felt or seen before pins me to the ground, and I wonder for an instant if this is how she feels while she's tied to that bed.

HER

I open the letter knowing only too well what it's going to say. Another bill. Another debt. Another lost chance to put right the money problems I've been trying to pretend don't exist. The truth is, I'm broke. Skint. Even bankruptcy won't save me now.

Ollie sits with his back to me at the dining table. I lean over his shoulder and reach for a slice of toast, cramming it into my mouth whilst studying the letter-the final demand before the balance on my credit card joins the others. 'In the red' they say when you're in debt, only the amount of debt I'm in can't possibly be covered by more loans or credit- I've tried that before. It's what got me into this mess in the first place. It's going to take a lot more than another handout to sort this kind of mess out. It looks more and more likely as each day passes that I'll have to take the last of my wages, buy a camper van and give the flat up.

Since me and Zack separated I haven't been able to afford the essentials never mind the credit cards, catalogues, loans, home insurance or utility bills. I can't even afford school clothes for Ollie. Since he went back after the summer holidays, he's been wearing trousers an inch too short and the same polo shirt with the faded collar that he sported the previous term. When Zack picked him up the other day he noticed, and still he didn't offer to contribute to the new uniform he so obviously needs.

Perhaps there is one option.

I graze the side of the newspaper lying on the dining table in front of Ollie. The paperboy delivers one to us every other morning though I've assured him we don't buy the paper. The page contains listings of escort agencies, and there's an advert for companions to accompany elite gentlemen to dinner parties, conferences, and the theatre. Though I'm sure these men are secretly looking for a daytime wife the adverts are worded in such a way as to give the effect that this career is above the phone sex chatline adverts, listed alongside them.

Escorting is the oldest profession. The only thing keeping me at arm's length from it is the little boy sitting in front of me, raising his lunch box, quizzing me as to why we haven't left for the school run yet.

'It's 8:30 mum,' he says, shaking his foot up and down in anxious joy.

'Let's go.'

I grab the car keys from the worktop and consider once more asking my dad to put the car in his name for a few months, just until things settle, just to be sure that when the bailiffs start knocking, they can't take my only source of income away.

I'm a delivery driver. A courier. A distributor. Whatever you want to call it, I drive around all day and drop parcels off to people who *can* afford to purchase things. Even things they didn't know they wanted or needed until they found the catalogue I'd slipped through the door.

I grab Ollie's coat from the hook, wrapping my own around my waist, and close the front door behind us.

The day is mild. The sun peaks beyond the trees and promises nothing.

Ollie slides into his seat and fixes the seatbelt himself as soon as I open the door. I check my watch, run around to the other side of the car, slamming the door shut behind me before revving the engine. My foot slams down with such force on the accelerator that the almost bare tyres skid and mud splatters upwards, landing on the freshly polished black Jeep that has just parked behind me. I know who it is before I turn the corner and catch sight of the tow truck parked around the bend in the road.

We reach the school in less than three minutes. I kiss goodbye to Ollie, wave him off and drive quickly away, peering into my rear-view mirror every so often, hopeful that they haven't yet decided to come searching for me. I know how they operate. If they see a car they want it for any money owed. Even something as worthless and old as this.

I push my foot down hard and only slow as I near the corner of Southmead Road, where the police station sits on the corner, beside the chemist. When I see a car that appears suspiciously like the kind CID would be using I slow down.

Only when I reach Shirehampton, creeping down the road past the shops in the twenty miles an hour speed limit zone, do I feel my shoulders relax and my foot ease its pressure on the pedal.

I didn't used to speed. I didn't used to be so afraid of debt collectors arriving at my door late at night. I didn't used to worry over answering the phone, and now it seems all I'm capable of is distinguishing between the people who I must speak to now, and those who can wait another week, or if possible, a month. When I get paid I don't think of what we can do this weekend now that the money's in the bank. I think *will I have any money left?*

I turn the sharp left down a narrow road which leads into a small housing estate. There's a hairdresser, and a primary school opposite. I follow the road along until it curves down towards the Portway. The lights change instantly for once and I cross the *A* road, continue over the humpback bridge where below the trains pass infrequently, and I stop the car beside the corner shop.

As soon as I'm out of the car I step inside the shop, grabbing a chilled pasty and a bottle of water, stepping back outside with just enough change left for dinner tonight. When I leave I walk back, away from the car, and in the direction of the always open gate which is the route I take when Ollie is with me. We've had many picnics here.

My footing is unsteady. I'm wearing the last remaining pair of shoes I own. Three inched high heeled black denim boots which desperately require new soles. I walk slightly off-balance, right leaning on both legs, having worn the heel down that way somehow.

I leave the grass as soon as the thin path appears, following it right, towards the river. Ahead of me, the grey sky mixes with the factory fumes from Avonmouth Docks. The beginnings of the Port sit astride the park and the tiny lighthouse, no bigger than the height of a van sits between overgrown shrubs and nettles, and beyond where I stand, the water ripples and sways in the light breeze.

It's no longer summer, but not yet cold enough for me to equate this with autumn. October is yet to arrive, and still, I haven't managed to fulfil my promise to be debt-free by winter, and to be able to afford Christmas at home this year, with my son.

I cannot bear to remember last year. The lack of presents sitting below a deformed tree that had been left out to rot for weeks, given away in the end because the man selling it was sure it would never leave the car wash forecourt on Gloucester Road if I didn't take it.

'Be kind to it,' he'd said. 'It's his first and only celebration.'

It had been our last too.

There was no birthday card for Ollie this year. Not from me. Only two decorated the sparsely furnished mantelpiece, over the unused electric fire, to save on heating. One from his dad, and another from my parents. The nan and grandad who dote on him. Who buy him everything his own mum should be able to provide.

I draw a breath of the cool morning air and stand watching a lone duck bobbing along the surface of the overstretched green muddy water. He looks hopeless and lost, much like I'm feeling myself in this moment, just until I look up and am met with the most wonderful sight.

A large willow tree brushes its leaves together in the wind like fingers gently tickling the underside of its own arm. Outstretched and free, caressing the hazy sky. The tree is lit from above by a golden halo, the sunlight bursts through the small lime green leaves and dazzles my eyes intermittently. Reminding me that there is a purpose - whatever it is - for this life. The changing seasons. Rebirth and growth. There has to be more than work and worry.

I follow the path down through overgrown bushes and along the fenced off area, where before me lie two paths. Two choices. More than I'm used to of late. I decide to follow the river towards the port on the left, knowing dog walkers and muddied grass verges lie along the right path. I decide against slow walking. Rushing along seems to calm me and focuses my thoughts as I hurry down towards the red bricked derelict factory, where the greenery gives way to a wide open square. If I remain on the road I'll find myself in the children's playground opposite the recovery centre for drug addicts. If I turn left I'll enter the council housing estate. Turn right and I'll soon end up beside the old Brunel college buildings in Lawrence Weston (once deemed an unsightly place to live, but now building its own signature in the city). I cross the square and continue down towards the port. Where thick smoke climbs the skies leaving a traced outline like a staircase in the clouds. The cold air from the murky silt water sweeps the hair from my face. The smell filling my nostrils, making me queasy.

I look across the River Severn and see the faint outline of Wales. The buildings look as though the diesel fumes from cargo ships docking between ports has created a helter skelter of smoke around them. The buildings are all but disappearing behind it, like ghosts.

I step back on the path to allow a lone man wearing a khaki trench-coat to pass. He doesn't look up, much preferring to keep his eyes on the ground. Before I turn around to continue on towards the main road where the motorway climbs ahead of me, leading in two directions: Wales or London, I see the man bend down and collect something from the ground. When I examine him closely he jolts as though pushed by an unseen force, gives a surprised look my way, and drops the item to the floor. Falling to his knees he scrabbles along the path until he finds the item and stuffs it down into one of his large pockets. It's only then that I notice the few spotted cigarette butts dropped to the ground around his feet.

Do people really do that?

I force a smile out to him. He must be financially worse off than I am. I don't pursue a conversation. Instead I continue to walk the way I intended, along the port, and back towards the square. Circling myself until I find that I'm standing on the pavement in front of the park. I take a seat at the bench facing the road, where the buses turn around to head back into the centre of Bristol, and unwrap the pasty. Swigging back water with every bite.

I could have eaten lunch at home. But then, I could have been there to receive the bailiffs. I could have stood there and watched as they took my furniture away. I could have seen every last piece of me leaving through the front door. Just as *he* did.

When Zack and I were still living together we earned enough that we didn't need to worry over affording a luxury Christmas tree, or a day trip to the beach every summer weekend. That's when it started.

My first credit card, became four, 'just for emergencies'- though I can't fathom now what kind of emergency would require payment from four separate cards. A broken washing machine does not cost four thousand pounds either.

These are but details. The fact is he left me no option but to disregard anything I'd been taught by my parents: not to rely on the state to support myself, not to use doorstep loans, to borrow from family instead of friends. I used them all, and still found myself unable to pay any of them back.

I've learnt my lesson. Listen to others who've been there. They have the experience to justify their advice- I don't. Well, I do now.

I walk past the recovery centre and away from the square, glancing up at the stone buildings on which the figures of saints and famous nineteenth century men stand looming above me on shop fronts and the old church building, now renovated into a tea room.

I imagine the steel workers being told they were being made redundant back in the eighties- how did they cope with the sudden loss of a career? What happened to them? I wonder too if they retrained or joined the fishing vessels until they were once again forced away from a career in the nineties.

I look around and notice how empty the area is. Envisioning the once densely packed space filled with men on their way to work, at varying shifts, women taking their children to the park after shopping for tonight's meal. I'm now but one of three people visible in the area, and by the look of it- the only one sober enough to remember where to go from here.

I leave the village shops behind me, following the main road back down towards the post office. I grab some wholegrain pasta, sundried tomato bolognese sauce, and a reduced packet of grated cheese in the Co-Op before heading back down the winding road towards the humpback bridge.

When I get to the car it's clamped. A notice has been stuck to the windscreen declaring that I'm parked on double yellow lines. When I look down to the ground I notice the faded outline of one of them, just three foot long on the dusty grey road.

I kick the car fiercely, instantly regretting it when a burst of pain shudders up from my toe. I look down at my boot and see the scratched rubber front has been stripped away from the black denim fabric.

I could force the chains free with the metal cutter I've still got beneath the spare tyre in the boot, but being arrested for driving illegally today would just top everything off in a way I don't wish to deal with right now, so instead, I head back up towards where the old Woolworths used to be and wait for a bus.

I'm in Broadmead by 11:20am and follow the underpass down through the Bear Pit over to Stokes Croft to meet the number 75 bus back up the Gloucester Road into Filton.

The letterbox is flooded with post when I get back, but no sign of a notice from my visitors this morning.

They got what they wanted. I'm carless, and soon to be jobless. I dump the pile of unopened letters and home delivery service leaflets on top of yesterday's, beside the microwave and sit in the chair. Not daring to weep in case I can't stop. It wouldn't do to collect Ollie from school red-eyed and washed out. No. I have to consider this the worst day so far this week and build on from here. The only way is up, as they say. Only 'up' doesn't look very easy to get to right now.

The flat is ours, for at least another month. The rent is paid and the council tax so we're not going to lose our home- yet.

The carrier bag containing dinner, our only source of food this evening, sits alone on the worktop. The cupboards above it, bare, except for a small jar of unopened peanut butter, and two bananas.

I consider calling Zack to ask him to take Ollie tonight just so I don't have to grapple with the idea of sending him to school tomorrow morning with the only source of conflict spread inside his sandwich. Anything containing nuts in a lunch box is frowned upon and results in an article inside the school newsletter, reminding parents that at least one child may have a severe nut allergy because they were never offered any before the age of four. I've read the research. I hate being seen as the one and only parent who refuses to abide by their strict code of lunch box criteria. A sandwich, yoghurt, at least one piece of fruit, and an oat bar. That just isn't feasible right now.

Zack wouldn't take him anyway. It's not his day. His days of contact are Saturdays, justified entirely on the fact that his partner wouldn't be able to cope with a weekday sleepover due to her ever so busy schedule. Being a beauty therapist requires a lot of work apparently.

I hold my face in my hands, praying for a miracle,

knowing that I must return to my original plan, but not really wanting to go down that road. You never know where it might end.

It was last Thursday as I skimmed the pages of a magazine, bored, with nothing left to read on the bookcase, having been unable to buy any new novels from Tesco for months, that I found the star signs on the final page.

You are at a crossroads. Two directions await you. Neither are easy. Follow through on your decision and see your finances sky-rocket. Don't and you may find yourself remaining where you are before Neptune releases its powerful energy in November. Something that will cause eruptions elsewhere in your life.

Opposite the star signs there were the usual listings for psychic readings and tarot card lines. Above them, to the left were the lads ads. *Chat and date; Granny wants to talk dirty; Young, hot blonde likes it in the morning.* It was then I realised why these adverts were placed in newspapers, and TV magazines, as well as Retro Ford and Nuts. It was as much for women in my position as it was for the men seeking a dirty conversation in their lunch break. Otherwise, why place the helpline number beneath the date line?

Before giving myself the time to think on it any longer I pick the phone up from its sleeve and dial. A woman answers after three rings offering me her most charmingly feminine voice.

'Daisy here, from *Cheap Chat*, how can I help you?' she says.

'Hello Daisy, I'm not sure if I should have called this number but I was wondering if you were looking for anyone at the moment, to take calls?'

'We're always looking love. Have you ever done this

kind of work before?' she says.

'No. But I'm looking for something new.'

'Give me your name and number, and I'll set you up with a telephone interview,' she says.

'Claire Donoghue, 112 Sycamore Drive, Filton, Bristol.'

'How does 10:00 tomorrow morning suit you?' she says.

'Fine. Do I need anything?'

'Just yourself love, and a quiet house if that's possible,' she says.

'Of course. Are there any upfront costs, because . . .'

'No love. You work from home, from your own landline, when you want. No need for anything but an open mind and good telephone manners. Karen Jones will call you tomorrow. After a brief informal interview, she'll ask you to take a call to practice. She'll be listening in so make sure you appear relaxed and non-judgmental. It's rare we don't employ a girl with a kind voice like yours. You'll do well on the young line,' she says.

'Young line?'

'Age is nothing but a number in this business love,' she says.

I'm a little pleased to think that somebody who's never met me considers me young.

'How old are you love, if you don't mind me asking?' she says.

'Thirty-two.'

'Mature line is not as busy at the moment. You could pass for nineteen,' she says.

I think she may be my new best friend.

'Do I have to work set hours?'

I ask this only because some of the lines I researched online ask you to work shifts.

'No love. Work as you please. Our busiest times of day are 9:00am-1:00pm and 8:00pm-12:00am. As long as you log on for at least sixteen hours a week you can do as you please,' she says.

All this knowledge is new to me. Though I read up on the subject that Thursday from the laptop before the broadband signal died. I can't afford to pay the Sky bill either. We've only got the landline for an extra fortnight because I lied. I told the call centre woman that my son was disabled and required urgent medical attention from a specialist who wouldn't take kindly to us making another phone call to 999.

I've educated myself on dirty talk, BDSM, taboo subjects, and the legal requirements of a sex chatline worker. All in all, I think I've got a good basis to begin this new career- which has become a necessary avenue of work much sooner than I'd anticipated.

'Goodbye Miss Donoghue,' she says, ending the call on a high. Much unlike my own emotions which seem to be swarming between nervousness and bewilderment. Terror and relief.

I've read that logging on to the line for six hours a day (whilst Ollie is at school) will enable me to take approximately forty calls. If I can keep them all on the line as long as possible I could earn four hours work, at 15p a minute. I could be earning £36 a day. That will cover the loss of earnings from my other work. £180 a week. I'm just not sure how to explain such earnings to the tax man. Do I term my employment call centre work from home or self-employed sex chatline worker? Either way, I still don't know whether I've got the job yet, though as far as I can tell it's pretty much a given that I have. My only qualm is that it will take precious hours away from my current work. And without a working car, the chatline would be a good extra earner but I'm not sure I want to do it full-time.

I fill the kettle and wait for it to boil, surveying the penalty notice that was stuck to my car. They want £220 pounds within seven days to unclamp it. Or I could let it go, put up without it for a couple of weeks and save up for a cheap runaround. Ensuring that it's not registered in my own name or to this address. Though the insurance would have to be wouldn't it?

When I look up I notice the clock has stopped. I twist my watch around and see that it's already 3:05pm. I haven't had time to make a cup of tea and now I'm going to be late collecting Ollie- again.

When I get there, having been forced to jog the ten minutes it takes from our house to the school which sits in the centre of the 1930's houses, I'm met with a sour-faced Mrs Pritchard waiting eagerly at the gates for me to arrive.

I knew before she spoke that Ollie had got himself in some kind of trouble. Only this time, I wasn't expecting it to have been quite so awful.

'He's been stealing again Miss Donoghue,' she says, taking the seat in front of me, offering me with her hand the plastic chair used for primary school aged children in the classrooms.

I'm sure she believes everybody to be below her in worth as well as IQ.

'Ollie has stolen a pencil case from one of the other boys in his class,' she says.

I force myself not to laugh out loud.

'Well, It's not as though it's . . .'

'I doubt it's worth anything Miss Donoghue. The fact is we can't accept such behaviour in this school. Ollie is already on his final warning for what happened last week. We take theft very seriously.'

'What happened last week?'

'You mean you don't know?' she says.

I shake my head.

'Ollie was caught stealing from the school nurses cabinet. She usually locks it but he caught her somewhat off-guard that morning.'

'Why was he with the nurse? Was he ill?'

'Headaches, tummy sickness. The usual Miss Donoghue.'

'The usual?'

'His father-'

'Zack knows about this?'

'Oh, I'm sorry. I assumed you'd discussed this with him,' she says.

'You shouldn't assume anything. I'm his mother. I have sole custody of Ollie. This is not like him.'

'No, Miss Donoghue. It isn't. Tell me, how is everything at home?' she says, crossing her legs offering a classy show of her slightly tanned skin beneath the smock style skirt that teachers must buy in specialist shops.

'What did he take?'

'Pardon?' she says.

'You said he stole something last week. What was it?'

'Money,' she says. 'About forty pounds.'

The air is instantly sucked from my lungs, and I find it difficult to catch my breath back. I can feel my heart pounding against my ribs. My chest tightening; constricting.

'Why is it kept in the nurse's room?'

'That's really not our concern here. The point I am trying to make is that-'

'Excuse me.'

My skin is burning with both embarrassment over Ollie's actions and fury over Mrs Pritchard's formal address towards me and her obvious disregard for the safety of belongings within the school premises.

'I really feel Miss Donoghue that-'

'If the money wasn't there do you really think he'd have taken it. It was an opportune moment. A moment of madness. It won't happen again. I can assure you that my

29

son is not a thief and I'll be having words with him as soon as I get him home. You mark my words. But in future I'd like to be notified of anything that occurs within the school, however trivial. Is that okay with you?'

'Yes, of course, Miss Donoghue. But there is the small problem of the police.'

'The police?'

'Jacob Darling's mother is furious about the pencil case. It's the second time something as expensive has been taken this way, and well, she-'

Darling. I should have known.

'She called the police about a stolen pencil case?'

'That isn't all, Miss Donoghue,' she says.

I'm sure she enjoys addressing me by my title. 'Miss' is far less superior than 'Mrs'. It suggests that you are either on the shelf or no longer wanted.

I shake her away from me and cross the narrow, dimly lit hall, shoving open the door to her oak panelled office, entering when I see that Ollie is sitting slumped over on the chair in the far corner, opposite a uniformed officer and a worried looking woman holding a child. I don't ask her name. There's no need.

I hold out my hand for Ollie to take and as we near the door, passing her, her overgrown son flexed on her lap, I shake my head whilst forcing myself to hold her gaze.

'There was no need to call the police Mrs Darling. There was really no need.'

The officer moves aside to let me pass without so much as a second glance, knowing only too well how harmful her actions were on the under-resourced staff of the local constabulary. He too looks as though he considers this as much of a wasted journey as I do. I only hope that she doesn't make him take a statement from her. Saying that, Ollie caused her sensitive child such distress he is unable to return to school for several days as he has nothing at all to write with though I'm sure she didn't call them for the pencil case, as it appears to have been returned. Mrs Darling held it in one hand as she cradled her immature son with the other.

No. It wasn't the theft she contacted the police over. It was the bruised eye Jacob was wearing, as I caught a glimpse of him while I tore away with my own son, who refused to look up from the ground as we walked through the open office door.

Mrs Pritchard was about to say something as we brushed shoulders in the corridor which lead to the now deserted playground, where only moments ago the clique of mums from the vegetarian bistro book group, WI grandmothers taking their turn to collect the children of extremely busy parents, and the occasional young mum who hadn't yet found the perfect job usually permeate.

As we came around the corner of the gates that the dutiful caretaker has left open for two more minutes, allowing us out of the building, I turn to Ollie, noticing he's still sporting the sorrowful look of the ashamed. He feels my glare on the back of his head, reaches back and scratches the nape of his neck peering up at me standing behind him when this doesn't suffice to rid the tingling feeling of being watched from his skin.

I stop walking. He's holding my hand so has no option but to fall in line with me.

'Ollie, why did you hit Jacob?'

The flash of a memory crosses his face. An instant of recognition over the thoughtless act, in yet I detect the slightest hint of a smile. Curved for just a few moments on one side of his lips.

'He hit me first,' he says, offering me his most honest gaze.

I must admit, he does appear to be telling the truth. I want to be tactful yet not accusatory.

'Why did you hit him back then?'

'Because he said something to me,' he says, swiping a small fly from the air as he looks up to me for confirmation that it was the right thing to do.

I can't bring myself to imagine Ollie would hurt anyone without just cause.

'What did he say?'

'I can't tell you, mum,' he says, sounding slightly exasperated by the sheer effort it's taken him to confess what he has done so far.

'You can tell me anything.'

He considers this for one moment - his six-year-old self appears to be grappling with difficulty to find the right words -, and then turns away to impart this final piece of information. His voice is but a murmur, but I get the gist of it.

'He said what?'

'Jacob said that you and his dad were having an affair. I don't know what kind of fair it is, but I'd like to go someday,' he says.

HIM

Amy's death was unfortunate. She was weak; too ill to cope with the possibility of living. Drugs stole her life. I merely tried to intervene to save it. But you can't save everyone. That's the first lesson I learnt.

The second lesson I learnt was not to take it for granted that I hadn't been caught. There is always a yet or maybe. Perhaps next time I will be, but I'll think about this later. There will be plenty of time to think in that cell. Right now though I have to move quickly.

There isn't time to procrastinate. Everything must be approached with caution. I know that. But I must think fast. I must do this right. I must consider every possible thought or action of my next companion. She too is slight-framed and giving off the tell-tale scent of heroin. A bitter-sweet combination of sugared doughnuts and vinegar.

She has deep lacerations across the insides of her arms. I suspect that this is merely a cry for help rather than a direct plot to end her life. For she's fighting me with every breath she is able to summon.

She has light, ash blonde hair and wide terrified eyes.

Her eyes are murky blue. A similar hue to her complexion.

Her skin is slick with sweat. There are red patches behind her ears where she's scratched so hard that she's broken the skin; still unhealed, kept so by itching away the crawling sensation of withdrawal. I can see her veins below the skin, above her collar bone. I doubt she weighs more than seven stone.

Her chest rises and falls in quick succession, with fear or anger I cannot tell. Only now as I approach her to apply a single cuff to her bony wrist she flinches, draws away from me, and howls like an injured animal. I move forwards, catching her hand in mine.

'Get off me. Let me go,' she says.

Her lips are chapped. Dry skin causes them to crack as she speaks.

'You know I can't do that.'

'Why? What are you going to do to me?' she says.

'Nothing. I'm not going to do anything to you.'

'You're sick. You're a sick freak. You lure me here with false promises and then what?' she says, looking down at the cuff still in my hand. 'You're going to tie me up?'

'It's the only way I can be sure you won't leave.'

She shoves me in the chest, expecting me to fall backwards or become winded. Instead, I grasp hold of her other arm, the one with the scars, and it's easy then. I cuff the wrist of her obviously weak hand to the bedpost and make my way over and go up the basement steps and into the kitchen. A sandwich will do for now-something bland and easy to digest with water.

I've got to work my way around the dozen or so bottles of water to find the cheese and bread. I keep the ready sliced loaves here to stop them from going stale.

When I return to the basement she's trying desperately to haul her arm free of the handcuff.

Bruising her wrist in the process. It doesn't take long for her skin to develop the appearance of self-made marks. Something I'd rather avoid if she's going to be difficult to subdue.

I can tell that it's not going to be long before the steady signs of crack withdrawal shows its full, and complete ugliness.

'If you're going to rape me just get on with it. I'd far rather die, but if you're going to keep me here like some kind of sex slave I'd rather you get the nasty shit over and done with so I can think straight,' she says, resigned to her fate all of a sudden.

Or is this a ploy for me to untie her? Will she jab her shoe into my groin and run the moment I release her? I can't take the chance.

'That's not what you're here for. If I wanted to have sex with you I'd only need to pay you enough to score, wouldn't I?'

She refuses to answer me, taking on a solemn vow not to speak to me any longer. I'm sure she understands that human contact involving communication is an important facet to the kidnapper/victim relationship. I can tell she's been in this position before.

'I want to help you, but in order for me to do that, you must begin to help yourself. You must want to change. Otherwise, this is going to take far longer than I've made the provisions for.'

She begins to groan again. Though it's less as an attempt to cry for help, and more of a plea to her own body for failing her.

'Are you in pain?'

'What do you care?' she says, darting me that evil glare I've learnt comes with all female addicts.

'I do.'

I don't offer her an explanation. It's not as if I've got the time to make polite conversation.

'I've got to go out for a bit. I'll have to give you this.'

I hold up the scarf I've grown used to using as a gag.

'You're not leaving me here,' she says.

'I have things to do.'

'You're not putting that on me,' she says.

'I'm sorry. But I can't trust you not to make too much noise while I'm gone.'

'You're mad. You're fucking crazy,' she says, tugging on the handcuff; her voice increasing in decibels as I inch my way towards the door.

'I'm sorry.'

I take the other cuff from my pocket and snap it in place over her other wrist.

'How am I meant to use the toilet?' she says.

'There's a bucket behind you.'

'I guess I'm supposed to have to figure out how to pull my knickers down whilst tied to this fucking bed, am I?' she says.

I don't retaliate. She's not in the right frame of mind. She wouldn't understand even if I tried to explain it to her. I lunge forwards before tying the scarf across her mouth. Hoping that by doing so quickly she won't have time to react. Once it's fastened in place I turn to leave.

She kicks out involuntarily, slamming back into the side of the bed. I hear her spine hit the metal, but she doesn't make a sound. She winces from the pain and chews one corner of her lip. I wonder if she does that a lot.

I close the door behind me, listening out for the sounds of jagged breaths as she attempts to tear herself away from the solid metal cuffs securing her to the bed, but it doesn't come.

Outside the air is crisp with the tang of early autumn. A light breeze rustles the leaves on the tree overhead as a lorry bounces up the road towards the common. The day is mild and carries with it the realisation that we're nearing winter as each day arrives. The problem with this is two-fold- the basement isn't warm in winter, in fact, it's overheated in summer and deathly damp and icy as it nears the holiday season.

Last Christmas brought mould and mildew. It took an age to rid the smell after white-washing the walls again and cleansing the floor with bleach. I don't want to have to concern myself with purchasing extra fan heaters. Besides electric heaters are dangerous. If they tip over they can cause a fire. If left in the hands of a pissed off whore who's been incarcerated for several weeks going through the worst symptoms known to any addict, she'll be more than determined to slam it down onto my head.

I prefer to walk. It's quicker by car, but cars are traceable. People aren't so unfortunate. They can alter their appearance. Change their pace, clothing, and hairstyle to suit their needs. People are also fallible. Especially those who are paid to stare at screens all day in those large CCTV operation rooms.

I know where they are too. Since I had that contract to plaster and paint the walls I helped to rebuild beside the old ITV television studios off Park Street, I've known where they are, and I've even become familiar with one of the intelligence operators. Susanne her name is. Though I doubt very much she remembers mine.

I continue down the path which leads to the bottom row of houses at the lower end of Redland Green. The traffic is heavily laden since the Residence Parking Zones were granted council permission. I don't think anyone has the ability to park outside of their own homes now, whereas before, it at least, was a probability. A small one at that, but still possible.

Colston Construction is a facilities management and buildings maintenance service. I joined the firm back in 1990 when it was then known as Regal Property Services. A legal battle ensued over the name, and they became known as Colston Construction after securing a contract on Colston Hall. Whilst I was working there, me and Ricky Jones, managed to meet several famous faces from theatre, and the music hall. The Who, UB40 and several other well-known faces have sold out concert tickets there.

Of course, the revision of the Health and Safety Act was made in the same year, so we were still working to the 1974 Occupational Health and Safety Act then, which meant ladder safety was simply knowing how to use one, and a qualification was based on two years prior experience of building or painting to get onto a site. Work was always available, and the only thing that kept us lads off the job was the recession cutting our bus fare vouchers by 30%. Most of us had to walk. Which is probably where I found my love of being out in the open. Fresh air and sodden shoes means a good day of graft to me.

I turn the corner at the bottom of Park Row and enter the office to collect my rota for the week.

'Ewan,' says Hayley, from behind the desk.

I nod, take the sheet of paper from her outstretched hand and sign the declaration.

Mitchell trumps through the doorway at the mention of my name, hoping to scam a lift from me.

'No such luck mate. I haven't brought the car.'

'Suppose we'll have to walk then will we?' he says, smiling.

Mitchell prefers walking. He gets to pass the University of Bristol on the way down the hill. He likes young, sweet, brunettes. His last girlfriend was young enough to be his granddaughter.

What they see in him I couldn't say. He's not exactly sugar-daddy material. That is, he doesn't earn half as much as us. He works less hours a week than the cleaners. I think he does it less for the money and more to get away from the house he shares with his son Ben. Not that he earns enough money to live. He's more like the rest of us than he'd ever admit, barely surviving on the crusts of wages since the coalition government was used as a ploy to cut every sector of society, except of course those in a position of power. Money breeds greed and hatred. Something England doesn't need right now.

No, it isn't money that attracts them to him. I thought once that it might be a daddy complex. You know, daddy divorced mummy, daddy is an alcoholic, daddy is emotionally distant, and so these college faced girls clasp eyes on an older, rougher face with a beard, and they want some of that. But again, I don't think that's possible either. Perhaps he's good in bed though they wouldn't know that until they'd begun to date him. I very much doubt date rape can last several weeks. Other than these possibilities I haven't a clue as to what would provoke a beautiful woman, twice old enough to be considered his daughter, into sleeping with him. Unless he lies about his age, which again is fairly obvious by looking at him. Perhaps they meet on dating sites. Maybe he claims to be loaded and they're too naive and desperate to believe him.

'Quit daydreaming and hurry up. We've gotta be there by eight o'clock,' he says, slapping his palm down hard on my shoulder.

I can already feel the heat of my skin rising at his aggressive manoeuvre at jolting me back to reality forcing me to take notice of my surroundings. There's no need for such aggression.

I spend the morning talking to a new apprentice named Billy. I doubt that's his real name because he comes from Poland and his surname is rather difficult to pronounce.

We don't worry so much over surnames as long as the job in hand is done well, and we can all leave on time. I don't want a repeat of the last girl, Devon her name, who I was forced to leave tied to the bed for over ten hours. Suffering from the full effects of heroin withdrawal and not having been administered a sedative or anti-convulsant since seven o'clock that morning she'd shit herself. The smell was worse than the mess I'd been forced to clean up and she wasn't too pleased that I hadn't been able to return on my lunch break.

She suffered from Delirium Tremens, and had, it appeared, been not only in excruciating pain for several hours, but had also suffered some kind of seizure, I expect due to the sudden withdrawal of drugs, and not from any form of epilepsy. It was difficult to ease her into a feeling of safety after that. Something I think she felt owed after an abysmal life on the game from the age of fourteen.

At lunch I leave Mitchell and Billy to eat together on one of the stacked piles of ceiling boards, someone has carelessly left to rot from the unsheltered body of the building and head back up to catch the bus, knowing I've only got enough time to let her use the toilet and to offer her a few slices of toast and a bottle of water to go with her Librium. I know it's meant to be used only for alcoholic withdrawal symptoms or extreme anxiety, but I'm not sure that I've got enough Naltrexone left in the cupboard. I'll have to call Piper to order in some more Methylphenidate and Propranolol too. All these things I have to remember, as well as to lock the basement door. Sound carries throughout these houses too well even with well-insulated walls.

I know this now of course, as I tread the steps down into the basement and see that she's exhausted her voice box to the utmost point that she can no longer speak. Instead, she croaks out a faintly annoyed sigh.

The gag has been stretched over her face and is now sitting on top of her head, causing her to look like an

40

eighties aerobics teacher. Her having freed herself from the only thing stopping her from screaming for help, however, is not enough to cause me anything but guilt.

'I'm sorry. I should have locked the door.'

She doesn't realise that I meant knowing you have a chance of freedom you're going to take it. Had I locked the door on the way out she wouldn't have rubbed away the gag so hard that her lips are now cut in several places, bleeding down her chin.

I want to offer her a sincere apology for the force I've had to use. I *am* sorry for her predicament. But, doesn't she know how much worse it is to watch somebody putting themselves through this each day, than actually having to cope with the addiction yourself?

'Does your throat hurt?'

She nods.

I'm not easily angered. I'm more likely to avoid confrontation. Funny now that I've placed myself into the kind of situation which warrants it, at such a scale, and on a daily basis. The things we put ourselves through to help another person. Sick, injured, tortured souls are my speciality now. I've grown used to them. Accustomed to their ways. Much like a prison officer, I've worked out how they tick. Body language says as much about a person as their words.

'It hurts,' she says, her voice breaking.

'Are you sore anywhere else?'

'Yes,' she says, faintly perplexed by my choice of words.

'Would you like something for the pain?'

She nods, backs away into the bed, she's now crouched in front of, and waits.

'Heroin or crack?'

'Both,' she says, her eyes lighting up as though she's a child being offered a bag of sweets.

'I've got the legal ones.'

She doesn't return my smile. I turn and leave the basement in order to seek Soothers and a couple of Ativan. Guarding against the idea that she'll scream by closing the door firmly behind me. Whatever she's shrieking is inaudible.

I bring with me a bottle of Evian and a paper plate containing two slices of thinly buttered toast. It won't help the cravings if she doesn't eat.

'What's your name?'

I ask her this as soon as I enter the room, dropping down to her level as though speaking to a child. I learnt this from my mother who never once raised her voice to me. She made sure to literally get on to my level as she spoke to me. A brief flash of my mother's golden hair and wistful expression moves towards me as I blink back the memory and place the bottle of water and the plate on the floor in front of her.

'You don't have to tell me. I just thought it would help. You're going to be here for some time, I want to make this easy for you.'

'I don't want to be here,' she says, her voice now a gruff whisper.

'I know. But you'll be glad once the drugs wear off. You may even become appreciative of this situation.'

'Circumstances can't alter preconceptions,' she says, quoting something I read when I was studying from Baxters theory of opposition.

I'm bewildered how a philosophy student can possibly have become so broken down and involved in the illicit world of drugs.

'I studied at King's College,' she says.

'What was your thesis based on?'

'Stockholm Syndrome,' she says.

Quite fitting given the circumstances.

'Why did you offer to pay me for sex if you had no intention of sleeping with me?' she says.

42

'Would you have preferred me to have sex with you?'

'I'd rather that than this,' she says, looking around the room.

I cast my eyes to where she rests her gaze. The metal box with the key to the handcuffs I left on the floor beside her. A reminder that she can be trusted not to escape if she behaves.

'Let me go. I promise not to tell anyone,' she says.

That's what they all say.

'I can't let you leave yet. You're not ready.'

'But-'

'Take this.'

I offer her an Ativan, and the two remaining Subutex I've saved especially for the occasion.

'It'll help you with the withdrawal, and if you turn around you can lie on the bed and rest.'

'You're not going to leave me again?' she says, her eyes darting around, unable to focus on any one thing except for the knowledge that she is soon to be left alone. Something else I am learning that no addict likes very much.

'I promise I won't be long. This house doesn't pay for itself you know.'

I'm beginning to sound like my mother now too.

'Please, I'll be good,' she says.

'I know. But I can't stay here any longer. I won't have a job to go back to if I don't hurry up.'

I hold out my hand for her to scoop up the tablets with her tongue from my palm. Such a sensual act is lost on me. Her tongue is cold, like a lizards. Are all addicts cold blooded?

Her torn lips scratch my skin as she slithers her tongue along the surface of my dry palm and tips her head back, ready to swallow the tablets down with the bottle of water I hold up to her with my other hand. She shakes her head and draws back from me, turning away

43

to spit the tablets out onto the concrete floor.

I'm not going to pick them up for her. They'll be contaminated with germs. Infected. Unclean. Like my hand feels now after her mouth has been all over it.

'Do you think I'd trust you?' she says.

I shake my head.

'Do you think I'd accept pills from the man who abducted me?' she says.

'I didn't abduct you.'

'You are disgusting. A vile creature who needs putting down. I'm not going without a fight. You've picked the wrong woman for your depraved fantasies,' she says, snarling and retching.

I want to say something but the words stick in my throat. I want to say that this is only short-term. She won't be here forever. I want to tell her that I'm doing this to give her back the life she's so thoroughly fucked up until this point. I want to tell her that there is no other reason for this, other than my wanting to help her. To give her the chance to start over. Clean, unspoiled, pure, new. But whatever it is that she thinks of me is so far from this truth that I leave the basement, lock the door, and return to work without so much as a second glance at her sad little face.

She wasn't expecting to be ignored. Something else I've learnt recently is that this causes extreme reactions.

When I return to the house later she's curled into a ball sobbing. I feel wretched. Like I've done a bad deed. Though I know I'm doing it for all the right reasons, she isn't aware of this fact.

'It hurts,' she says.

'Where?'

'Every-fucking-where,' she says.

'There's no need to swear.'

She's staring at the pills she spat onto the floor earlier.

'I want them now,' she says.

'I should have cleaned them up. They'll be contaminated now. I can't give you those.'

'But I want them,' she says. 'I need them.'

'I'll get you some Methadone. Just this once. After that, you're going to have to put up with Zopiclone and Codeine.'

She looks up to me with a pained expression.

'That's not enough,' she says.

'It's all I've got until Friday.'

A while later I'm holding the bottle up to her lips. She takes several large gulps, retching from the sudden intrusion of liquid in her almost empty stomach to line it ready for her one-off dose of narcotics.

The toast lies on a plate on the floor untouched. How somebody can survive an entire day on only a cheese sandwich and 30mls of sweet green Methadone is still beyond me.

'Why are you doing this?' she says, calmed from the placebo effect of having swallowed the liquid. It'll take several minutes to ease her pain and calm her trembling limbs.

I want to tell her, but it's too early. She isn't ready to hear it. She's not yet willing to accept that she has a choice. When she's better, she'll be more likely to understand, so I ignore her.

She doesn't take kindly to this but I see her shoulders drop and her face begin to warm from the drugs entering her body. The liquid is working its way through to the dopamine receptors in her brain. Making her think she's taken the illicit version. She smiles, turns her head to the side and throws up on the edge of the bed.

'I'll change your sheets.'

I leave the room, find a polka dot duvet set and a navy blue sheet, which I use to cover the mattress.

Before I leave the room I make sure she has enough water and a couple of slices of freshly buttered toast, hot from the grill.

'How are you feeling now?'

'Better,' she says. 'Thank you.'

HER

Why would a father tell his son that he'd been having an affair? How would a child know what that even meant? And, perhaps more importantly, what would saying something like that achieve for anybody?

'There is no affair or fair sweetheart. I don't know where Jacob got that from, but it's not true.'

Jacob's father Steven, is a football coach. He runs an adult team for people with learning disabilities. In his spare time he works for the PTA. I can't imagine what he was thinking coming out with that, but then again, I never have been very good at understanding people.

What could his motivation be, I wonder? It's not as though the mere suggestion of such a thing would make me want to sleep with my son's nemesis' father. And such a ludicrous idea is not something a child would just invent. I have to speak to Jacob. I have to know what is going on in his father's warped mind.

Back last summer Ollie was interested in joining the team. I still have his father's number somewhere.

I run upstairs to find the notebook I used to leave beside the handset in the hallway. That's where I had to keep it from Zack.

Towards the end of our marriage he began to suspect that I was having an affair. He used to check my text messages. I had to keep anything I'd recorded away from his prying eyes. I think the jealousy began as a substitute for love. We'd outgrown each other. He was simply looking for a reason for the abrupt termination of our relationship. A way out. If I'd slept with somebody else it would have been easier for him to hate me.

The mere mention of an affair will ignite his passion to blame me for the end of our union. He'll see it as confirmation. His suppositions will fuel further debate over whether or not my unfaithfulness was what drew us apart, and cover the fact that his strange behaviour was actually the culprit. It will both propel his divorce papers through the door and convict me for something I haven't even thought to do. It won't help our situation one bit.

I have to speak to Steven. This idea must be quashed.

The notebook is lying on top of the address book, and a photo album from our trip to Ireland rests beside it in the drawer of my bedside cabinet.

The ferry crossing was awful. I suffered from seasickness the entire journey. Ollie was small and it was a struggle to contain the teething cries of a young baby whilst hanging my head over the side of the boat.

I leaf through the pages of the notebook and find his number written beneath the plumbers. I take the book downstairs and dial Steven's number. It goes straight to voicemail and I decide not to leave a message. It's better to get these things sorted out face-to-face, though thinking on it, perhaps I should have left a message telling him that it was something to do with the football team. He'd have called back then. I'll call again later and ask to meet him at the school gates in the morning.

I'm about to follow Ollie's voice trailing from the kitchen into the hallway, begging for something to eat when the phone rings. I answer immediately, preparing myself for what to say.

'Hello?'

'Claire, it's Steven. I missed your call. I was just hanging Jacob's kit on the line. How are you?' he says.

'Actually. I needed to talk to you.'

Formal and straight to the point; gives him less chance to consider his moves.

'Oh?' he says.

'It's about Jacob.'

'What's he up to now, the rascal?' he says.

'He told Ollie today that you and I had been having an affair'

'A what?' he says.

Clearly this is news to him.

'An affair.'

'Where the hell did he get that idea from?' he says.

'You told him.'

'Claire, I . . . I don't know what to say,' he says.

'Put it right, for both our sakes. If Zack finds out, I'll never hear the end of it.'

'I'm so sorry. I had no idea.'

'Talk to Jacob. Tell him he's made a mistake. This can't get out. You really don't want Zack to hear this.'

'I'll tell him. I'm sorry,' he says.

So am I.

I hang up the phone just as Ollie appears in the kitchen doorway with a thick coating of chocolate around his mouth.

'Biscuits?'

'Cake,' he says, licking his lips.

'Where did you find that? I haven't been shopping yet.'

'It was on the kitchen table,' he says, passing me a small card. 'This was next to it.'

I turn the envelope around and see my name written

in delicate letters, like music notes.

I know instantly who it's from.

Claire,
I thought you might like to know that I haven't
forgotten. I found this in a delicatessen. Enjoy.
Zackary. X

How could we forget?

'Is it from dad?' says Ollie, sucking on his icing coated fingers.

'Yes.'

'What did he say?' he says, cocking his head to one side as he always does when awaiting an answer.

'He hopes you have a wonderful birthday. He's sorry he couldn't be here.'

'Is that my card?' he says, grabbing at the note written inside the small, otherwise blank card, with the picture of a small bear, dressed in blue, wearing angel wings.

'No, love. It's mummy's. Why don't you go and take your uniform off and I'll get the dinner on?'

'Okay. But, then can we go to the fair?'

'There is no fair Ollie. It was a mistake. A big mistake.'

'I'll ask daddy to take me. When is he back?' he says.

I don't know what to say. Does he mean when he's coming home or when he's moving back in, with us?

I divert the conversation by asking him what he's been doing in school today. Though I wish I hadn't asked as he gives me a run-down of every subject he learnt and conversation he had with everyone he remembers seeing today.

'Why are you taking tablets?' he says, watching me with the curious expression of a six-year-old.

'I have a headache.'

After dinner we seat ourselves in the position we take up most evenings. Me at one end of the sofa and Ollie at the other.

He reads from the book he chose in the school library. I try to catch up on placing orders using the online system of my sole trader's account. I've earned almost two hundred pounds in commission this week. I'm going to log on to the chatline later too, for my second evening 'shift'.

Last night I spoke to a retired police officer who wanted me to whip him while he wanked, and an Indian fellow who was considering starting his A-levels in London next year. I devised a place of birth, age, hairstyle, body shape and size, as well as a place of work as the evening progressed. They all seemed to want to know where I was speaking from, and were less interested in who I was. I suppose it's all a learning curve.

I jotted down my minutes as soon as I logged off for the night, curling up beneath the blankets in the living room, falling asleep downstairs through exhaustion more than laziness.

With my earnings from the chatline I've earned £225 so far this week, and it's only Tuesday. Though I won't see any money from the chatline until next Friday. Like most cash-in-hand work I get paid a week behind. Still, it's enough to keep the debt collectors off my back for another fourteen days.

Ollie falls asleep with the book lying on his chest. The pages rustle with his breath. I lift him up, feeling the full weight of him as I trundle out of the living room. He looks small for his age but he weighs a tonne. With my arms securing his neck and the backs of his knees I carry him to his room. The curtains are left slightly open in the middle to allow the moonlight to creep through the window and leave a shimmering glow across his little body.

He sighs in his sleep, like his father.

I leave the door ajar in case he wakes in the night to use the bathroom. I creep down the hallway feeling the plush carpet sink beneath my feet.

This flat was made to be lived in. It's the kind of place that felt like home the moment we chose it.

It was my decision to move out of the house we shared with Zack. It didn't feel right to be living under the same roof until the place was sold. It's a good job we did leave, considering he still hasn't put it on the market. We'd still be living there now if I hadn't have saved up for this place. I don't think he really wanted me to leave. He probably would have liked it if our arrangement included sharing a bathroom and kitchen. If he could still keep an eye on my daily activities. He'd have a heart attack if he knew what I was doing for a living.

I'm about to resume my position on the sofa when my mobile phone rings. I collect it from the coffee table where I leave it permanently on, in case an emergency event occurs in the middle of the night. The screen flashes causing flickers of aqua light to skim the room.

'Steven?'

'I know it's late. I thought I should let you know that I've spoken to Jacob. He's very sorry for what he said. I don't think he understands. He seems to think that a conversation he overheard was about me and you because the woman had a son and . . .'

'It doesn't matter. As long as he's not going to mention it again. The school mums will have a field day over such gossip.'

'It's all in hand. By the way, will Ollie be joining us for practice on Thursday?' he says.

'No. I don't think so. He's into his computer games at

the moment. He says he wants to be like Mario.'

'It'll do him good to get out. We've an extra two seats if you want to join us,' he says.

'I really don't think so.'

'Can I mummy, please?' Ollie says.

'I think we have a spy,' says Steven.

'Ollie go back to bed.'

'I can't sleep. The music woke me up,' he says.

'I'm sorry, I have to go.'

'So, Thursday, shall we pick you up around five o'clock?' he says.

'I can't Steven, I'm working.'

'Oh. I thought you worked when Ollie was at school?' he says.

'I do. I just . . . I've got a lot to do.'

'Haven't started a second job have you?' he says. 'Veronica is training alongside the care work. That's all we need- overworked mums,' he says.

I'm sure he means well, but I'm really not in the mood.

'Steven. I have to go.'

'We'll speak soon,' he says, before I hang up.

Who's Veronica?

If he's dating again at least he'll have his mind elsewhere from now on, if it was something to do with him. Though I very much doubt Jacob was fed this information through the television screen. It's much more likely that he overheard an adult conversation taking place between his father and . . . well, I don't know.

'Come on Ollie, back to bed.'

He dawdles along the hallway back to his room. I watch him pull the covers up tight around his head, leaving just enough of a gap to breathe through.

'Can you tell me a story?' he says.

'It's late.'

'Just a little one,' he says.

'There once was a dinosaur called Dino. Dino the dinosaur lived in a forest. The trees were tall, and his friend was small . . .'

I watch him sleeping, as I did when he was an infant. It took an age for me to wean him away from his dummy. And then he began to suck his thumb. After that, he developed a swift rocking movement to calm himself long enough to sleep. That's when we first noticed.

The problems began around the age of eighteen months. Being our only child his often strange behaviours were normal- at least to us. By the time he entered playgroup it was obvious that something was wrong. Our GP made a referral to the pediatrics clinic where he was diagnosed with hearing loss.

His odd acts, such as cocking his head to the side when listening for a reply, or calming himself through thumb sucking and then rocking, was all to rid the watery sounds flooding in one of his ears. The specialist likened it to being underwater. Ollie was both distanced from our voices, and hoping we wouldn't talk for the noise it made in his ears when we did.

I look back on those first years of his life wondering what of it he can still remember. Does he share the same memories as me over days out, our several short holidays to Ireland, Zack's sister's wedding?

Sophie. I haven't heard from her since the split.

Was it something to do with our sons loss of hearing that kept me and Zack glued to each other for those early years of his life? Or was it during those times that things started to go wrong? It's not something I wish to concern myself with now. It can't be fixed. It shouldn't be fixed. It's a chapter in my life I will neither look back on with regret nor wanting. We shared moments with our son that can never be forgotten or replaced. But I wouldn't want to repeat them. Those memories are in the past, just like us. I only hope Zack is able to move on, as I have. Though it doesn't seem that way. Not when he is letting himself into my flat and leaving cards and cakes on my dining table. I'll have to stop leaving the spare key in such an obvious place.

Since we moved in I've been afraid of locking myself out of the flat. After all, I don't have a friendly locksmith neighbour around here, or a husband to deal with such things anymore. I've been leaving the key beneath the Buddha in the back garden. A present from Laura. A friend of mine who's now deleted me from her Facebook friends list.

I'm not sure what I've done to offend her, but it must have been bad though in all honesty I doubt it has anything to do with me at all. I expect that Zack must have said something to either offend or perturb her from re-commencing our friendship after I left. Something he'd grown accustomed to doing during dinner dates with friends or family meetings and greetings. He used to sit and seethe, silenced by a couple of glasses of wine with a meal.

He was never cruel. I don't think he ever spoke a vicious word to me. He didn't need to. All he had to do was ask me a couple of questions it was impossible to answer and then he'd sit back and smile as though the very act of having gotten me aroused and ready to explode was his only intention. He didn't want to argue. He didn't want a fight. He wanted to unsettle me. And I couldn't live like that anymore. Treading on eggshells, not really afraid to speak, more afraid to say the wrong thing, and when I did he would remain quiet and passive.

I believe the term is passive aggressive. It's something narcissists use to emotionally charge individuals when wanting to create an atmosphere of distrust.

He wanted me to feel insecure, illogically unsafe of a quiet, kind natured man with the demeanor of somebody who loves his family. It's a perfect concoction of psychological torment. Mind games, I've learnt, are like emotional torture. The only person who appears genuinely unhinged is the individual who is continually challenged by their reflex to bite back.

I'm sure his mother isn't the only one who blames me for the separation. Nobody was expecting it. Neither of us had slept with anybody else. There was no mention of a domestic dispute. We wouldn't say a bad word about each other. We grew apart, we said. But I don't think anybody believed me. For when I took Ollie from the house he spent his first years in everybody was asking me how I was feeling. I thought it odd at the time. But looking back on it now I wonder if he said something. Did Zack impart some information that could have made them suspect I wasn't taking the break-up quite as easily as I was? Or had I given them reason to think I wasn't feeling quite myself?

I don't remember being emotional. But I do remember trying to convince Laura, Sophie, and even my own mother that I would not find it difficult to live alone.

At the time I thought it was my mother's over-protective instinct to tend to her daughters wounds, and my caring friend's need to feel duty-bound in ensuring I didn't feel alone (throughout) this; that I had people to lean on, that I only need ask for help and it would be freely given. But was there more to it than that?

I fall asleep peacefully beside Ollie, allowing his deep breathing to lull me into the darkness.

HIM

She still hasn't told me her name.

'You're not having any part of me,' she says.

'Make one up.'

It'll be easier to bond if we communicate openly. I too learnt a little about Stockholm Syndrome as an undergraduate of The Open University. I studied a BSc Psychology. This was back when I hoped to train as a clinical psychologist. When the only training requirement was an MSc and a voluntary post. I qualified just before my mother died. That was the end of any thoughts for such a career.

I'd recently completed a thesis on the pharmacology of mental health disorders when my mother died. I'd also gained accreditation with the British Psychological Society, but I never got to practice. Instead, I gave up my volunteer post at St. Peter's Hospice as an assistant Psychologist, and fell into a bout of depression. I was signed off work for six months, then twelve, until finally going back to such work was no longer an option. The new accreditation scheme fell into place meaning that I'd have to enrol on a doctorate in order to practice, having completed my MSc ten years before.

I never left the paid job. Building had been in my blood. I returned to full-time hours, and slipped from the ease with which I'd lived my life until then. I kept myself busy. Preferring the company of my thoughts over others.

I tried to make friends. To find companions to share a night out at the pub with but none of them could hold their promise to join me. They all had families to go back to. I had nobody. That's how it's been ever since. Of course, now that's all changed. I guess it's ever since I met Amy.

It wasn't a plan I set out to complete. Far from it in fact. Amy was my girlfriend. We met in a bar, round the corner of Redcliff. Where St. Mary's sits on the crossroad. I'd always wanted to see inside the place, but had never dared. It seemed strange to drink somewhere only other lonely souls seemed to be. I didn't want to be one of them.

Amy was playing a game of pool with a young lad who she seemed to have never met before. I found her enthusiasm for the game endearing and her confidence attracted me to join them. Both me and the lad, Barry, lost to Amy and another wanderer who joined in. Seemingly known to Amy, Jo played very well, even with a broken arm. They won fair and square.

Amy offered me a drink and we found ourselves cooped up in a corner of the grubby pub with half a pint of bitter and a packet of cheese and onion crisps each. She seemed very forward. Not hesitating to take out my wallet and leave me waiting for her to return from the bar with another glass. I didn't realise until I got home that ten pounds had gone missing.

Blaming her actions on the alcohol I hoped to see her again the following evening to let her explain her theft to me. I was willing to hear it, open for anything. What I wasn't expecting was for her to tell me that it was a ploy to get me back to the pub. I haven't been there since.

'How's the pain?'

'What do you care?' she says.

The same words Amy used.

'Do you need some more Codeine?'

'Like that's gonna work,' she says.

'It'll help.'

'How do you know? I haven't seen you writhing around in agony all night. I haven't heard your teeth chattering so much they snap in your mouth.'

'You've broken a tooth? Show me.'

'Why? So you can tug it out my mouth?' she says.

'No. So I can get you to a dentist.'

She pauses, imagining the possibility of escape.

'Yes. I want a dentist,' she says.

'Does it hurt?'

'I can't tell. Everything does,' she says.

'Where's the tooth?'

'I think I swallowed it,' she says.

'You don't know?'

'How the fuck am I supposed to know. Everything hurts. I can't feel anything over the pain,' she says.

'I'll get you some more pills.'

I leave the basement, returning with her third bottle of water and the tablets. Once again she licks them from my hand, only this time, she glides her top front teeth alongside the thick skin of my palm, causing an involuntary shiver from the tingling sensation that now runs down my wrists, right up to the crease of my elbow. Then she bites me.

Her teeth sink down hard into my skin. I jump back from the pain but she snaps her teeth tighter around a small nip of skin beside the finger I wear my only ring and doesn't let go until she tears off a piece of my flesh.

'I've got AIDS,' she says, smiling afterwards.

The small flap of skin she tore from my hand sits in one corner of her mouth. The blood from her broken lips meets my own in a curdling mess around her chin. It's the most disgustingly erotic thing I've ever seen. Like a lady of the night becoming a vampire killer from biting the skin of a man. I wonder if she's going to eat it until she spits and splutters, tugging once more on her handcuffs.

'You shouldn't do that.'

'Why not? Who's going to stop me?' she says. 'You said so yourself that I'm not here as your play thing. Then what is it? What do you want me for? Why are you keeping me here like this?' she says.

It's a good question. One that deserves an honest answer.

'I'll tell you when you're ready.'

'I'm ready now,' she says.

I look into those red-rimmed eyes, vacant and haunting at the same time. I wonder briefly if she has a mother and father at home, desperately trying to look for her. Wanting nothing but the safe return of their daughter. Do they know she's destroyed herself this way?

I look down at the scars covering the insides of her arms, travelling in width way slants from her wrists to the insides of her elbow. Did she cut herself to cope with life or to erase her feelings? Numbing the pain or as another way to feel alive?

Her composure is drawn, beaten down. She looks as though she is cowering, rather than struggling to keep warm in just a T-shirt and jeans that look as though they cost a fiver in the market. She looks as lonely as she believes me to be. Well, I'm not lonely any more. I have her. Does she realise that she has me too?

'Why am I here, you fucking fruitcake?' she says.

I admire her tenacity; her ability to remain obstructive and disobedient, even when it's clear that it's I who holds the reins. Her life is in my hands.

'I want to help you.'

'Why?' she says, irritated by my diffusion of her comments.

'I believe you have a problem, and I want to help you fix it.'

'My only problem is you,' she says.

She can only see the object of her hatred as responsible for her current situation. If she wasn't here, with me, she'd be free to use.

'I want to help you, but you have to trust me.'

'How can I trust you?' she says. 'You're keeping me locked in a fucking basement for Christ's sake,' she says, tugging once more on the cuffs that secure her wrists to the bedpost.

She's beginning to sweat. Her limbs will tremble soon and she won't be able to eat or drink without being sick.

'You need to eat something. Your body is going into withdrawal.'

Suddenly her attention is diverted to the very real possibility of freedom; from her head.

'No it's not. You've got pills.' she says.

'They're not a substitute. They're to help you cope.'

'Cope with what? What are you talking about?' she says, dying to itch her face. To scrub it raw with her filthy fingernails.

'Withdrawal. You're going through withdrawal.'

'I'm not clucking yet,' she says.

She can't fool me. No matter how much strength she wants me to believe she has, no addict can handle the sudden withdrawal from a substance without the aid of something. That's why I've been holding out from using the Codeine and Zopiclone until now.

'I'm not withdrawing,' she says, more to herself this time, than to me.

'I've got stronger substances. Medicinal. It'll help with the symptoms. But you have to let me treat you.'

'Treat me? You're not a fucking doctor. You're a psychopath. Is that why I'm here? You want to medicate me. Keep me lucid, so you can get your mates round here for a free fuck?' she says.

'No. that's not-'

'If you're going to do something . . . something bad to me, then I'd rather be out of it. So get me some real drugs. Not pills or Methadone. Just get me the real stuff, now,' she says.

'I can't.'

'You can't or won't?' she says.

'I buy everything from a pharmaceutical expert. He doesn't sell illegal drugs.'

'It is all illegal. Even legal highs are illegal now, you idiot. Even I know that and I only buy my shit from . . .'

'That's enough swearing young lady. Get your act together. Pills or not you're staying here.'

'Stick your pills up your arse,' she says.

Later as I'm running the shower I hear a faint knocking sound from below. I run the water until it's warm, not too hot, and stand beneath the shower head, feeling the tiny droplets of water dancing on my skin. Even with the water running I can still hear the occasional tapping from downstairs.

The bathroom is directly above the bed. I knew this when I arranged the basement furniture- what little of it there is anyway. I thought that by being able to hear her, I might find some comfort in knowing that she's okay down there. It must be hard being alone for so long, having nobody but me to talk to. And even that cannot result in complete solace. Knowing that the man who's keeping you here is doing so only by being able to listen out for every sound you make, recording every movement. I'm not sure I'd cope very well with it myself.

I turn the shower off and instantly feel the draft of cool air filtering its way through the bottom of the door. I still close the door when I'm naked even though I tend to usually live alone. I do this more out of respect than anything else. For if she did manage to escape the confines of the basement and flee up the stairs to leave I wouldn't want her seeing my bare flesh though I doubt she'd be able to do that. I've fixed her cuffs securely. They're the same ones the police use. I got them at a good price from eBay though how the individual selling them came to get hold of them in the first place is something I'd rather not think about.

I know I'm late for work. I know the boss is going to be annoyed over my absence this morning. But I had to do it. I had to make an appointment with my doctor. I'm having my first ever HIV test, and to be honest, I'm growing increasingly anxious by the minute.

I've never had to worry myself over such things as HIV tests. Not even with Amy. We never slept together. We didn't need to. We were content in getting to know each other. Of course, at the time I didn't know she was an alcoholic. I didn't consider this for one minute in the bar that night. She didn't seem the type.

I think they call them functioning alcoholics; those people who are able to hold down a job, a career, take care of their children, their home, and themselves whilst continuing to drink themselves into an early grave. Only when you look closely at such people can you see that there is something wrong. Something sitting beneath the surface of their eyes. They are wounded. Troubled minds hidden beneath mascara and eye-liner. The shadows beneath their world-weary eyes are coated in make-up, so that nobody will be able to see the pain they are masking.

I dress quickly and leave the house. I drive only because it'll get me there faster, and not because I particularly want to.

Diesel fumes and the smell of damp moss from the trees to my right fill the car through the open window. The houses are masked in a faint hue of mist that's emanating from the river.

The suspension bridge isn't far from here. I sometimes go there when the summer heat has all but disappeared. The place has an ethereal feel to it in autumn. By then the flowers have dried up or died off and the ferns have begun to shed their leaves. The ground is moist and the smells are clear and fresh; river water and grass.

I navigate my way between dustbin lorries and a few parked caravans left on the side of the road, blocking the sight of the pedestrians attempting to cross the busy road.

Gypsies tend not to stay for long. This part of the Downs is more a resting place; a pit stop before they move on to their next site. Nobody minds them being here. In fact, I envy them their ability to live amongst the world yet simultaneously not have to interact with it. They keep themselves to themselves, just as I do.

The car park is surprisingly empty when I turn into it.

Inside the waiting room I sit with my hands, palm down on my lap, waiting for my name to appear on the screen.

I'm both dreading the conversation and yet find it almost humorous that I've found myself in this position. Requiring a HIV test at the age of forty-seven when I've never actually had what one would call a 'committed relationship.' Or is that worse?

Beep.
I look up at the screen.

Ewan Carter, Room 7: Dr. Radmond

Here goes.

I enter Dr Radmond's office. The room is light but claustrophobic. The desk is piled high with files and the shelves are filled with a compendium of reference books for various forms of illness and their appropriate medicinal treatments. I doubt he knows any more than me about pharmaceuticals but I wouldn't dare mention this to him.

He sits with his hands drawn to his sides and his chest puffed out as though he needs to air his authoritative position within the confines of this confined room.

'Mr Carter, how can I help you?' he says, his voice kind, and instantly reassuring.

I know he'll understand my concern and won't show a hint of judgment.

'I would like a referral to the GUM clinic. I think I may have come into contact with somebody who has AIDS. She says she's been diagnosed and I don't doubt her.'

'Have you had sexual intercourse with this person?' he says, unflinchingly.

'No. She bit me.'

I raise my hand to show him the deep cut. Her teeth marks are still visible though it's been hours since the incident occurred.

'I see,' he says, wearing a slightly puzzled expression for a brief moment before turning to tap away on his computer.

'In case you have become infected with anything else I shall print you off a prescription for some antibiotics.

These are especially for skin infections. Though it's rare for an individual to pass the HIV virus onto somebody through a cut to the skin it's not impossible so I will refer you on for an appointment today. You should receive a phone call within the next day or two from the clinic. They'll book you in at your earliest convenience. In the mean time what is it that you do?' he says.

'I'm a builder by trade.'

'Try not to do too much with that hand, keep it covered, and perhaps in future take a lighter approach to your sexual encounters, Mr Carter,' he says, jokingly.

I can see that Dr Radmond likes to take a light-hearted approach to life. A definite positivist personality. I wouldn't put it past him to have undertaken some courses in NLP or wellbeing. He seems the sort of person to do such a thing.

I leave the surgery at 10:45am and drive straight to work. I only hope that I'll be allowed to take a lunch break with the rest of them. It wouldn't do not to be able to return home and check on the woman, even if she did cause me a morning's pay.

HER

I'm awoken around 7:00am by a hammering sound which jolts me awake. I reach out my hand, running my arm down the length of the bed from the pillow to my own leg before I realise that Ollie is no longer curled beside me. I look over to where he'd been lying fast asleep all night, dreaming, as I lay beneath the covers beside him, basking in the heat of his warm little body.

'Ollie?'

'In the kitchen mummy,' he says, calling out from the only room I beg him not to go into when I'm not with him.

I tug the covers from my hot skin and pad down the hallway to find him standing beside the toaster with a knife dripping with butter in his hand.

'Ollie, what are you-?'

Bang Bang Bang

'Somebody's at the door mummy,' he says.

'Yes, I know. Come here.'

I pull him close to me, swiping the knife from his small fingers and wrapping my arms around him. Shushing him with a single finger to my lips.

'We don't know who it is.'

I say this hoping he'll understand, but knowing he won't.

'Open the door then,' he says, innocent to the way in which the world operates.

'I can't. I'm not dressed.'

'I'll do it then,' he says, pulling away from me.

'No, Ollie. Be quiet and stand still. They won't know we're here if they can't hear us.'

'Why?'

'Ollie, shush.'

He stands awkwardly, staring at the door, with his hand curled inside mine.

I don't want him to be frightened, but if it's debt collectors, I really think this is preferable than him witnessing bailiffs taking away our belongings. It's too early for it to be anyone else.

A note slips through the door, but I won't read it until we're on our way out. We'll take the back door, just in case.

The new car is in the garage. I very much doubt they have the rights to jump over an eight-foot high fence and start creeping around the garden peering through the windows looking for a vehicle.

I hear footsteps moving away from the front door and down the concrete path, back on to the road.

'Come on, Ollie. They've gone now. Let's get something to eat, and get your packed lunch ready for school.'

Silenced by my dismissal he refuses to budge. It takes every effort not to tell him to move out of my way and to stop gawping at the door.

'There's nobody there. There's nothing for you to see. Don't worry about it. Let's have breakfast.'

'You're worried mummy,' he says.

'You're too grown-up. I'm fine, Ollie, really. Now go

and sit yourself down at the table.'

We eat in silence.

When we leave the house I bend down to pick up the note that was shoved through the door.

Amira & Sons.
Total debt: £2,150 owed.
Please pay in full or contact our customer service
representatives to make payment arrangements
to clear your outstanding balance. Your account
has now been issued with a default notice.

That was the only credit card I had left. I thought I'd paid it.

'Ollie, wait. I have to make a quick phone call before we go.'

He resigns to sitting on the dining chair beside the window birdwatching as I enter exit the living room, closing the door behind me. I don't want him to overhear me.

We arrive at the school late. I start work even later, and by the time I take notice of my growling stomach it's time to leave for the school run once more.

It's not the first day this week that I haven't had time to eat. I can already see the difference working two jobs has made to my waistline. I only manage breakfast and a late dinner once I've put Ollie to bed. I'm sleeping on a full stomach and eating barely a thing all day. I've gained four pounds in a week. If I keep this up I'll be as fat as a turkey before Christmas.

Ollie's face is drawn to the ground where his feet are perched one on top of the other. His hands are twitching beneath the table and he doesn't look up when I call his name.

'This can't go on,' says Mrs Pritchard. 'He has barely eaten his lunch. He won't talk or join in classroom activities and he won't tell us what the matter is. Perhaps we could assist you in a referral to a . . .'

'I don't think that's necessary, is it Ollie?'

He doesn't look up, instead he twists the frayed edges of his royal blue school jumper between his hands, not daring to look away from the ripped laces of his shoes.

'I really think-'

'It doesn't matter what you think. We're doing fine, aren't we Ollie?'

He continues to ignore me as I pass in front of Mrs Pritchard and bend down, taking his chin in my hand.

'I don't think Ollie is very happy Miss . . .'

'You think?'

'We only want to help you-'

'You can't help me because I'm not in need of help. My son is unwell, can't you see that?'

'He seems fine to me, but maybe a good rest will do him some good,' she says.

'What is that supposed to mean?'

'I didn't mean to offend you Miss . . .'

'Enough with the *Miss*. Come on Ollie, we're going home.'

He doesn't move.

'Ollie, I said come on. We have to go.'

He looks up from the floor and refuses to meet my eyes. His face is tear-stained.

'Oh, honey, there's no need to cry.'

'Will they be there when we get home?' he says.

'Who?'

'The bad men. I don't want to go back if they're still there,' he says.

'There aren't any bad men, Ollie.'

'Yes, there are. The ones that were at home this morning. I saw them while we drove away. One of them was wearing black. I don't like his face,' he says.

'Come on, enough with this nonsense. Let's get home and have something to eat.'

I take his hand and ignore the concerned expression on Mrs Pritchard's face as we pass her.

As we're getting into the car I wait a few moments before setting off, taking the time to look into the rear-view mirror and study Ollie's worried face; pale and drawn, as though he's carrying the weight of my problems. A burden I have no intention of letting him take.

On the way home I can feel the thudding of my heart beneath my ribcage. I grip the steering wheel tightly, praying they won't be there when we get back.

The phone call this morning didn't exactly go well. I ended up screaming down the phone, forgetting Ollie was only on the other side of the door.

'How dare you come to my home and frighten my son within minutes of us getting out of bed. You ought to be ashamed of yourselves sending people round in the morning when children are at home. At least wait until they're in school.'

I recount the rest of the conversation in my head, knowing that in seven days time I will have no credit score left and am at risk of losing my main occupation; a business I grew from scratch without the help of anyone else or the financial back-up of a loan. Being a mumpreneur is now going to have been another fad. A pipe dream, left at the wayside for being a single parent. A mother who can't even afford to keep a self-employed job.

The credit system with the retail company is dependent upon your credit score, checked randomly throughout the year. If it shows red I won't be entitled to a credit facility any more. I'll have to purchase the products from my own money. I won't be able to continue to work that way.

My only hope now is to pay off the default sum and collection fee, a total of £2,400 by next Tuesday or go full-time on the chatline and hope for a miracle. A few regular callers are all I need to boost my income.

Who am I kidding? I'm not getting paid for another eleven days. It's highly unlikely that's going to work. I really do need a miracle.

As it happens, small mercies do appear at the strangest of times and in the least plausible places. I manage to acquire £175 from deliveries, meaning I've just over four hundred pounds in the bank. Enough to cover some of the debt. I'm hoping this will keep them off my back for an extra few days, only when I call them to make the payment they inform me that it covers only the legal costs of applying for bailiff action. I've still got to pay the remainder by Tuesday or else I can expect a repayment fund through the courts.

I can't risk a County Court Judgement. I can't see myself in the dock of a civil court begging for extra time to enable me to cover the food costs, now that I've spent all of my available funds on bailiff fees.

I've always put Ollie first. He'll never go without. It's only pride stopping me from calling my mother and ridiculing myself with another explanation of the finer details of my financial situation in order to beg for a hundred pounds. I know full well she'll give it to me, but not without hesitation. Not without wanting to know the ins and outs of my income and expenditure. Writing off my credit card and catalogue payments as being of unnecessary importance in the grand scheme of things. Rent and council tax must come first.

What she doesn't realise is that without petrol in the car to work we'll have no food to eat. I often wonder at the naivety of people's logic when it comes to understanding others needs. Can't they see how broke I am and how desperate I am to put things right? Without anyone on side how am I meant to get myself out of this whole shitty mess?

When my mobile phone rings I'm about to explode with tears. I want to shout down the phone 'don't bother me with your crap, I'm trying to piece my life back together. The one my ex-husband managed to ruin,' but I freeze when I see in the caller display that it is in fact him.

'Hello, Claire?' he says.

'Zack. I'm in the middle of something, can you call back later?'

'How's Ollie?' he says, dismissing my words.

'Fine. We're both fine.'

'Good. Listen, I'm going to have to pass on having Ollie over this weekend. I'm a bit strapped for cash. Is there any way you could bring him to me for the day on Saturday instead?' he says.

'That's impossible.'

'Are you busy with your little paper-round?' he says.

Great. Undermine me.

'It's a lot more than that-'

'Sure. So can you?' he says.

'Not really. I don't think I'll have the petrol-'

'I didn't realise things were that bad. Look, you know I'd help, only I'm in the same situation myself. In future though, if you need to borrow anything let me know okay?' he says.

'Right, well, I really have to get on now so . . .'

'Saturday. Drop him off around nine. You can pick him up at six, if that's not too much trouble?' he says, hoping I'll agree.

'I really can't promise anything.'

'Why are you being so difficult?' he says.

73

'I'm not. I just-'

'Forget it then. I thought we could spend some time together too, but I can see that's out of the question as well,' he says.

'Zack, we're separated. I'm not expecting to spend time with you.'

'Found someone else have you?' he says.

'Like I have the time.'

'You've got plenty of time. You choose when you work. I don't,' he says.

I can feel the hostility pouring down the phone like some essence in a horror movie. I imagine it's green smoke oozing from every pore of his olive coloured skin.

'I can't believe you.'

'You're still my wife. I just thought we could make it easier on Ollie if we got along, but I can see that's not something you need now that you've found yourself someone else,' he says.

'There is no-one else. I'm not interested in a relationship with anyone right now. We've been apart for . . .'

'I know. I know how long it's been. I thought you'd come back. I thought you'd have second thoughts, realise what you're missing. Now I see that you don't feel that way. It's okay. I understand,' he says.

'I'm sorry.'

'I know,' he says. 'So am I.'

Why does he always make me feel this way? As though I've done something wrong. As if *I* have something to apologise for?

'You have Amanda now.'

'It wasn't working out,' he says.

'You've split up?'

'Yes,' he says.

'I didn't know. I'm sorry.'

'It's okay,' he says.

Again, what am I apologising for?

'Goodbye, Claire,' he says.

'Goodbye.'

He hangs up instantly.

Do I regret leaving him? Do I truly feel that I somehow caused the breakdown of our marriage? Somewhere hidden within my unconscious, is there some part of me that regrets my decision to leave, though it was an equal ending? He wanted something from me I couldn't give. I wanted out. Or is that only how *I* remember it?

Ollie eats at the table, barely able to make conversation. I'm sure he feels awful for his little outburst at school earlier on today, but there really was no need for him to have told the headmistress about our visitors this morning. I don't doubt that he was feeling upset, fragile even, but was there really any cause for him to concern himself over adult business at all? That's something I resent Zack for.

He used to include Ollie in any and all communication relating to the running of the household: bills, taxes and other such nonsense a child doesn't need to have their heads filled with. I suppose in his own way he was preparing him for maturity. He is a very clever young lad. But not old enough to be able to comprehend what we are saying. Such conversation doesn't need to be freely explored with such a young mind.

Ollie puts down his fork, and asks to leave the table. Something too, that I feel is unnecessary given that his father is no longer here to care. I never did see the need for it. Manners are one thing, but strict obedience quite another.

I don't want Ollie growing up hardened to the world,

unable to enjoy his childhood for the few short years that it's here, or worse; hating us for it. I don't want to wind up cooped up in some care home with no visitors when I'm old. I'd rather we re-established the kind of relationship I wanted with my son now, rather than it disintegrate before my eyes, just as my marriage has.

Ollie doesn't know this yet but I've planned a holiday. As soon as I've cleared the debts or set up a manageable payment plan, and we have a little money spare each month, I'm going to take him to Disneyland. Florida is far too expensive so I've set my sights a little closer to home. France is but a tunnel away. My only hope is that the immigrant protests have ceased by the time we take the trip.

I'm sure Zack won't mind. And it will allow Ollie the time to remember what it is that being a child is all about. He should be having fun, playing with friends his own age, taking part in after-school activities, not becoming increasingly nervous every time someone knocks on the door or listening through the paper thin walls for one half of a conversation his mother is having on the phone to a debt collection company without knowing what it's all about.

'Ollie, you know those men only wanted to collect something. They're not bad people. It's their job. And it's mine to make sure they get it. Do you understand?'

'I think so. But why are they following you?' he says.

'What do you mean?'

'The man in black was in the van behind us. He waited while you left me at the gates,' he says, not realising the implication his words have on me.

My palms sweat and my hands begin to shake. I push them under the table so that he cannot see.

'What else did you see, Ollie?'

'He followed in the van behind you when you left the school,' he says.

76

The room begins to circle around me. My arms are prickling and a distant humming begins to sound in my ears. My skins crackles with whatever it is that causes me to jump up from the table and sink my hands down into the bottom of the cold, steel sink. I run the cold tap and splash the water over my face hoping to cool my cheeks and rid the horror from my eyes.

Why on earth would they be following me?

HIM

The woman is crawling along the floor like a demented dog. She has been screaming all night though I've told her nobody can hear her. She's refusing direct speech and has now become immobile. She is suspended from the chains I allowed her to use, giving her extra room to eat, sleep and pee.

Instead of enjoying her new freedom she believes that shouting through the wall and wearing away her voicebox will give her some chance of escape. She's sorely mistaken. A plea for help cannot be heard through the insulated walls.

'If you don't calm down you'll have a panic attack.'

She lets out a fierce low moan, as though she is a woman in labour, bearing down to give birth on the floor of this revolting smelly space we share.

She messed herself on purpose. I had to clean it up this morning. She had plenty of room to use the toilet, but instead chose to use the floor. She then proceeded to smear it up over her calves and now it is coating her knees and hands as she writhes around like a dog playing with mud on the concrete floor.

'Why are you doing this?'

She looks up at me and smiles. I fear I have lost her. She is in the throes of substance withdrawal, and it is much worse than I had anticipated.

'You don't need to do this. You can get through it. I can help you.'

'I don't need your pills. I want to go home,' she says, exhausted.

'So you can use?'

She nods.

'I don't want you to. I want to help you, but you have to let me. I know what to give you to ease the symptoms. If you'll let me it will work.'

She shakes her head, refusing my offer. She's taken nothing from me since she bit my hand two days ago. The cut has almost healed. A nasty scar will be left in place of the triangular shaped flap of skin that she has taken from me. It is dark pink and ugly. Something I'd rather have done without, but it can't be helped.

I can see her distress, but I'm not sure I will ever understand why she is acting like an animal. Prowling around the floor.

'Let me help you. I can see that you are hurting. I don't want you to feel like this.'

She is a fighter. Perhaps she was born that way. But I truly believe that nurture, rather than nature, causes people to act the way that they do. Biology can only create something, it is set off through circumstance and adversity. Environment and conditioning.

I wonder if she is always like this when she is suddenly forced clean from drugs or if this is the result of her current situation? I guess I'll never know.

Later I decide to dine with her. It can't be very nice to eat and sleep alone while you are resident in another's house. I can imagine her sitting here late at night listening to my TV through the ceiling wishing she was

79

with me.

I bring the plate of food and a bottle of water down from the kitchen. Along with two tablets: Subutex. In the hope that she will take them when I have left the room. I place her paper plate on the bed beside where she sits, rocking back and forth.

She doesn't look up acknowledging my presence, but she does stare down at the plate with recognition. Does she realise how little she has eaten in the past three days?

I take my own plate of sausage and mash with onions and gravy from the floor and begin to eat, hoping that the smell and sounds will stir within her something that will cause her mouth to water and her digestive tract to restrict. Seeing somebody eat while you are hungry makes you want to eat too.

She continues to rock, back and forth, back and forth, whilst gazing at her untouched plate of food. Is she losing her mind?

I hadn't considered that she might not only be withdrawing from heroin and crack cocaine but perhaps some medicinal compound for her obvious distress. Does she suffer from some kind of mental health disorder? Is she withdrawing from anti-psychotic medication? Is she dangerous to herself or others? Why hadn't I thought of this? Had all of my training and experience been for nothing?

Her face is clammy. Beads of sweat rise up on her brow. Her clothes cling to her skin, and she's taken on the ash coloured hue somebody suffering from cancer might whilst being treated with chemotherapy.

I am reminded of my time as an Inpatient Unit Volunteer for the local hospice whilst I was studying. Some of the patients there looked no different to the way this woman looks right now. Is it the appearance of death that I am seeing?

Her movements are fluid, and her features lucid as though she is no longer contemplating survival or a means to escape, but has instead resorted to some semblance of acceptance for her unfortunate circumstances.

She wants to be left alone. She no longer wishes to interact with me through the form of head-nodding or the occasional twitching in my direction. The primal groaning has ceased- finally. She is but an unrecognisable version of herself. Without wailing or swearing she appears feeble and broken. Torn beyond repair.

What have I done to her?

I sit alone with the TV turned down low so that I can hear the steady rhythm of my own heartbeat.

She looked peaceful when I left her. Finally giving in to rest her head back on the pillows.

I don't know if she's taken her tablets yet, but I left them there in case she changed her mind and realised that it is kinder to accept any form of relief, however small for now. Just until the true drugs leave her system completely.

She has at least two days left of the awful pain and inability to coordinate her actions. The involuntary bowel release and jerking movements will subside by Saturday. Sunday she will be ready to eat a good hearty meal. I've planned steak and chips for us both to celebrate.

I bought the beef especially. Thick cuts from the butchers. I'm going to make my own chips, and a sauce my mother taught me to make though I'll leave out the red wine for obvious reasons.

I fall asleep blissfully unaware that tomorrow is going to bring with it something completely unexpected.

I'm tired.

A building labourer failed to arrive this morning so I had double the work to do. Lifting and carrying large bags of cement from one floor to the other by wheelbarrow.

I wasn't thinking straight.

She must have taken the pills because she's calmed.

Her limbs no longer shake and her ragged breaths have quietened down.

'Who was she?' she says.

'Who?'

'The woman who made you this way. She must have hurt you badly for you to be doing this,' she says.

'She didn't hurt me.'

'Aha, I knew it was true. There was a woman,' she says, pleased with herself. 'Is she the reason for all this? Are you doing this to compensate yourself against whatever it is she caused you?' she says.

'It wasn't like that.'

'Right,' she says.

She thinks for a moment.

'Did you lock her up too?' she says.

'I'm not having this conversation. It's making me uncomfortable.'

'Guilt,' she says.

'She died.'

Her body tenses at this.

'You're a builder aren't you?' she says, a while later.

'I told you that, yes.'

She offers me a knowing glance.

'You actually build?' she says.

I'm unsure where this conversation is going.

'Yes, I do.'

'Then you know how to build walls in houses,' she

says.

I nod.

'Then you buried her here,' she says, her eyes taking on a mystical glaze.

I refuse to answer any more of these single answer questions.

She lets out a faint cry.

'You buried her beneath the floor and covered it up,' she says, walking up to the far wall, running her hand along the stone grain. Her fingers slip and she moves away from it, stepping back into the side of the bed.

'She's in the walls,' she says. 'I can feel her. I can hear her whispering in the night.'

She looks over to me then.

'She's here, isn't she? In this house. You buried her in this house,' she says.

Whatever I say will only confirm the way she died, and that I played some part in it. Regardless of where she's buried, this woman doesn't need to know.

I shake my head, not quite able to meet her eye.

'I have to get some food in. Do you mind if we discontinue this conversation?'

She blinks several times.

'I won't be long.'

'Wait,' she says, as I turn to leave the basement. 'I've come on my period.' Then as an afterthought: 'Can I have something to read, please. I'm going out of my mind with boredom here,' she says.

'Sure.'

I close the door behind me, locking it with the key and the double bolts; one at either end of the heavy steel covered wood.

'Is that her?' she says.

I cannot dismiss her concern yet equally I'm unable to

gaze into the eyes of the woman who looks back at me from the photograph.

'You took her didn't you?' she says. 'What did you do with her?'

'Nothing.'

This comment infuriates her further.

'You give everything away with what you don't say. Did you know that?' she says.

'I didn't do anything to her.'

'It's her though, isn't it?'

I'm not having a repeat performance of earlier.

'You killed her,' she says.

I bite my tongue to stop myself from blurting anything out.

'Did she fight you back? Did she escape? Did she threaten to tell the police?' she says.

I turn away from her, feeling my knuckles clench. The jagged nails I forgot to cut yesterday are digging in to the loose skin of my palm.

'I'm not sleeping another fucking night in this hell-hole if she's buried in the walls of this basement,' she says.

Her face is crimson. I can feel the heat of her anger from here.

'Stop it, now. This isn't good for either of us. Can't you see that?'

'She whispers to me in the night. I can hear her. I can smell her,' she says.

'No.'

The room begins to buzz as though an open electricity cable is pumping energy through the air.

'She's rotting away in there,' she says, pointing to the thick stone wall. 'Her flesh is being eaten by maggots. I can hear them climbing over her skin. They're eating her heart. They make such a noise,' she says, dropping to her knees with her palms covering her ears.

'Enough. No more. Just stop this now.'

She looks at me then, with a new found confidence. As though she understands me more.

She stumbles backwards then, falling onto the bed.

'Is that what you're going to do to me?' she says.

'No, of course not.'

'I'll fight you. You won't hurt me like you hurt her,' she says, a determined expression taking over from the previously unruffled features her face has worn for the past few days.

'I didn't hurt her. I wouldn't do that.'

'You can't even admit it to yourself, can you?' she says.

I didn't think. I bought her a copy of *The Post*, Bristol's local newspaper. I should never have given it to her.

She reads it aloud to me once more, in case I haven't heard a thing she's said.

'Amy is presumed dead though no body has been found. It is thought that she may have been in a relationship with a local builder. She was last seen wearing-'

'Enough. No more. There is no need for you to concern yourself with that. I didn't hurt her. I could never do that.'

'You kept her chained to the bed like me, and then you buried her, where? In the walls of this basement? What did she do, refuse your drugs? Try to fight back? I'm not going to be that woman. I'm not-'

'I didn't kill her. I didn't hurt her. There was nothing I could have done . . .'

I sit with my back against the cold hard wall. I bring my palms up to my face and draw them down over my eyes so that I can feel the scarred tissue of the hand where she bit me graze against my lips.

How am I going to explain to this woman who Amy

was, what happened, how she died, if I don't even know who she is?

'Tell me your name.'

'No. I've told you. You're not having any part of me,' she says.

'Please, tell me your name.'

Then I will tell you mine.

HER

Payday has arrived! And with it comes enough money for me to cover half of my debt or to book our tickets for Disneyland. I won't have enough to cover the entire debt so they'll pass it off to the courts any way. If I can get away without the trading company knowing about my awful credit score I'll be able to keep working for them for a few months longer. That will give me a bit of time to figure out a money making strategy.

I'm aware that I could get a part-time job, but I can't afford the childcare, and I don't know of any work other than within a school that would allow me to work from 10:00am until 2:00pm Monday to Friday, at term times only. Making a name for myself on the chatline is my only feasible option right now.

Ollie returns from school looking more and more withdrawn each day. He slides into what I can only describe as a form of childhood depression. He misses his father. He's missing his home, and he no longer feels included at school.

It breaks my heart to see him this way when it would all be so much easier if we had the money to enjoy the time we spend together.

A holiday is something I need just as much as him. And we're going. Whatever it takes I'm going to make sure that he gets to experience some normalcy.

I hurry into the kitchen at the smell of burning emanating from the saucepan on the stove where the rice has now turned black and has stuck to the bottom of the pan in a milky tar-like sludge.

'We're having a McDonald's for dinner Ollie. Get your coat and shoes on.'

He takes no persuading to leave the house and jumps onto his booster seat at the back of the car with an excited smile I don't think I've seen for a long time.

'Can I have a happy meal?' he says, his face beaming.

'You can have whatever you like.'

I use the drive-thru and order us both a meal deal with a milkshake made from ice-cream. I take the short-cut road straight from Eastville and along past the Glenside campus of the University of the West of England.

There are groups of students leaving their days activities in huddled familiarity at the bus stop or waiting for the lights to change so they can cross over and cadge a lift from their parents who are waiting eagerly at the other side.

I'm at once envious of their obedient parents nurturing taxi skills, something I was not able to experience during my college years.

I didn't get the GCSE's I needed to take the light vehicle mechanics course I wanted to pursue. My parents wouldn't have transported me to University and back, and I certainly couldn't afford a bus pass, even with the student discount. Ollie is going to have so much more than I had.

Growing up was hard in the eighties. Protests over government funding cuts, demonstrations over unfair pay, Union enterprises going into liquidation along with the organisations they supported. It is the music and clothes that lasted long after the recession.

It's going to be different for Ollie. I'm going to ensure that he has a good education after enjoying a carefree childhood. He's not going to fall into debt, working a minimum wage job. Zack wouldn't allow that either.

I park up in Snuff Mills where the sun always seems to find a place to shine between the trees, even in winter.

The moss-covered trunks of ferns and chestnut trees to our left, and the high running water of the stream to our right leave a fresh awakening scent in the air, making me feel light-footed and my senses slightly aroused.

Ollie is dazzled by the glare of the sun peeping out from behind a deep grey cloud overhead, but this doesn't discourage him from slipping away from me to climb the dry muddied hill, disappearing into the undergrowth where he stops suddenly at the top, all too aware of the prying eyes that watch him from below.

'No climbing.'

He doesn't answer me. Instead he gazes down at something which has caught his attention and screams. I run as fast as I can up to where he stands crouched now, with his hands holding himself upright on the sturdy branches of a gnarled tree, its leaves somehow turned as black as ash.

'It's dead,' he says, wearing a panic-stricken face.

'It's okay. Nothing to fuss over. It's going to be all right Ollie. Everything is going to be all right.'

I catch the symbolism in the notes of my voice; meaning all of our problems.

'We're going to be all right, Ollie.'

I bend over, stroking his hair as it begins to rain. Small trickles drop down between the branches of the trees, leaving sap and sprigs of broken leaves on our cheeks and hands.

'Come on. Let's get out of here. We'll eat our meal in the car.'

He doesn't move.

'We have to bury it,' he says, looking up at me with hopeful eyes, filled with tears.

'It's only a squirrel.'

'It's a baby. We learnt in school that smaller ones have a thin white line down the back of their tail from when their fur changed colour. We have to bury it,' he says, matter-of-factly.

'Okay. But you're not touching it. They're rodents. Full of disease. Let me do it.'

And so I find myself digging the earth with a small stick I find amongst the bracken surrounding the ground we stand on, burying a dead baby squirrel in the rain. The things you do for love.

He seems pleased with my pathetic attempt and takes my hand without a word, asking the sky to grace him with a peaceful afterlife. I'm not sure where he heard the expression from but he seems to know what it means. For when we get back to the car he looks up to the heavens and exclaims a warm thank you to the sky for looking after his friend, who he claims now is a boy called Sammy.

We sit in the cramped car with the heaters on full blast, set to a medium heat to dispel the condensation that's appeared since we left it only half an hour before. Once we've finished eating I drive us home to the sanctuary of our meagre existence where I find that the electricity has gone out.

Now that I've paid for the tickets, and booked us both a hotel room in Paris I haven't the money to cover the pre-payment meter.

I run my hands over my brow and down the length of my hair in exasperated resignation. Surely it can't get any worse.

'I'm taking Ollie away, Zack. It's all been paid for.'

'It's not Butlins. This is abroad,' he says. 'Besides, I thought you were strapped for cash.'

'I've just been paid.'

'Enough for a holiday? What are you doing, moonlighting?' he says. But there is no humour in his voice. 'You can't take our son to another country on your own. I'll come with you. We'll go as a family. I'm sure my mother-'

'Zack, we're not a family anymore. I'm taking our son away for a few days. Besides it isn't as though you tell me everything is it?'

'What's that supposed to mean?' he says.

'The school-'

'I don't want to hear another word about that. Our son is not a thief. He was being bullied,' he says.

'He lied to us Zack. He involved the school in something that was no business of anyone's.'

'When was this?' he says.

'It doesn't matter.'

'I dislike you keeping things from me Claire,' he says, his tone serious, his words uncompromising.

'Me keeping things from you? Do you want to see him before we go or when we get back?'

'I'll take him out Saturday,' he says.

'We're leaving Friday.'

'Tomorrow? Why so soon?' he says.

'Because . . .'

'Because what, Claire?' he says.

I detect a hint of something unpleasant behind his voice. Something I don't think I've ever felt before comes over me in waves. For the first time, I find I'm actually frightened of upsetting him.

'I've bought the tickets at a discount. The hotel has already been paid for.'

'I see. Well, enjoy yourself, Ollie's staying with me,' he says.

'It's Disneyland Zack. I can't go alone. What kind of lunatic goes there on their own?'

'The kind that can't even take care of herself least of all her son,' he says.

'I resent that Zack. There's no need for this.'

'A child needs both of their parents, Claire. I thought you of all people would understand that,' he says.

There it is again. The hints to a prior life. He seems to enjoy such moments; raking up the past. Can't he see that I am trying to do my best on a limited budget?

'Things are hard at the moment, Zack. I haven't the income to afford holidays and I thought-'

'You thought what? That you'd spend what little you do have on taking our son to another country for a weekend, without his father?' he says.

'I just think that it's time we enjoyed ourselves. Me and Ollie need to spend some time together to-'

'You weren't able to enjoy yourself when we were together you mean. That's hardly my fault. And besides, you need to start acting more responsibly,' he says.

I can feel my lip trembling. My chest begins to tighten. The muscles in my hands flex and burn as I try to keep myself composed. I cannot bear to cry in front of him. I do not want him to think that I'm weak. That I brought all of this on myself.

'I have to go now, Zack.'

I manage to speak without a tremble or a flicker of frustration being detected.

'Whatever,' he says, before hanging up.

I lean against the wall to support my weight. I feel as though I'm sinking through quicksand, and there's nobody here to save me.

'Mummy, are you okay?' says Ollie, appearing in the doorway.

'Yes, I'm fine. Go and sit back down and eat your dinner. I'll join you in a minute. There's something I have to do.'

He puzzles over my need to ground myself in this moment by pushing the full force of my body against the wall. My legs cold against the radiator that I can no longer afford to use.

Was it always like this? Had I just stopped trying to please myself, giving in to his every request, whilst we were together? Have I always been so accepting of Zack's behaviour?

I settle down in front of the TV, not watching it, but comforted by its low hum.

Ollie is settled. I left him to sleep off the excitement of our upcoming trip to Paris. He's looking forward to meeting the people dressed as characters from some of his favorite films: The Jungle Book. His little face has been beaming all night.

He's such a knowing lad. He always has the need to keep telling me that the characters we are going to see aren't the real ones. Repeating over and again that the real ones have families to look after and jobs to do according to their particular characterised careers.

I distrust that he is a first-timer on this Earth sometimes.

I've only just logged on to the chatline when the man on the other end of the line tells me that he's been thinking of me. He is one of my regular callers. He has a broad cockney accent and a hearty laugh. Brash, honest, and genuine.

The evening continues much the same as it usually does. I list the minutes I've taken in calls down one side of the notebook left open on the soft leather sofa whilst adding the total for my day beside it each time I put the phone down before having to pick it up again quickly so as not to wake Ollie when it rings again.

I wouldn't say I enjoy the work. Not in the sense that I get anything out of it other than a bit of adult conversation and some money at the end of each week, but I do find it easy. So much so in fact, that I've now been promoted to another line. Young and kinky I am, apparently.

It's fun sometimes though especially when my dirtiest clients of the night begin to call. David likes to wear his wife's clothes when she's out shopping. He particularly enjoys parading around in her underwear until the last moment when her car pulls up in the driveway. I wonder if he's ever been caught?

Then there is Gerald who wants to be treated like a bitch. I have to make him feel worthless and cheap. He comes quicker when I tell him to behave. I suspect he's married too.

I don't feel any less for men now that I know their darkest desires. If anything, I empathise with them more, knowing just what it is that makes them tick. It's a shame I don't share such a skill with ex-husbands.

I really don't know what Zack's thinking sometimes or where he gets his ideas from. It's as if he likes to live his own life to the full without considering anyone else, but dare I do the same, his wife still, and mother of his child, all hell will break loose. I'm beginning to suspect that he resents me for something. Though I haven't a thought as to what it could be.

I log off after my final caller of the night and make my way into the bedroom, passing by the door to Ollie's room where I watch him sleeping for a few seconds before I allow myself to head off to bed.

I wonder sometimes if he isn't sleeping at all but hoping that I will be passing by to offer him a goodnight kiss and to tuck him back inside the blankets he kicks from his little screwed up body.

I leave his door ajar and leave mine wide open in case he awakes from a night terror and wants to come and sleep beside me, like he used to. It doesn't matter how many years have passed I don't think these behaviours ever change. My own mother still leaves the bedroom door open and the light in the hallway on, even now.

I toss my dressing gown over the back of the chair, but it slips and falls to the floor. Brushed cotton on polished wood. I wait until I've settled down beneath the duvet before switching off the olive coloured lamp perched beside a small bird cage candle lantern. Black and ominous looking in such a light room.

From this angle I can see that the moonlight glows ethereal and bright even through the pale duck-egg curtains. There are no stars out tonight. I was searching for them before I put my coffee cup down in the kitchen and made my way towards Ollie's room.

It sounds like a cat at first. Scratching against the front door. But as I reach behind my head to fold the pillow in half I see it. The shadow of a person shifting in front of the glazed door, visible even from here. Illuminated by the streetlight.

HIM

Her name is Elise. She didn't tell me, of course. I read it on her thigh.

She wears a deep blue entangled heart tattoo, covered in ivy. On the top right-hand corner of the heart is the name Elise. Below it is another: Kieran. I guess he's a past boyfriend. If they're still together I very much doubt he'd approve of her continual drug use. Though of course, she is clean now.

Today she accepts a single white pill from my hand.

'What's this?' she says.

'Solpadol. It's all I could get. It's the most potent opiate you can have on prescription other than morphine.'

'What's in it?' she says, scrutinising the thick round white tablet in her hand.

'30mgs of codeine.'

'What am I supposed to do with this?' she says, flicking it onto the floor beside my foot.

'Swallow it.'

She doesn't like it when I answer her in a direct way. She much prefers a metaphorical conversation. I expect it has something to do with her philosophy classes or perhaps she is a poet at heart.

'Do you like to read?'

'I read the magazines and newspapers you bring don't I?' she says.

'Books. Do you like to read books?'

'I used to enjoy crime,' she says.

'Not any more?'

She raises her hands offering me the chance to catch the point she's trying to make. Why would you want to read crime if you're effectively living your own crime story?

'You should be a comedian.'

'I don't find this situation in the slightest bit funny, Ewan,' she says.

'You're clean.'

'How can you tell?' she says, quite honestly oblivious to the lack of shadows drawn beneath her eyes or the puffiness across her cheekbones beginning to form once more.

'You look better.'

'That's because you're looking after me is it?' she says, not wanting to contain the laughter which causes her shoulders to jump up and down.

'No. It's because you no longer have crack or heroin in your body.'

'Only the legal ones,' she says, smiling.

'I'm weaning you off those too, though not as quickly.'

She walks right up to me then. Much closer than we've been since I applied the handcuffs on her the first night she came to be here.

She stands so close that I can smell her rancid breath as she edges her face closer to me so that our noses are almost touching.

'Am I supposed to appreciate this, you making me

live like this completely sober. Nothing to take the edge off.' she says.

'Uh...yes.'

'Are you nervous?' she says, not giving me time to answer.

She draws back her face and looks me right in the eyes.

'You should be. You've no idea what I'm capable of,' she says.

It's my turn to smile.

'What, you don't believe me?' she says.

If she could find the strength to fight now then why didn't she before?

'I don't doubt for one moment, given the opportunity you'd kill me Elise, but I don't believe you would do so now. Now that you know the truth.'

'The truth about what?' she says, stepping back into the wall as though attempting to scurry away like a frightened mouse between the open bricks.

'Amy.'

'The woman you . . .'

'Yes. I'm going to tell you everything.'

'Why now?' she says.

'Because you're ready to listen. Because you will understand.'

'I don't know if I . . .'

'You want to hear it but you're afraid. I understand that Elise. But if you want to go home-'

The confusion instantly causes her to raise her eyes and when she does a faint line appears along one corner of her forehead. The first signs of skin degradation. Wrinkles which begin when an individual reaches their thirties.

'I'm not sure if I want to.'

'Elise, listen. I don't want you thinking I'm some cold ruthless killer. That's not who I am. And, I think you know that too. Don't you?'

I see the words I've spoken tumbling around inside her head. Jumbled and split between the other warped ideas of her brain.

'If I'd have wanted to kill you before I could have. You know that. I only want the best for you Elise.'

I forget for one fleeting moment where I am, who I am talking to, what we both are to each other. I raise my fingers up to her face, but no sooner have I rested my forefinger against the cool skin of her cheek does she pull back and lash out at me with sprawling hands. She lands one punch on the lower part of my nose attempting to stun me. I turn and catch her other hand, about to lunge for me in a clenched fist, which would never in a million years knock me to the ground, when she trips forward into my arms. She tugs herself away from me, shoving hard against my chest but I manage to placate her.

I sit back against the bottom of the bed feeling the harsh ice cold metal board against my spine. My arms wrapped tightly around her body, unable to let go. She's fallen slack in my grip. No longer fighting. No longer trying to get away.

She is lying with her back against me. Her breasts beneath the bare skin of my arms, covered in a loose fitting T-shirt. She fell into me with her eyes closed, her head twisted to one side. Her breath is no longer loud, raspy, and filled with burning hatred. It is undetectable. Unheard.

I wonder what it is like outside of these four walls tonight. Is the moon a large, full luminescent ball, glowing in the sky? Are the dark pavements black from the rain; slippery, and shining in the streetlight? What is the cold doing to the homeless and the wild animals which roam the area? Will I have to charge the car battery tomorrow morning? Get my neighbour to jump start the car for my trip to Leigh Woods?

I slip the ring from Elise's finger easily. She barely weighs more than a bag of cement, and I can hoist them about all day long without much thought. I'm careful to lay her down on the bed without damaging any part of her. She looks peaceful. I thumb the indented skin of her finger where the ring has been sitting for so long it's left a dirty mark where the water cannot penetrate when she washes her hands. I see that inside the ring there is an engraving.

With love x

I wonder if Kieran bought it for her. If it holds some sentimental value other than that of a gift from an ex-boyfriend. An engagement ring perhaps? It doesn't matter now. I push it down into my pocket where it sits against my leg. A piece of her. Something of hers that I can own. I will hold it sacred. Keep it protected with the only other piece of jewellery I own which belongs to another.

Amy wore a thin gold band. Elise's is much stronger, made of sterling silver. It's well worn, but I'll treasure it just the same. I'm wondering whether to leave it inside the small tray in the jewellery box upstairs. Hidden behind a selection of ties at the back of the wardrobe.

Even from the basement with the open door I can hear it. Somebody is knocking on the door. Nobody ever calls on me, especially at this hour. I don't have anyone who cares enough to visit.

HER

I hoist the bags down the hall from where I packed them in the bedroom last night. Ollie sits on the little stool beside the front door, tapping one foot against the laminate floor in impatience.

'Ollie, come now, we have to get this lot in the car.'

I don't know if it has anything to do with our late night caller yesterday but he wears a world-weary expression as though waiting for something to happen that will ruin our plans of leaving this morning.

He jumps up and bounds over to the door. I carry the two bags, heavier than they should be, out of the door and towards the car. As I'm about to use the key fob Zack's car screeches around the corner and parks on the kerb in front of the driveway, blocking our exit from the flat.

'I was hoping to catch you before you left,' he says, jumping out of the car and slamming the door behind him.

'Zack, we're in a hurry, can't this wait?'

'I managed to get hold of a set of tickets for Disneyland. I booked a hotel. It might be the same one as you,' he says.

'I thought you had no money?'

'Daddy, are you coming with us?' Ollie says, beaming with delight.

'No, Ollie.'

'Why?' says Zack. 'I thought you'd enjoy some adult company. Besides, Ollie needs both his parents for a trip like this. It's special.'

'Zack, this was meant to be just the two of us.'

'One more won't hurt,' he says, turning to Ollie. 'Right little man?'

I open the boot which creeks with rust, as I dump the bags down into it, slamming it back down hard.

'If you'd rather I didn't come . . .'

'No daddy, please come with us,' says Ollie.

'Why do you always do this Zack? I can't enjoy one thing, share one single memory without you there to-'

'Fine. I'll stay, but you really ought to have said so when I spoke to you,' he says.

'Zack, I told you not to bother us.'

'Okay, I get it,' he says. 'Who is it Ollie, who else is coming with you and mummy?'

Ollie squints his eyes.

'You daddy. You said you were coming,' says Ollie.

He shakes his head and turns to me, whispering so that Ollie can't hear him. 'I thought it would be a nice surprise, but I can see that you don't want me ruining this once in a lifetime opportunity to screw me over so-'

'Zack, that's enough. You're upsetting Ollie.'

'No, you are,' he says.

As he moves to walk away, back to his car, I grab the sleeve of his jacket but it slips through my fingers. He turns to look back at me and shakes his head.

'I thought better of you, Claire,' he says.

'What is going on, Zack? Why are you doing this?'

'If you'd rather I wasn't here just say it. Don't lead me

102

on. It isn't fair on little Ollie,' he says.

'I thought I made myself clear when you called. This is something for me and Ollie to share. An experience I'd rather not-'

'Have me around for?' he says. 'I get it. I do. I just thought it would take you a bit longer to find somebody else, that's all.'

'There is nobody else, Zack. I told you that.'

'So who else is going with you? Ollie said-'

'He meant you Zack.'

'Oh,' he says, halting with his hand on the door of his car.

'Well, maybe I've been a bit hasty. I just thought-'

'No Zack. You don't think. You never think. You just do, that's your problem. You act, then consider it later.'

He pauses for a few moments, shakes his head and opens his car door.

'Daddy, wait. Please come with us. I want you to.'

'I can't Ollie. Your mother has made that perfectly clear. She wants to take you on her own,' he says, slamming the car door behind him, and starting the engine up. Ollie runs towards the car just as he speeds off down the road.

'Ollie, come back here.'

'Why can't daddy come? Why do you always have to fight?' he says, tears welling up in his eyes.

'We don't fight Ollie, we-'

'Yes you do. I always heard you back home,' he says, running back inside the house.

'Ollie, we have to leave now. We'll be late.'

'I don't care mummy, I'm not going without him,' he says.

It took me almost twenty-five minutes to convince Ollie that we had to leave or we'd lose our booking. That if we didn't make it to the tunnel on time we wouldn't be able to go to France at all. He eventually walked out of the house and seated himself down in the car without a word. Refusing to look up when I spoke to him.

The entire journey was broken only by a single stop in the services near Poole in Dorset while we took the coastal route towards the channel tunnel.

Back in our hotel after the first day of activities, including a 'meet and greet' by some of the iconic characters from the Disney films, and a journey through the making of Cinderella, Ollie grew bored and decided he was too tired to continue walking through the grounds, so we're sitting in the large dining hall waiting for some creamed chicken and potatoes when my phone rings.

'Claire, I'm so sorry to call you, but I have to tell you-'

'Oh God Zack, what is it?'

'There's been an . . . an incident,' he says.

'What do you mean?'

'Your flat has been broken into. I'm not sure what's been taken, but someone has definitely been in there. Did you lock the door when you left? Because -'

'Of course I did. I wouldn't forget something so important.'

'Are you sure, because when the insurers look into it-'

'What have they taken?'

'I don't know. It's a mess Claire. The place has been bulldozed,' he says.

'Call the police.'

'Claire I-'

'Call the police, please. Can you deal with it? I don't want Ollie to come back to that.'

'What is it mummy?' he says.

'Nothing love.'

'It's hardly nothing Claire, the flat looks like a bomb's hit it,' says Zack.

I draw in a large breath of air, releasing it at length.

'Please Zack, can you call the police and deal with everything, I really don't want this to ruin our holiday.'

'You mean you're staying, after this?' he says.

'I hardly think that wasting all this money and coming back to that is worth ruining Ollie's holiday over, do you?'

'Well I suppose I can tidy up a bit and-'

'No Zack, the police need it left alone for fingerprints. Can you call them first, before you do anything else?'

'Who's your home insurance provider?' he says.

'I haven't got any.'

'You're not insured?' he says.

'I didn't have the money for that on top of everything else.'

'Claire this is so irresponsible of you,' he says.

'I don't need a lecture from you Zack, I just need you to deal with this for me until I get home.'

'I'll see what I can do,' he says.

'Thank you Zack, I really appreciate it.'

'I think you should consider coming back sooner. This isn't going to go away you know. You can't keep burying your head in the sand,' he says.

'Thank you, I know.'

'I'll deal with it Claire, but when you get home you need to prioritise-'

'Yes, thank you. I'm well aware of where my priorities lie.'

'This isn't my fault. You've brought this on yourself,' he says.

Don't I just know it.

'You've made your point Zack.'

'If you hadn't have gone in the first place then this

would never have happened,' he says.

'How can you say that? What am I supposed to do? Ollie needed this. *We* needed this. I thought a break would do us some good after everything we've been through.'

'Like I said Claire. You've brought it all on yourself,' he says, before putting the phone down.

'Really? Really. Well I . . .'

I look down and see that Ollie is bent over rubbing his eyes with his hands balled up into fists.

'Oh Ollie, don't cry sweetheart.'

'We shouldn't have come. Daddy said . . .'

'What did daddy say?'

'He said we shouldn't be going away when . . .'

He leaves the words hanging in the air, with a faraway gaze in his eyes.

'When what? Ollie, I won't be angry. Please tell me. What did daddy say?'

'He said we shouldn't be going away when we have things to pay for, like bets,' he says.

'Debts?'

'Yes,' he says. 'Don't be upset. Daddy cares about us, that's all.'

'I know he does Ollie. I know.'

I take him in my arms and hold him close to me feeling his tearful breaths causing his body to jerk at each inhalation. How does Zack know I'm in debt? I haven't told anyone the state of our finances, not even my mother.

We spend the rest of our meal avoiding the issue, hoping that neither one of us will speak about it, but it doesn't stop Ollie from asking me why I was talking about the police.

'It's nothing to worry about Ollie.'

Though, I am worried. Our home has been broken into and I'm not there to sort it out myself. He waits until we're seated in the open-plan hotel restaurant before he brings it up again.

'Why do the police want to talk to daddy?' he says, forcing another spoonful of the thick creamy herb sauce into his flushed little face.

I glare at the nosey woman on the table to our right who's been listening in to our conversation since we arrived. I'm hoping she'll look away, but the tenacity of the woman causes me to flush with unreleased venom when she creeps her chair forwards to hear better. I lower my voice in response to Ollie's question and continue to offer the woman an evil stare.

'It's nothing to worry about. Just eat your food and then we'll head upstairs to our room. It's been a busy day hasn't it?'

Ollie doesn't answer. Instead, he attempts to finish his plate of food, his mind wandering over each and every possible reason for his father's call, until he looks up and says: 'I think we should go home tomorrow. We've been to Disneyland now,' he says, standing up from the chair and pushing his plate into the centre of the table.

'No Ollie. We can stay. I promised you a holiday and that's exactly what you're going to get.'

'But mummy-'

'Come on, let's watch a film in our room and eat the sweets we bought earlier.'

I stand up, pushing my chair beneath the table just as the waiter appears behind us, smiling.

'Did you enjoy your meals?' he says.

I hesitate long enough to offer the nosey parker beside us an obviously fake smile, which she doesn't return, before looking back into the waiter's eyes.

'Yes, thank you.'

'Come on Ollie, let's go.'

He stalls with his eyes on something behind me.

'What is it, Ollie love?'

'That man looks like the one that was following you the other day,' he says, nonplussed.

'I doubt that anyone was, but even so, they wouldn't follow us here.'

I trace his wandering gaze over to where a couple stand beside the cashiers desk.

'No,' he says. 'It's not him.'

Ollie walks in front of me on the staircase, up to our room.

Later we're nestled beneath the duvet, having folded out the sofa bed which faces the TV, with our hands brushing each other's inside the rustling bag of popcorn. We fall asleep with the crisp wrapping of it between us. The streaks of moonlight through the window leaving a faint hue silver blue sky on the skin of our arms as we lay side by side in peaceful slumber.

HIM

Elise Fitzgerald is no longer here.

The house seems quiet and unloved without a companion, and so, determined to see this through I vow to find another lost soul to help once I've completed my fishing trip.

I've always enjoyed a spot of fishing, having learnt from the best teacher a man can have- his father. It's something I use now to tame my mind when it begins to wander back to that fateful day. The day I lost my mother. The only woman who ever loved me unconditionally.

It's funny now, looking back, I can see what my father was attracted to for all of those years. Having been married for thirty years my father was often asked 'what keeps it ticking along then old boy?'- to which he'd reply 'love, passion, mystery and a little help with the washing up.'

I can see his point now. I really can. Though it's too late for me. For us. Too late for me and Amy. She was taken from me.

'Only the good die young' is not something I'd ever

thought on before. Now I believe it fits. Elise was good too. It's such a shame having to let her go, but I know it's the right thing. She didn't want to be here. She wasn't cut out for living like the rest of us. I did my best and now it's time to move on. Refocus on my aim. The goal that has kept me sane for almost two years now. Whoever said good can never be given freely without the giver wanting something back was speaking some truth. For I wouldn't be where I am today if I hadn't have offered any of these women my assistance. It is really up to them if they take it or not.

I've been home less than an hour when someone begins knocking on the door. I consider doing as I did last time and ignoring it. Whoever it is is probably trying to sell me something and I'd rather not give them the time of day.

The hammering is persistent and I can't think straight with such urgent noise and so I go to open it, only when I do I find that there isn't anybody there. I check the letterbox for a note but there isn't one. I can see straight down the path to the road from the open doorway and there doesn't appear to be anyone around. There is no car parked haphazardly on the pavement nearby and no sign that anyone has even been here.

I close the door and stand for a few moments wondering who could possibly have managed to leave the area so quickly when I hear the tell-tale *beep* of an instant message alert on my open laptop. It's leaning on the edge of the chair in the living room where I'd been sitting, before deciding to tidy up the basement, putting anything away that Elise has used or touched.

I sit myself down on the chair and place the laptop onto my thighs, feeling the warmth of the monitor instantly on my bare legs. I always wear shorts indoors. My mother used to say that I was hot blooded- I do believe it's true.

The woman I'm speaking to is Katherine. I haven't been talking to her for very long. We met on one of those chatlines. Something I'd always associated with dirty old perverts wanting a quick fumble over the phone before their secretary returned to the office on their lunch break, but now that I'm using them myself it doesn't seem as sordid as I once thought.

I began to use the chatlines and instant messaging service when Amy passed away. I was lonely and wanted an adult conversation with an intelligent beautiful woman. It seemed appropriate under the circumstances. The anonymity it afforded us both.

I don't call them for sex. Perhaps they prefer my calls to the others. It can't be easy feigning an orgasm every ten minutes. I wanted to talk- that's all. And now I call regularly, speaking only to those who are of a mature age- say thirty plus, somebody who I can share my experiences with and who does not feel obliged to share their own with me. Whether theirs is truth or fiction I couldn't say, but we all keep secrets from one another. Life would be dull if we were honest with each other at every waking moment. Sometimes it's nice to hold back. Of course, I have to really don't I? It wouldn't be right to divulge my interests to a complete stranger.

One of the women I speak to isn't a complete stranger. We've been talking regularly since she joined the line. Claire, her name is. I don't know if that is her real name, but I hope that it is. Claire: original and modest.

She is not a Tara or plain Jane. Claire is a mother and soon to be divorcee. Of course, I haven't asked her why she decided to leave her husband or why her marriage broke down, but I get the impression that it was a little more than a simple 'we fell out of love' and that it wasn't entirely 'a mutual decision', though I didn't pry. I told her that it was okay. That I wasn't expecting complete honesty from her. Her marriage is her business. Though I did insist that as we were both protected from harm as conversing solely over the phone that she could be as honest as she felt she could be with me. That was when she told me something that made me question whether the end of her marriage truly was an amicable ending or if something else had caused it.

She told me that her husband was very protective over her, even going so far as to purchase tickets to join her and her son on a trip to Paris, which she refused. Until the burglary, her and her son had been enjoying themselves on their first holiday in years. Only when she mentioned that, did I begin to doubt his need to play the protective ex-husband and doting father. Because you see, I couldn't understand how he believed that she could have brought it all upon herself. Surely nobody asks for such bad fortune.

Circumstances are often unfortunate and most situations such as a burglary are out of our control. No matter what our actions may be, the consequences are rarely caused by pure negligence on our part. There is always something else at play or as I suspect somebody else. I think somebody is out to hurt her, but I don't yet know who.

Claire isn't working tonight so I choose to speak with Karen next. She's a forty-year-old brunette from Leeds. Her broad accent is bright and fluffy. She is always pleased to hear from me and takes great interest in all of the things I've been up to.

'So, Claire is somebody you particularly like on this line,' she says, once more, teasingly. 'Can't be much fun only having one favorite,' she says.

'Oh, I don't have a favorite, I value her honesty. She is loyal to her callers and yet doesn't give too much away.'

'I always thought you enjoyed the mystery Ewan,' she

says.

At the sound of my name I realise she's being more truthful than I am right now.

'Yes, I do Karen. You're right. You're always right.'

I can hear the smile in her voice. I enjoy her company but not as much as Claire's. We're not as close as we could be if she gave a little more of herself away. Still, I suppose I'll have to accept that a job is a job, and Claire cannot be expected to be logged on at every minute of every day. Especially as she has that young lad to look after.

I've always wanted children. Some part of me knows it's probably a little too late in life to be worrying about marriage and children now, but starting a family of my own is something that I've always wanted. I wouldn't take such a decision lightly, and I know that it is unusual for a man to be saying this, but I'd feel whole if I was to come home from a busy day at work to find my wife and child waiting for me.

I don't believe in old fashioned values. I respect a woman's decision not to choose to settle down straight away, but I hope that one day I will meet somebody who wants that too. What my mother and father had was very special. I believe I deserve that as well.

I thought I had found the right woman in Amy. Before her, I often felt unwanted, unloved or was deeply disappointed in the way a woman felt the need to treat me- as if I was less than her. The women I dated would change overnight, altering their personality to fit with their outward appearance. Bold, brash and seductive.

Before Amy there was Susanna. Susanna didn't want children, much preferring to spend her time on a career in medicine. She became a doctor in the end, and ended up marrying one too. Before her was Jade. My childhood sweetheart. The woman of my life. The one who left me for a worldwide round trip on her gap year and never returned. I heard later that she'd met a lifeguard called Brad during a trip to Australia. Of all the cliché's . . .

Still, I've lead a solitary existence until now. Comforted by my regular calls to Claire and Katherine and sometimes Karen. But especially so to my female companions, who I hope will one day feel the same wave of peace as I do once I let them go.

I know I'm not as good-looking as the men these women usually date. I've never thought of myself as attractive. I've had a lazy eye since birth and a small scar which runs down from one corner of my chin towards my throat. I don't have much money, but I've got a good heart. I've just had nobody to share it with.

HER

I've been thinking about it for the past two months. How much easier it would make things if I put the final end to this bitter arrangement. I'm taking the day off work, having dropped Ollie to school half an hour ago. I find myself growing increasingly anxious at the thought of such finality but it has to be done. I know this now. I can't put it off for much longer.

I park opposite the solicitors which sits on the corner of the street which takes you straight down to Queens Square or if you turn left into the county court.

There are cars parked along the side of the road and the busy street is bustling with commuters on their way to work. That's one thing I don't miss since I began working for myself; having to deal with other people. Working alongside those who you wouldn't otherwise give the time of day for, having to force a smile and adhere to a dress code, sharing a Christmas meal with them all at the end of the year whilst pretending to be interested in their new house renovations or recent trip to the Canary Islands.

I cross the road and step up onto the kerb, pressing

the large automatic button to slip through the wide glass doors. I walk up to the reception desk and hover over a leaflet offering information on the abolition of Legal Aid for civil court suits.

'I'll be with you shortly,' says the short woman behind the desk.

She has faded dark hair that I assume was once dyed and wears a royal blue cotton M&S blouse over a lime green smock top with trousers to match.

She puts the receiver down, having had no luck it seems in getting hold of whoever it is she wishes to speak to, and slides her chair towards me to take my name.

'Claire Donoghue. I'm here to meet Mrs. Beresford.'

'Take a seat over there and she'll be with you in a few moments,' she says, clearing her throat then turning away from where she'd pointed to flick through some files on the shelf behind the large beechwood desk.

I take a seat in the waiting area, collecting a magazine titled *Home Sweet Home* from the table, and begin aimlessly flicking through it, oblivious to the woman who has appeared, standing in the entrance to my left.

'Miss Donoghue, I'm Mrs Beresford. Please come this way,' she says, just as I look up and am greeted by a much younger version of the woman who I spoke to less than a minute ago, who now sits at the desk sliding paperclips onto folds of paper.

I wonder if this is her daughter.

I follow Mrs Beresford on through a large open corridor where several rooms sit numbered at either side. She opens the door to room six and I follow her inside.

There is a large notepad on the table and a small silver tray containing two glasses and a large container of water in the centre of it. A slight chill envelopes me from the air conditioning vent above us so I decide to leave my coat on as I sit down.

Mrs Beresford takes a pen out of the pocket of her trousers and seats herself opposite me. She smiles warmly, but it doesn't shake the feeling of unease that continues to grow inside my chest.

'Miss Donoghue, how can I help you?' she says, placing both elbows on the table and clicking down the pen nib ready to take notes.

'I'd like to file for a divorce.'

'Okay. May I ask what reason you would like to give?' she says.

I consider this for several seconds before she leans forward, and placing her hand on the arm of my coat, she offers me an awkward smile.

'It makes things easier if we can offer a reason for your decision to the judge,' she says.

I know she's trying to make me feel more comfortable, but my skin begins to tingle with heat.

'I'm not sure what to say.'

'Let's start from the beginning and then work our way back to that shall we?' she says.

I nod slowly, feeling the full weight of what it is that I'm about to do for the first time since I made this decision.

'How long have you been separated?' she says.

'Just over six months.'

'Do you still live together?' she says.

'I live with my son Ollie in a flat in Filton. Zack, my husband, still lives in the house we shared in Henleaze.'

'And are you considering obtaining a residency order?' she says. 'For your son,' she continues when she notices my confusion.

'I don't think . . . what is it exactly?'

'It's an order given by the judge based on the recommendations of both parent's representative's to decide where your son will permanently live,' she says.

'He's with me already. Is there any need for it?'

'Some parents find it easier to have written documentation displaying their rights to ensure that no party can go against the court's recommendations,' she says.

'So it offers a form of protection?'

'Exactly. And it can be done at the same time as you obtain your decree absolute,' she says.

'I don't think we need to worry about that.'

'Okay,' she says, glancing down at the notes she has begun to take before looking back up at me with empathic regard.

'Was your separation amicable? No domestic disputes, violence etc?' she says.

'Yes, amicable. And, no. Not at all.'

'Finally, why are you seeking a divorce now?' she says. 'This might be easier to answer now that we've discussed some of the other factors.'

'We weren't getting along. In fact, we haven't done so for quite some time now. I guess we just drifted apart. I know it's a bit of a cliché, but that's really how it was.'

'It's more common than you think,' she says, smiling.

Then she sees it. The little glimmer of unease I've been trying to contain. She can tell from the way my eyes blink and my lips tremble, so slight she'd have missed it if she wasn't sitting so close to me. She can see that I'm not taking this as well as I've been outwardly expressing.

'It's okay,' she says. 'This is both an ending and a new beginning. Birth, marriage, death, job loss, and moving house are the most stressful events anyone can go through, and in these circumstances often two or three of them are occurring at the same time. It's completely normal to be a little upset,' she says.

I force myself to remain constrained.

'That is it, isn't it?' she says.

'Yes. Of course.'

'You know, if there is anything else we have guidance representatives here. If you need somebody to speak to?' she says.

'I don't need marriage counselling.'

'Oh no. It's for individuals who are in the process of separation or who are obtaining an absolution of marriage,' she says. 'Think of it as a form of mediation.'

'No, it's fine. Really. There's no need.'

'Well, if that's all?' she says.

'It's all just so final isn't it.'

I meant to keep this thought in my head but it slips from my mouth before I have the time to think.

'I guess I knew it was going to happen one day. I just assumed it would be *him* filing the papers to *me*.'

She doesn't respond to this, but her body language shows that she understands me. That there is something behind her eyes that suggests she too has felt the aching knowledge that she's made a mistake, done something wrong, and is now paying the ultimate price. In my case literally. These things cost thousands, unless concluded quickly. There's no reason why it shouldn't be. I only hope that nothing more effects Ollie, he's had such a restless summer. I don't think he could mentally cope with any more upheaval.

And then she just comes right out and says it. I wasn't expecting somebody in such a position of non-judgmental authority to be so forthright.

'Was there somebody else?' she says, holding my gaze. I feel she is doing so as if waiting for me to snap.

This is not a confessional. She is not a criminal barrister. This is a civil case, where neither party ever has to attend court.

'Perhaps you would like me to forward on some information regarding residency orders just in case,' she says.

I open my mouth but nothing will come out. Her words have anchored somewhere deep inside me and are burrowing beneath my skin. I feel as though if I move it will pierce me and then she will see the wounds I bear beneath my composed exterior.

And then it happens again. It's as though I can't stop myself. She really would be very good retraining in criminal law.

'There was some jealousy on his part. It became quite overbearing. We both decided to separate. It's been hard. Especially recently. I'm beginning to think that he might still hold a small flame for me.'

'You're sure you want to do this? You've taken the time to consider everything?' she says.

'Yes. I want to make this final. I want a divorce.'

She takes a few notes and then looks up at me with the same open expression she's been wearing throughout our conversation.

'Is there anything else you would like to discuss before I request the papers for you to sign?' she says, waving her notes between us like a fan.

'No, I think that's it.'

'Help yourself to some water, there is rather a lot of forms to read through. I'll fetch the papers from upstairs, and be with you in a few minutes,' she says, leaving the room and closing the door behind her.

No sooner has she left is there a knock on the door.

'Come in?'

A tall blonde woman who doesn't appear to be a clerk pops her head round the door and flicks back her hair before she speaks.

'Would you like a couple of biscuits. These things take a long time and it's almost lunch,' she says, smirking.

'Please.'

When she returns Mrs Beresford is standing behind

her with a thick pile of papers and a blue folder beneath her arm.

'Thank you Millie,' she says, taking the plate from her and leaving it on the table beside me.

'Help yourself,' she says, as Millie closes the door behind her with a wink. 'I'm a diabetic.'

I understand this to mean pig out on the lot, and so I do. These things always make me feel hungry. I stifle a yawn as Mrs Beresford explains what some of the legal terms mean and leafs through the sheets of paper, picking out the ones I have to read especially carefully before signing and handing them back to her.

When we're finished I look up at the clock on the wall behind me as Mrs Beresford takes the tray containing the empty plate and half filled water beaker from the table, and notice that it's almost twelve o'clock already.

'Grab yourself some lunch from the Costa across the road. They do a lovely cheese and caramelised onion toast,' she says, as I take the door from her hand and follow her back out into the reception area.

I nod goodbye to the receptionist who greeted me earlier, now seated behind the desk crushing a sandwich into her mouth, leaving lipstick prints on the bread. She waves to me as I shake Mrs Beresford's hand and walk out of the double glass doors into a surprisingly warm afternoon.

I pass the cafe as I turn the corner to collect the car, knowing I'm almost fifteen minutes late and the ticket has run out. One of the parking Gestapo appears waving a ready prepared ticket in his hand as I jump inside the car and reverse before he has the chance to apply the sticky pouch to the windscreen of my car. Parking inspectors are not the enemy, but they come close.

I leave the centre of the city in time to place a ready meal of macaroni cheese in the microwave and boil the kettle for a cup of tea, still feeling anxious over returning to the flat that less than a week ago some stranger was leafing through my things, having broken in. The flat feels violated.

When I'm done brooding I can't help but go over each page that I had to endure reading whilst signing my divorce papers this morning. I am now the petitioner. He is the respondent. The dissolution of our marriage is now in process. I wonder when he will be served the papers? The papers will be filed to the court this afternoon, and the summons and complaint must be served to him by post.

I don't know what his reaction is going to be but I can't see him being very pleased at the finality of my decision. Though of course it was initially both of us who decided that, for Ollie and ourselves it would be best to separate. I'm not sure Zack realises the true implications of our decision. Does he know that this is the end? That one of us should have applied for a divorce by now? Or was he intending for it to be me? Deliberately waiting for me to be the one to serve him so that he wouldn't appear to be the bad guy in all of this.

Well, I shall find out soon enough.

I have two hours to pass before I have to leave to collect Ollie from school so I log on to the chatline to pass the time and credit my account with enough funds to cover the added expenses I've now racked up by my decision to file for a divorce this morning. Who knew legal expenses were so, well, expensive?

HIM

It's too quiet here. There is not enough extraneous noise from the street. No police helicopters overhead. No airplanes heading away from or towards the airport. There are the occasional group of students heading down towards City Road where they've now redeveloped many of the three storey high houses and filled them with student lets now that most of the Afro-Caribbean shops have gone into administration. Just as many of the clothing shops in Cabot Circus have taken over from the ones in the centre of Broadmead. Some of the buildings of which remain empty several years on.

I look out of the window at a deep grey sky overlooking the hill where my house sits neatly back from the road, contained in shrubbery I have no intention of clearing away. Gardening is for the elderly folk. Retired and with no other commitments to absorb their time.

I don't mind decorating. I run my hand along the wall of the kitchen recently altered to a lemon white which brings out the shine of the white cupboards from the spotlights in the ceiling.

I drag a chair over to where I'll sit leafing through the newspaper at intervals between dishing up a microwave meal and thrusting dried out spaghetti onto a plate which will sit in my stomach far longer than is healthy. I open a bottle of wine I'd bought for the steak meal I was hoping to prepare for Elise, that I never got to make, when my eyes strike the familiar picture I have imprinted into my retinas.

Amy.

She sits on the edge of a walkway where a potted plant is visible to her left. Her right arm is draped around a white dog. Some kind of terrier. She looks into the camera with an infectious smile planted onto her face that doesn't look fake. She is happy there. Her home it says in the small print.

Her love of animals and regular visits to Cornwall for a seaside trip with her fiancé were broken when she disappeared one night on her way home from work. She told friends she was meeting somebody. It is believed that she never had the chance to get to her lover as CCTV footage shows her last movements to be between 5:15pm and 5:26pm on June 12th 2014. She was last seen wearing a duck egg coloured sweater and cream jeans. She was a known drug user with two convictions for shoplifting. She had a spell in prison for six weeks during the winter of 2013. Her parents are appealing for new information due to a spate of missing person cases being unsolved in recent months, even though the women often return home, unharmed, but refusing to tell police where they've been. Most recently Elise Fitzgerald and Anne Dixon who re-appeared within two months of being reported missing. Both have since remained drug-free.

At least there is some reprieve from the often dark subject matter in the media. Missing people almost always turn up one way or another. My girls have been given a new lease in which to lead their lives. I only hope they continue to do so wisely.

I fold the newspaper in half and feel the stomach-churning fear that often catapults me across the room to retch into the toilet bowl. But it doesn't come. Not today.

I pour the wine so that it froths and spills in tiny droplets which cascade from the rim of the glass. Mopping it up with a clean dishcloth left on the side of the sink.

I tossed the bag from the basement into the bin. Now that Elise has returned home I doubt anyone would be interested in leafing through the rubbish bins outside the house fronts searching for clues, so I've left it at the bottom of the bin, beneath several bags of unwanted clothes I thought wouldn't be fair to give away to a charity shop.

I sit back and take a sip of the wine. The bubbles fill my nostrils with the fizzy liquid and I cough, spluttering, and drop the dishcloth on the floor. When I bend down to pick it up I see a note that must have fallen from the table when I came through the kitchen earlier after depositing the bags in the bin. I bend forwards to pick it up, turning it over in my hand, and steadying myself on the table as I read it.

You are going to pay for what you did.
Keeping me here was wrong. I might be clean,
but that wasn't a choice you gave me. I'll be
coming back, and when I do I want assurance
that you won't ever do that to anyone again.

Elise appears to want to blackmail me. The only thing is she is aware that I don't have a lot of money, so what else could she want from me?

The long evenings draw out at such an unreasonable pace that I have to find many ways of keeping myself occupied.

I could complete the 1,000 piece jigsaw of the Bristol cathedral I began yesterday but my heart isn't in it tonight. Instead, I find myself calling the chatline to see if Claire is about. It's that time of the evening when children are being sent to bed after supper and mother's and father's throughout the United Kingdom are settling themselves down for the night to watch recorded programmes they are unable to watch while their children are awake or to log on to the chatline they use to work from while their children head into their bedrooms to sleep off yet another tiring day of schoolwork and playground games.

Being a child is fun. It's growing up, taking responsibility and maturing into an adult that's the difficult part. When all is said and done it doesn't get any easier once you are officially labelled an adult, you just have a lot more paperwork to complete, work to do, and people to please.

I pick up the phone and dial the number to speak with the busty, long-legged blonde with a size 38-24-28 figure, as advertised on her intro. What the numbers mean I've no idea, but Claire answers on the second ring.

'Hiya, Ewan. How are you today?' she says.

'Very well. I've just opened up a bottle of fizz. Would you like to join me?'

'Sure. I could do with a nice cold drink. What are we having?' she says.

I very much doubt that we're drinking the same thing, but I can hear her shuffling about, her footsteps padding into the kitchen where the carpet meets the linoleum. I can hear a fridge door being opened and the tell-tale sound of a bottle of wine being reopened. The sloshing sound of the liquid as it hits the glass. The bottle clanging against the shelf as she places it back inside the fridge, and then the sounds of her feet re-entering the living room where I imagine she has her feet up, seated on the left hand side of the grey velvet sofa, with her back against the armrest and a cushion placed on top of it to steady her neck. She sips quietly and then begins to tell me about her day.

'Do you call this work?'

'Yes and no,' she says. 'Yes I get paid, and I do have to log on for at least sixteen hours a week, but it doesn't feel like working. I can relax, open a bottle of wine and talk to some lovely people. Especially you, Ewan. You always make me laugh.'

I'm slightly offended by this. I don't deliberately make her chuckle- that cackle she's acquired from many years of having to feign happiness in an unpleasant marriage. I don't consider myself humorous at all. And I don't take kindly to being considered one of the many 'lovely people' she speaks to. But I'll let her comments pass. It isn't her fault. She doesn't realise how she comes across sometimes. I suppose we must all learn to change our ways at some point though.

'So why did you decide to join?'

I'm expecting a fictionalised account, but she actually sounds as though she is offering me a real glimpse into her sometimes depressing life.

'I was really struggling to pay the debts and then I saw this advert. One thing lead to another and, well, here we are,' she says.

'Would you ever consider meeting one of your callers?'

'For sex? No,' she says.

'That's not what I meant.'

'Oh, no. That's not allowed. I'll get kicked off the line. Besides, knowing my luck, I'll meet the one weirdo who locks women up in his basement for sadistic sex games.

So, no. I won't consider it,' she says.

That's a shame. I'd really like to meet her. She has such a kind spirit and a lovely voice. It would be good to know if the image I have of her inside my head is a match to the real thing. I wonder if the real Claire wears her shoulder length blonde hair down. And if her nails are really painted the pale rose and silver glitter she tells me they are.

'I'd love to know what you look like. If I sent you a text would you send me a photograph of your face. Just a portrait so that I can look at you while we speak?'

'We don't offer those services. Besides if they heard you reciting your private number to me I wouldn't be allowed to use the line,' she says.

'Why? We're adults.'

'Yes, but, you see-'

'I know. I know. It's against the rules. I'm actually not a rule-breaker myself. I just get the feeling that you are.'

'My manager says that if we swap numbers then we could call each other off the line. That way they wouldn't be making any money would they?' she says.

'What if we swapped email addresses instead?'

'I'd have to-'

'Create a new separate one so I wouldn't be able to search for your personal details?'

'I was going to say, I should ask my line manager, but perhaps it is safer for me to keep my job if I don't mention it. Besides these lines are listened in on occasionally for safety purposes. If they heard this conversation it would be my job on the line,' she says.

'No. I completely agree with you. It's a shame, but it could cost you your job. And by the sound of it you really can't afford to lose this stream of income. Have you contacted the Debt Advice Board or your local Citizen's Advice Bureau? It's free and they do all the leg-work for you.

'It's a three to six months wait here, and besides, as long as I'm careful I can pay everything off before Christmas,' she says.

'But it's only three months away now.'

'I know,' she says. 'I'll figure something out.'

HER

'But mummy, everyone else is going?' says Ollie, backing away from the door so that we can leave the house in record time- early by ten minutes for the first time in a year.

'I'm sorry darling, but I haven't got the money for this school trip on top of everything else.'

'I could help,' he says, nervously twisting his hands together.

'And how are you going to do that?'

'I could say something to daddy,' he says.

'No. It's nobody's business but mine. Besides, he hasn't got any spare money either. Anyway, you shouldn't be worrying yourself over this. You're too young. Now let's get going.'

We arrive at the crossroads to be met by a heavy stream of traffic. An ambulance is parked on the corner with its doors open ready to welcome its new guest. I turn the radio down in respect as we drive past it, turning left towards the school. I leave Ollie in the playground with Jacob and another boy around the same age.

It doesn't matter where they are, when Jacob is

around they always tend to huddle together as though plotting something. I only hope that for all of our sakes it isn't anything to do with money. Another bout of thefts from the school will most likely lead to a suspension this time, and I can't manage with Ollie at home for a couple of days.

When I get back to the flat I pull all of the letters that I've so far managed to ignore for the past six days from the drawer in the kitchen and take them into the living room, where I sit on the edge of the sofa sorting each notice into piles of importance. After a while it seems obvious that the ones in urgent need of being dealt with have passed their expected payment dates. The next pile contains letters that could be dealt with now if only I had the money to pay them.

Ollie's school trip is the least of my worries. It seems that unless I can make enough money to cover the necessary legal fees and minimum payments as well as food I'll have to miss the rent and vice versa. I can't afford it all.

I look up at the ceiling and take a deep lungful of air, hoping to cleanse myself of this never-ending tiresome chore of sorting through mail that I have no intention of paying from my measly wages. I place the *urgent* pile on top of the *do it now* pile and apply them to the bottom *doesn't matter* pile, resting them all on the coffee table beside the phone.

I'll start making calls to debtors after I've made myself a slice of toast and logged on to the chatline for an hour.

I'm sitting with the phone in my hand and a fresh, hot cup of tea beside me on the table. I look over my right shoulder when I feel pins and needles shooting down my arm. That's when I see them. They flit past the glass door, blocking out the light so that their shadows fall on the carpeted floor of the living room in front of me.

131

I don't need to get up and look. I know it's the same men who were following me before we went away. I know because they've been here every morning since we came back. They hover outside for a while before knocking. Their insistent banging continues for almost twenty minutes. Usually, I'm in the kitchen so I can take the back door out and hide in the garage. But they'll see me tip-toeing down the hallway if I move so I remain as still as prey, hoping they don't walk across the small piece of lawn at the front, holding a hand above their head to examine inside the window, searching for movement.

They must know I work from home. How else could they know when to call? It's too much of a coincidence that every time they come here I'm at home, whatever the time of day. I'm only glad that Ollie is not here. It will only frighten him again.

The police never asked me for a statement about the burglary. I had expected to hear from them by now, but Zack assures me that he's told them everything. How they were able to gain access through the front door without anyone seeing them enter the flat. How they didn't break anything, including the door, and that nothing appears to have been taken.

I've searched the flat several times, going through cupboards and boxes hoping to find something that they dropped or misplaced. Evidence such as a hair or a receipt that would indicate who it was that managed to break into a property in broad daylight, but I haven't found anything. It's as if they were looking for something they were unable to find. Something of such importance that whoever was credited with the job was skilled and knew how to enter a property without leaving a trace.

I meant to call them yesterday but decided against it. Besides the police must have been and searched for fingerprints as soon as they were called because Zack has tidied everything away. He even took the time to clear the bedrooms of the boxes I still hadn't bothered to throw out. There were seventeen of them in total, lined up against the wall of both mine and Ollie's bedroom. Zack replaced the lock on the front door, or the police did, because he was here when we arrived home. He was sat in his car as I turned the corner. He got out and handed me a new set of keys and he helped us haul the bags out of the car, along with some souvenirs we'd picked up in Paris. He didn't stay for lunch though I invited him too- for Ollie's sake more than mine. I haven't heard from him since. I expect he's already received the divorce papers and is now sat mulling over them.

When the shadows of the men move back, I know that they've stepped away from the door and are about to leave so I jump up from the sofa and run through the hall towards the kitchen, hoping to escape through the back door, but as I turn the letterbox lifts up and I catch one of the men smiling up at me as I stall in front of the washing machine.

'Mrs Donoghue, we have permission from the high court to obtain money from you or to seize goods. May we come in?' he says.

I stand there with the full realisation over what I've been desperately trying to bury my head from for the past three months.

'There's nothing for you to take. I was burgled while away . . . visiting a dying relative. They've taken everything.'

'That isn't strictly true is it Mrs Donoghue. Your husband-'

'He's not my husband. Not any more. And I'm no longer Mrs Donoghue.'

The man stands upright and backs away from the

door while the slimmer one, the one I suspect is the one responsible for following me to the school and back, steps forward, crouches down and peers through the letterbox, offering me a sympathetic bow.

'Claire, we have one hour to do this, well fifty minutes now. If we can't gain access after that we will have to call the police. I can see that you're distressed. You're perfectly within your right to be upset, but this is out of our hands,' he says. And to prove his point I can see the other man behind him raise his hands in the air through the mottled glass.

The half-glazed front door is the only thing at this moment preventing them from taking everything I own from the flat, including Ollie's bedroom furniture.

'Have you got anyone you can borrow a thousand pounds from. That would enable you some more time to find the rest,' he says.

'No. I don't have anyone. Since I separated from my husband, my son's father, I've lost my home, my car and if you take my laptop I'll lose my job.'

'We understand, Claire. We really do. But we don't want a conviction of obstructing the law on top of that do we?' he says.

'You're not the law.'

'No. But we're working for the courts. We'll have to call them soon if you don't let us in,' he says.

What are my options, really? Let them in and face the consequences, praying they don't realise that the car parked outside on the drive is mine too? Run into the shed and hide the laptop? I can't do that now I've told them I own one can I?

A small part of me still believes that there is hope. That I could find a way out of this if I'm able to bide my time.

Think Claire. Think.

'Can you give me an hour?'

He turns his head and repeats my question to his colleague who I can see from here is shaking his head.

'I'm sorry. That's not possible. Every time we return it's adding further fees to your account,' he says.

The rebellious part of me refuses to budge from the kitchen doorway. The logical, mature part acknowledges that this will only make it worse. It's like a fight between my conscience and my inner teenager. I want to run, hide, throw shoes at them, do anything but face up to this and let them into my home to take away all that I own. I equally want to just let them in and get on with it. I know I won't win, but I'm determined to try.

'Let me see your papers.'

I run over to the front door and place my hand in front of the letterbox waiting for them to hand the envelope to me. I unfold the signed, stamped and sealed documents and see that I may have found a small reprieve.

'It's null and void.'

The slimmer one sighs as though he's heard this a hundred times too many this week.

'I assure you it's very real and-'

'It's dated tomorrow. You'll have to come back tomorrow.'

I pass it back to him through the letterbox and watch as he gazes down at the papers in his hand, shuffling them towards his friend who nods in agreement before he crouches down and looks at me through the narrow opening of the letterbox in the door.

'Right you are. We'll be back tomorrow. Sorry to have bothered you, Claire. I do hope you will be more accommodating when we return,' he says.

'Oh, I will be prepared.'

I watch them waltz down the path and back out onto the road, leaning against the wall and waiting for the hammering in my heart to slow before I settle back down on the sofa, hoping to finally be able to begin work.

They didn't mention the car. The one I bought from our old neighbour's son who owns a garage in one of the backstreets on the way down Kellaway Avenue. I managed to knock off two hundred pounds from it as it'll need some work doing to it before its next MOT.

I paid £250 for it. The problem is, it's still in his name. I haven't dared to send the V5 off yet for the log-book in case any of my debtors check with DVLA if I own a car. It's technically off-road on the driveway- at least, I hope that's how they'll see it.

My first call is from an elderly gentleman who likes to be whipped by his mistress, who's currently away on an all expenses paid trip around the globe; trotting around, spending his money with her best friend. I often wonder if these men make up just as much of a story as I do on these lines.

My second call is from Ewan. And I must admit his offer seems tempting.

'I'm not asking a lot am I?' he says. 'Just think about it.'

'There's nothing to think about. I can't.'

'I'm offering you a lifeline here,' he says. 'The balls in your court, but take some time to think about it.'

Time's not on my side.

'I can't meet you, and I can't email you. I told you, I don't have any internet at the moment.'

This is another white lie to add to the others I've been forced to create since becoming a fully-fledged single mother.

'The shed is clean and I've planted three seedlings in the ground where Remmington Road sits at the bottom of Redland hill,' he says.

'What?'

'I said . . .'

'Oh, okay. I get it.'

'You get my little joke, do you?' he says.

'Yes. I'm not far off myself actually.'

And there it is. I have his address implanted in my mind, as he'd hoped it would be. Does he honestly think I'll turn up on his doorstep and go through with this plan of his? Quite possibly. He must be lonely, and not very good looking to be using this line.

'Check out Gumtree for that item we were discussing. It's listed beneath antique furniture. Eighth down from the list,' he says.

'Right. Okay.'

I don't want to continue this conversation but I haven't managed to get in many hours this week and I need all the money I can get. Holding him on the line for as long as possible is my goal though the conversation is leading in all kinds of directions I'm not completely comfortable with. And to top it off, I'm actually beginning to grow curious over what he looks like. That is if he's being truthful with me. He might be a psychopath stalker who's stealing men's photographs and using them to advertise old mirrors in order to get vulnerable women like me to visit his house.

'So, how are you anyway?' he says, turning the conversation away from his invitation to meet with him.

'My furniture is being repossessed tomorrow, and I'm not sure what to do.'

'It's that bad, huh?' he says.

'Yes,' I stifle a laugh.

'Offer still stands. I'd better go, I have some ironing to do,' he says.

'You do your own ironing?'

'It's not so unusual is it?' he says.

I can't remember a time when Zack helped me with anything around the house. 'Woman's work,' he used to say.

'Well, it's been a pleasure speaking to you, as usual

Ewan. Take care, and I'll speak to you soon.'

'Don't forget what I said, mind,' he says.

'I won't.'

I hang up the phone, slightly dazed. I'm wondering how I've come to be propositioned in such a fashion by a complete stranger when I couldn't even keep my own husband's interest during the final year of our marriage.

I log off the chatline, having earned enough for some petrol, hoping it will cover the entire week as I need to work extra hard in building some decent sales next week if I'm to afford Christmas this year. I place the receiver back down into its sleeve and ignore the post being dropped through the letterbox, slamming down hard onto the mat, where it will stay until I figure something out.

To while away the next hour before having to leave to pick Ollie up from school I flip open the laptop, finding myself instantly drawn to discover if Ewan has been telling me the truth.

There it is, in black and white; a photograph of a very, old, beautifully engraved mirror with a description beneath detailing its various registered owners throughout the years. One of which is Ewan Carter of number 3 Remmington Road, Redland, Bristol.

I can see that beside the advert is a mobile number, probably one of those given by the site to hide the identity of your phone. Then again, it might be real. Beneath the mobile number is an email address, which when I check it out appears listed on a reviewing website for coastal path walks. Beneath his review is a photograph showing him standing on the seafront of Clevedon with a fishing rod in his hand, and a khaki green bag containing what I believe are maggots and other disgusting equipment for the keen fisherman.

His smile is wide, his eyes bright and alert. Thick stubble covers his face making him appear older than he actually is. Forty-two isn't past my age range for a potential suitor, but it is ten years more than my own age. And he isn't the type of man I'd usually go for. If I was at all interested, that is.

HIM

Sometimes the lies we tell ourselves protect us. Sometimes they lead to us disclosing more of ourselves than we'd planned to. This is one of those moments.

I'm sitting in front of the screen staring at the photograph that I found in my inbox this morning. I rarely check my emails but I was hopeful that she had sent me one back. It seemed only fair to reciprocate. After all I've offered her a way out. Something I doubt anybody else would do, now that she's exhausted all other possible avenues in seeking a solution to end this downward spiral of debt.

The internet is a wonderful thing, but it enables us to never be fully private anymore. There are no secrets these days. Only ways to confirm others suspicions of us. Our online personas both trap us and label us as either trustworthy or dishonest. I hope I fall into the former description.

Her blonde hair falls around her face. She has a clear complexion and wide blue eyes, slightly lowered to stop the flash of the camera from causing her to squint. She wears a lilac long-sleeved top and her face is turned slightly to the side as though there is somebody behind her telling her to smile. Her lips are slightly pursed to cover a small overlapping of her two front teeth. She looks happy and confident. Something I look for in a woman.

She cannot hide the obvious nurturing side to her personality though, for I can just make out the first two letters of a pendant worn on a thin gold chain around her neck, that the camera angle almost disguises. It reads: Mum. A three letter word that shows how loved she is.

If she really is in trouble then I'd like to believe I have found a way out for her that doesn't require anything illegal, dangerous or worse than bailiff action. It won't stop them visiting her today, but it might enable her to get her stuff back or if she wants to- to buy new. Once her debts are cleared she'll see that this was a one-time thing that she needed to do because she was strapped for cash and in trouble. She wouldn't have to think about it again.

The idea of not being able to see her after this saddens me, but if she does go through with it then, at least I will have been able to spend some time with her. I will have gotten to know her, and perhaps altered her perception of the morality of such a proposition.

I pick up the phone and dial, hoping she's received my email and is sat waiting for me, looking forward to hearing my voice just as much as I am of hers. She answers after several rings when I'm half-expecting her not to.

'Claire, it's me. You look pretty.'

'Thank you, Ewan,' she says, chuckling.

'I can see that you're not offended.'

'No. Not at all. I find it quite flattering,' she says.

'What do you think about the advert?'

'Very pleasing. Do you work out?' she says.

'Not any more. There's no need. I have builder's

bones.'

I'm sure I can hear her smile at the other end of the line.

'Did you read it?'

'Yes, Ewan. I did,' she says, a note of tiredness in her voice from, I suspect, the act of dropping in one-liners of hidden metaphor to break up the sentences of our conversation.

She seems to take much longer to answer me now that she's playing along.

'What do you think?'

'The picture is very nice,' she says.

'And the invitation. Are you going to visit?'

Me I mean. Is she going to accept my invitation to come and visit me?

'It's not possible this weekend,' she says, rather quickly.

'Next?'

'I'm not sure. I'll have to get back to them,' she says.

I can hear the distraction in her voice.

'Is there somebody there with you?'

'Oh, no. Just the door. Will you have to go in a minute?' she says, knowing full well that it's her who has to end the call.

I can hear banging and raised voices.

'I have to go. But before I do, write these numbers down-'

'I haven't got a-'

'Grab a pen.'

I can hear rustling and somebody knocking the hell out of the door in the background.

'Right,' she says.

'One, five, zero, nine, five, six, seven, six, eight, one, two, eight, one, zero, two, five. The 18th of August 2014 and the 18th of August 2018. Backstreet, one, two, four. Have you got it?'

'You don't honestly expect me to pay using-'

'A gift. Speak to you later.'

I hang up the phone knowing that she might still need some convincing.

It was last night as I sat back watching re-runs of a comedy series on UK Gold that I ran through what to say to her over and again in my head until I finally wrote the email, sending it to her just before midnight. I offered to pay the debts- all of them, but in return, I wanted to meet her face-to-face. I wanted to check that she was real. That I had been feeling kindness towards this woman for weeks because she was genuinely in need of somebody to look after her, to protect her, and cherish her.

I'm not deluded. I know it isn't lust or indeed love that fills my heart with pleasure every time we speak. It's so much less complicated than that. It's a connection of sorts but not in the way a psychologist would interpret it. I'm not infatuated with her. I care for her.

I offered her one night with me in exchange for three thousand pounds. Enough to clear her debts, but not enough to leave her complacent. I'm not going to offer her a regular income. I don't want her to feel pressured. Only now I assume she will.

I assume that whoever was banging the hell out of her door was some kind of enforcement officer. If she gives him my debit card number and remembered to note down the start and expiry date as well as the last three digits of the code at the back of the card then she will have paid off the most pressing amount. We can work on the rest later.

I want to help her to help herself. There's a fine line between doing something for somebody to ease the pressure of a problem and being screwed over. It would be far too easy to say that I'm preying on her vulnerabilities in order to pressurise her into sleeping with me. Far lesser crimes have been committed. But that is not my intention. I want her to want to be with me. I want her to leave the rocky path behind and focus on her future with her son. If that means offering her enough money to sort herself out for a bit, in exchange of a date then so be it. I wouldn't have expected her to think I wanted nothing for it. Yet I don't want her thinking I'm a pervert or worse, taking the money and never answering my calls again either.

While I'm thinking all this the phone begins to ring.

I pick it up to be met with the raspy breaths of somebody who's been crying and moving things around at the same time.

This is the first conversation we've shared that hasn't cost me thirty-six pence a minute. It's also the first time we can speak without using our secret code.

'You didn't pay them did you?'

'I can't take your money,' she says, in obvious despair.

'Who are these people anyway?'

'Amira and Sons or something. They were here a couple of weeks ago and then they sent these men from the high court and now they're taking the furniture.'

'What have they taken, Claire?'

'Everything,' she says.

I can hear her slump down onto the floor of the living room.

I stand up and begin pacing. The doorbell chimes twice. I peer out of the curtain, half-drawn to cloud out the rain that falls in tiny splatters against the backdrop of a dark grey sky.

A woman stands, almost hidden from view by the protruding bricks that disfigure these 1930's houses. They sit below each windowsill; a constant reminder that architecture is no place for a man wanting a view of whoever is calling on him in the middle of the afternoon.

The woman holds out her hand to press the bell once

more and I freeze when I see that she wears the same beige leather jacket that Elise wore when she arrived here several weeks ago now.

It isn't her. It can't be.

The threatening note was written in haste. Her anger and resentment was burning a hole through the single page she used to spread her inky fingers on. She didn't mean it, did she?

She's gone now. But it won't be long before she comes back, and when she does I had better be prepared. In the mean time, I have more pressing concerns.

I turn the laptop towards me and the screen instantly brightens when I plug in the charger. I type in the name of the debt collection company that Claire gave me earlier and hope that when I get through to them they believe me.

'Amira and Son collection services, Marnie speaking, how can I help you?' says the woman who answers.

'I'd like to make a payment. My wife has just had her belongings taken.'

I hang up once I've given her my card details. She was obviously not expecting such a fast turn-around. People don't tend to respond after their things have been taken with kind words and a pay-off. I only hope that when they call her to make arrangements for her things to be collected from wherever it is they keep them, that she appreciates I wasn't joking.

I book a table at a moderately priced all-you-can-eat at the top of Park Street. Somewhere she can pick and choose whatever food takes her fancy. I wait beside the phone for her to call back. Expecting admonishment for making the decision to pay her debts regardless of the outcome. She doesn't call, and so, realising that she's probably left for the school-run already, I make my way into the kitchen to prepare dinner.

I must eat something healthy today. I have to stop relying on ready-meals to get me through the empty evenings.

I open the back door to allow a little air into the stuffy kitchen that seems to attract the heat and smells of every other room in the house. The lingering atmosphere containing the crisp smell of dried leaves and autumn rain is preferable to yesterday's dinner and a slowly rotting bin bag.

I'm about to put the half-filled sack of potatoes in front of the back door to keep it open so that I can throw the bin bag in the refuse outside when I see Elise walking away from the hedgerows that separate the back garden from the lane.

How long she's been out there I couldn't say, but it was long enough for her to leave muddied footprints along the path towards the gate where she exited, following the lane out onto the road.

HER

I put the phone down in disbelief.

How could I have been so stupid? Now I owe him. What the hell was I thinking? Of course, he was asking for the name of the company for a reason but at the time, I didn't twig onto it. What have I done?

Ollie stands beside me, visibly hurt that yet another planned trip with the school is unaffordable to us.

'Can't you tell Mrs Pritchard that you'll pay her back?' he says.

'No, Ollie. Not now. Let's talk about this in the car. We're late.'

He follows me out with his face drawn down, staring at the ground beneath his feet. My mobile phone begins to ring just as I'm about to close the door. I decide against answering it now, almost knowing who it is and what they want. Avoidance is the best strategy at this point, and it seems to be something that I'm very good at.

We arrive just as the caretaker is about to close the gates, forcing me to enter the school through reception with an excuse as usual, but we make it past him in time for registration. I watch as Ollie bundles his way into the building with his rucksack on his back and a packed lunch box my mother bought him, hanging from his fingers. I skip through the reception area where a couple of the other mums- the usual late arrivals, stand waiting to sign their children in.

It's one of those days where even if I didn't receive the call this morning telling me that the stranger I've been speaking to on the chatline had paid my largest debt off- something would still go wrong.

I have to find a way of collecting my belongings from the storage centre in the council depot, not far from where my car had been taken, when I managed to accidentally park on double yellow lines. I should really have appealed the case as those lines were so faint you'd need a magnifying glass to notice them, but at the time I didn't have the energy or the inclination for another debate to add to everything else.

I still haven't heard from Zack, but I don't suppose I'd want to contact my wife just a couple of days after she'd filed for a divorce either. Still, he could have been adult about it, called to tell me that he'd received the papers or written to me.

Though it's probably for the best that he hasn't, it wouldn't do either of us any good, and Ollie has suffered enough under the wings of our silent arguments and the discordant atmosphere that surrounds such events. It's better he doesn't know. Not yet anyway. At least not until it's all finalised and the signed copies of the decree absolute have been sent to us both. The certificate which will sit in a drawer somewhere, probably the same one as our marriage certificate, gathering dust, mainly ignored; a reminder that closure is not an ending, but the beginning to another life.

As Mrs Beresford, my solicitor said, 'sometimes a necessary denouement to a perfect life means making sacrifices you would never have otherwise considered.'

I twist the meaning of those words to enable me to complete the next task I've been hoping to put aside until I'm in a better frame of mind.

I ought to be grateful to Ewan for helping me out. He doesn't know me. I could be anyone. But something niggles in the back of my mind. Something my father once told me, 'nobody does anything for nothing.' Ewan will want something in return, and I already know what that is.

Ewan's invitation was simple. One night with him for enough money to pay off all of my debts. I'm sure he's prepared to offer me more money and is expecting my time in return. Though I very much doubt that it is my time he really wants.

I should've known something like this would happen. It's not every day that you meet somebody willing to go that extra mile for you, to keep you and your child fed and clothed. It's rare for them not to want something of you, that you feel obliged to give.

As I've said before, prostitution is the oldest profession in the world, and I'm about to make the ultimate sacrifice to pay Ewan back for his good deeds. If only there was something else he wanted. If only I had anything else to give.

This time, I answer the phone. I can't put it off any longer.

'Claire, did they call you? Did they tell you?' he says.

'Yes. I don't know what to say.'

'No need to say anything is there? I'm only glad that I could help,' he says.

'How am I supposed to pay you back? I don't have any money.'

'Like I said. Your time. Your company. Just to see your sweet smile. That is all I require in compensation.'

'I don't know if I can do that. I don't know you.'

'You already know that I'm one of the good guys. I'm not asking for anything you are uncomfortable with,' he says.

'When you say 'company' you do mean sex, right?'

'I don't want you to feel pressured into doing this. I want you to enjoy spending time with me. I want to see you Claire. Your photograph cannot possibly give you justice. It is the real thing I want,' he says.

'I have to think about this. I need time. This isn't something I ever thought I'd do.'

'You're unsure. Of course you are. That is perfectly reasonable. Perhaps you should sleep on it,' he says.

'It's just not the kind of proposition I've had to consider before.'

'I understand. Call me tomorrow, please,' he says.

Do I detect a slight bitterness to his voice?

'I have to go now, Claire. But you will consider this, yes?' he says, his voice losing its calm.

'I will. I'll call you tomorrow.

'Okay. Goodbye,' he says, ending the call before I have the chance to reply.

Something was distracting him. I have a certain knack now, since joining the chatline, of picking up on every sound and feeling. I take more notice of my own voice. The way I speak, the tone, the words I use, are all important facets to entertaining my clients.

There was something underlying my own discomfort though. The thought, however unlikely, that somebody would find out. That it would later be used against me. A fear I guess that the image others have of me would be of a desperate woman, a highly sexually charged mother who chose to have sex with a complete stranger for money.

If anyone discovered our secret I would surely be ripped apart. Not least of all by Zack, who already believes me to have been unfaithful towards the end of

150

our marriage. Though what reason he has for this idea I can't fathom.

I never once looked the other way while we were together. Even now I can't imagine being with anyone else. Certainly not somebody I barely know. Definitely not Ewan.

Later as me and Ollie dine on the sofa, watching children's programmes, we meet a similar conclusion to retire to bed for an early night. Without being asked, he places his empty plate into the sink and wanders towards his bedroom.

This would normally afford me the time to log on to the chatline but my heart's not in it tonight. Feigning orgasms is one thing, but acting interested in all of the callers private lives is something I feel unable to do. I don't think it would be right to pretend to listen whilst conjuring up some excuse not to repay Ewan for what he's done for me.

I paid a man with a van to drop the furniture off earlier. The only thing I haven't bothered to plug in is the cooker. I can't fathom how to apply the leads into each socket without blowing myself up so I bought us fish and chips from Filton Avenue on the way back from the park.

I hear Ollie yawn though it's barely seven o'clock. I leave the room to find him dressed in his pyjamas, curled up beneath his quilt. He sniffles and moves away from me as I perch myself on the edge of his bed, stroking my hand through the fair hair behind his ears.

'I think you've caught a cold. Why don't I bring you in a nice cup of hot chocolate?'

'I'm not thirsty, mummy. Just tired,' he says, turning around, burrowing his head inside the pillow.

I watch him fall asleep and leave the room quietly,

entering the living room to return to my seat.

Looking down at my mobile phone resting on the table in front of me which is flashing to let me know that I have a new message, I start to realise how far from the real world I've become since acclimatising myself to living like a hermit.

I really need to get out more. I can't remember the last time I went out with friends. The last time my mother babysat Ollie. I should really give her a call. Let her know that I'm still alive.

I pick the phone up and check the message before dialing her number.

Got the papers this morning. We should talk.
Zack.

It's odd not having an *x* applied to the end of a message from him. It's just something that we've always done. On notes, letters, and text messages. There is no kiss. There is no emotion in his words either. But that doesn't stop me from trying to read between the lines. Is he accepting of this or angry?

I call him first before I change my mind. I can't keep putting things down to chance, blaming the universe for everything that comes my way. And, I'm not going to sit here and talk to my mother about my decision to end a 'perfectly good relationship because I'm having doubts or going through an identity crisis,' as she likes to word it, without getting it over with and speaking to him first.

No, I'd much rather deal with the pressing issue of our divorce before I speak to my mother. Get it over and done with, then we can move on. We have the rest of our lives to live. There isn't time for regrets. Life is short. Too short to allow the past to get in the way of building a solid, happy future.

'Zack, it's me. You wanted to talk.'

'It's a big decision, Claire. Are you sure you're up for it?' he says.

What's that supposed to mean?

'It's for the best. Don't you think?'

'Shouldn't we have at least discussed it first? It's not like I've ever hurt you. We're adults. It's about time we behaved like them. I'm willing to put all this aside if you are. Can't we at least talk about this first?' he says.

'What is there to talk about?'

'Ollie. What about him? Have you considered how this is going to affect him at all? And us, how is this going to look? The most stable couple amongst our friends unable to live together, then divorcing . . . it's too much, Claire. It's all too soon. You need to think about this before jumping straight down *that* road.'

'I have thought about it Zack. I've thought of nothing else. Don't you think it's time to do this?'

'I don't understand though. We were happy weren't we? We were meant to grow old together? I don't want you regretting this decision in five years time when you realise what you've lost,' he says.

'I'm not losing anything, Zack. Neither are you. We're still parents. Ollie is both of our responsibility. We're just making this easier for us both. Do you know how hard it was for me to leave with Ollie and to see my married name on that passport?'

'Do you realise how difficult it is for me to explain your absence every time somebody calls around?'

'What do you mean? You haven't told anyone?'

'You know what my mother's like. She'll throw a fit if she knew you'd taken Ollie and left. I did it for you,' he says.

'Zack. What are you thinking? We're separated, surely they know I'm not coming back?'

'Well, that's for you to decide isn't it.'

'I've made my decision. In fact I made my decision

six months ago. Don't make this any harder for me, Zack.'

'You know what's hard?' he says. 'Knowing my wife, the mother of my child, doesn't feel the same way about me as I do her.'

'You know it isn't like that. You made it so . . . awkward. It was hard living under the same roof, sleeping in separate beds when all along you thought that I-'

'I know there was somebody else, Claire. But that's okay. I forgive you. I just thought we could put it all behind us. Let me know what you think, yeah?' he says.

'About what?'

'About coming back. You need to come home, Claire. Stop this nonsense now and pack up your things. Bring Ollie back to where he belongs. I'm not sure how much longer I can wait for you,' he says.

'And what about Amanda?'

'Never mind her. I told you it's over. I ended it. I realised what a mistake it was. It was too soon. It's you I want. We're still married, Claire. I still love you. I've never stopped loving you,' he says.

'You're making this too difficult.'

'No, Claire. *You're* making this harder than it needs to be. Just come over. We can work it out. It doesn't have to end this way. Besides you're hardly fit to live alone,' he says.

'What is that supposed to mean?'

Where is he going with all this?

'Next time your flat gets broken into I might not be around. What if Ollie was there with you? Next time you might not be so lucky,' he says, immediately regretting it when I ask him about the police.

'When are they coming to take my statement? It's been almost a week now Zack, and-'

'I've already done it. I gave them a statement when

154

the locksmith came to fix the door,' he says.

'You never told me.'

'I did. I told you I'd sort everything out,' he says.

'Yes, but I didn't think that meant I didn't need to give a statement.'

'You were on holiday. They can't take witness statements from people who weren't present at the time of the incident,' he says. 'I paid for the door to get fixed from my own pocket. I might not be able to do it again so you need to take care of your home. Look after yourself better. If anything happened to you or Ollie then-'

'It won't. I'd protect him with my life. I would never let anything happen to our son, you know that.'

'What if you couldn't save him. What if there was nothing you could do? What if . . .'

'There won't be a next time, Zack. It's not exactly a bad neighbourhood. It was an opportunist. A moment of madness from an impulsive teenager. I doubt it will happen again.'

'Is that what you've told yourself? Claire, these people, whoever they were, were professionals. There wasn't a mark on the door. Whoever it was, was looking for something. They knew you weren't there. They chose their moment carefully,' he says.

'You don't know that. How can you say there was more than one of them. Anyone could have done it.'

'Not everyone can break into and enter a home without being seen, leave with nothing and leave no trace that they were even there,' he says.

'But you said they left a mess. You said they wouldn't come back.'

'Of course, I had to tidy up. You better hope they don't come back. I can't have Ollie living somewhere like that,' he says.

'That's not your concern though is it? I'm not your

concern.'

'He's my son, Claire. I think it is,' he says.

'I mean, where I live is none of your business.'

'Well, we'll leave that for the courts to decide,' he says.

'What do you mean?'

'You didn't think I was just going to let him go too, did you?' he says. 'Like I said, you have a decision to make.'

'You don't have to be like this.'

'You're right, I don't,' he says. 'I've got to go now. Let me know your decision soon. If I have to find a solicitor I'd rather know sooner rather than later.'

I hang up the phone before he does.

My head begins to throb with the impending migraine I seem to get only when I have too many things on my mind. I have two important decisions to make. But I know my answer to both of them. I'm just not sure how I'm going to tell Ewan and Zack my answers. Or at what cost such huge choices are going to bring to mine and Ollie's future.

HIM

She was working the lines last night. It doesn't bother me that she wishes to continue such artificial conversation as much as it upsets me that she believes she still has a need for such work. I've tried to convince her to give it up several times during our conversations over the last three days but to no avail.

I don't tell her that I know when she's logged in. It wouldn't be right. She might think I'm stalking her, and that wouldn't do. She needs to feel empowered. I would never try to take her independence away. She is a mother, and a mother's instinct is something that cannot be disturbed.

When she asked me if I was into any kind of fetishes, if I enjoyed some kind of kink that I was unable to get elsewhere, I told her the truth. It is up to her now whether or not she believes me. I told her to take as much time as she needed, but that I had already, based on our most recent conversation, bought the food, and it wouldn't last long. Fresh meat and vegetables never do.

I finish work early hoping to prepare the house so that it appears more hospitable. I didn't really worry so much about that when Elise was here, or Amy for that matter. They weren't going to be worrying over the interior designs of a house they were never going to be spending time in.

I tried to make the basement appear presentable, but having to consider all possibilities of breaking down, attempted suicide, and accidents, I was forced to decorate the place as minimally as possible. There was no room for fancy bedding and ornaments: both potential weapons. One for hanging and the other for attacking me with. With Claire, it is going to be different.

I've sautéed the chicken and roasted vegetables with duck fat potatoes. Preparing a meal that I know she'll like. I make the gravy from the chicken stock like my mother used to do, and sift the greens so that no residues of water are left to cause the cheese sauce to thin and give the appearance of an amateur chef attempting to woo an attractive woman with food in order to lure her to his bed.

I took the time to ask Claire as much about her likes and dislikes as possible this morning, as I ran around the market searching for the best priced, but nicest looking ingredients I could find. She spoke in a hushed voice as though convinced that somebody was listening to her.

I think her main priorities remain in my sexual preferences rather than the food we are going to be eating. I've tried to reassure her that I'm not going to make her do anything that she doesn't want to, but I have the distinct impression that she's going to come armed with a knife in her handbag, just in case.

Now I sit beside the unlit fireplace with a glass of white wine in my hand, waiting for her to arrive.

HER

I'm running every possible conclusion over and over through my head as I leave the car and make my way to the first of my customer's houses.

This morning I have around thirty orders to deliver and two hundred catalogues to drop off. I'm trying to keep my thoughts focused on the task but when I look up and catch Mr Rogers giving me the same look that Ollie's teacher gave me this morning I'm starting to realise I need to get a grip.

'You alright love?' he says, placing his trembling hand over my shoulder in a gesture of support.

'Yes. I've got a bit of a headache, that's all.'

He takes his bag of products and shakes his head when I offer him the change from a twenty-pound note.

'Get yourself a packet of paracetamol with it,' he says.

I love the way the older generation think that all problems can be solved with a backbone or a painkiller.

I continue the morning round and head back to the car, hoping for a late lunch when my phone rings from the pocket of my fleece.

'So, are you up for meeting me tomorrow evening? I

thought we could talk about this. You've had plenty of time to make a decision. I'm offering you the chance to have your say, no strings,' says Zack, on the other end of the line.

It seems as though he's losing patience. As if he's been running over what to say when I eventually answer one of his incessant calls, for hours. The idea to have a polite conversation with me has now faded, leaving annoyance and irritation in its place.

'I don't know. What time were you thinking?'

'About seven. My mother said she'll have Ollie over to her house. It'll give you a breather too. It can't be easy doing everything on your own,' he says.

I'm slightly irritated by his sudden interest in my feelings. Since when did he care how I was? I've spent the past ten years, giving up a career for self-employment, coping on minimum wage jobs to support the family I have to also cook and clean for. Now he wants to show me kindness, support, and consideration.

'Okay. I'll call you to confirm tomorrow.'

'Great. I'll meet you at mine?' he says, sounding brighter. Then 'are you okay? You sound distracted,' he says.

'I'm working.'

'Oh, right,' he says. 'So, I'll see you tomorrow.' His voice more elevated as the conversation has progressed.

'Sure.'

I place the phone back inside my pocket, hoping that the rain won't soak me through before I find the keys. They were in my pocket, alongside the phone. How can they not be here? I'm sure I'd have heard them fall if I'd have dropped them when I was distracted by the phone call. Wouldn't I? Grabbing the final holdall of catalogues up from the front seat. But then how could they end up back inside the locked car? I don't really have time to think about this any longer. I run back to my last customer's house: Mr and Mrs Dawson and hope they have a spare screwdriver.

It's an old shitty car and I doubt it'll take more than a few jabs of the keyhole to twist it round and force the mechanism inside to free. When I do try though it doesn't budge. I consider pulling the windscreen wiper back, forcing the wiper blade free of its little nook and jarring it down hard through the window seal until I hear a click as I'd seen on a TV programme, but decide to smash the window with the screwdriver instead. Prising the door open, ensuring not to cut myself on the exposed glass protruding from the window seal, I jump inside and bring my arm back towards the seat to grab the keys.

It's a good job I didn't have to hotwire the damn thing too. I've never been any good with electricity. Almost killing myself once as a student, hammering a plug into the socket, having forgotten to secure the back to it properly. I ended up across the floor in a flash of light, the wooden hammer gripped tightly in my hand. My housemates told me later that my face was as white as my knuckles as we spooned spaghetti carbonara into our mouths; living off pasta being one of the parts of student life I won't ever miss.

I slam the door shut behind me and drive away, all the while the same nagging feeling of what I'm going to do later building and rising inside my chest and into my throat; anticipation or fear? Excitement or apprehension? I'm not sure.

I watch the shadow moving behind the glass for a few more minutes before daring myself to leave the car and walk up the path towards the red painted wooden front door.

The garden looks slightly overgrown. Dried out flowers are cascading from two flowerpots sat at either end of the short walkway. Red bricks cover the front entrance where a porch once stood. The turrets of which are still mounted on the cream painted wall. It's a 1930's house with a shed on the side that looks distressed and unloved.

As I walk towards the house I can see that the property has the impression of a woman's touch, noticing the net curtains covering the windows.

It's not too late to back out. I could offer him another way to repay his kindness without the need of spending an entire night with him. Maybe he knows this too. Perhaps he's testing me to see if I'll go through with it. I don't know yet if I will, but I raise my hand to knock on the door anyway.

If he was a psychopath I'm sure I'd have felt the signs by now. I read a report online once that suggested women are more likely to feel their way through situations whereas men are more likely to consider the logical options before doing anything. I wonder if that's true. Or if, like me, some women are just destined to attract the wrong kind of people.

I feel the strap of my handbag slip from my shoulder and pull my hand away from the door to place it back on to my shoulder when the shadow I'd seen through the lace curtains appears behind the door and opens it.

'Claire. I wasn't sure if it would be you?' he says.

'Are you expecting anyone else?'

'Not at all. Come on in,' he says, opening the door a fraction wider, only enough to allow me through before flitting his eyes about behind me as though looking for someone.

'I hope you're hungry. I've cooked enough to feed a family of eight. I've never been very good with portion sizes, I'm afraid. I'm an all or nothing kind of guy, I suppose,' he says, not realising that these words are most definitely not the kind I want to hear when meeting a stranger for the first time, in his house.

I have a feeling that he doesn't entertain people very often and is not used to female company. Especially so when I enter the living room while he pours me a glass of wine without inviting me to find somewhere to sit before he leaves the room.

I take a chair that sits in the corner, furthest from the door where I have a good view of the street. If I have to scream it would be much louder from here, I reason, as I shrug off my coat, leaving it folded on the back of the chair behind me.

Reaching out I take the cool glass from his outstretched hand when he enters the living room. He smiles and sits down beside me, questioning my attire with his eyes.

'I wasn't sure if I should dress up as though we were going out or not so I-'

'You look lovely,' he says. 'Radiant.'

The face-mask was a good idea then.

The nerves begin to evaporate as we get talking. The ease of the conversation surprises me.

'So have you always lived alone?'

'Since my mother died,' he says, his features darkening slightly as he mentions this.

'That must have been hard. But you've made something of yourself, haven't you.'

'I'm a builder. It's a trade I fell into I guess. My father was one, and my grandfather. In the family as they say,' he says, with added energy.

'You enjoy it though?'

'I like to build things from scratch. Start something from the bare bones. Seeing something you've created with your own hands appear upwards from the ground where there was nothing or something so awful it had to be knocked away is a moment to be treasured,' he says. 'But most of all I enjoy my own company. I don't miss

163

not having anyone to share an evening with. Well, I didn't.'

'But you do now?'

'I miss companionship. Having somebody to bounce ideas off. Having somebody to go out with, even just for a walk. I miss that,' he says.

'I'm just getting used to that myself.'

'I'm sorry, I should never have-'

I hold out my palm to halt him in his tracks.

'It's okay. I'm okay. In fact, I've sent him the divorce papers. He called me this morning and asked me to meet him tomorrow evening to talk.'

'What do you need to discuss? Sorry, it's none of my business. I put my foot in it sometimes,' he says.

I'm slightly taken aback by his enquiry but try not to show it.

'I didn't think we had anything to discuss, but he made it clear that he isn't going to make this easy for me if I decide to pursue it.'

'The divorce? But I thought you'd already made your decision. You're separated aren't you?' he says.

'Yes. I have made it clear to him that this is not something I've taken lightly. I've been thinking of nothing else since I left, in all honesty. It's just that with everything else - the debts and work - I haven't really had time to sit down and discuss it all with him. I guess I was putting it off.'

'But you're sure? This is what you want after all, and you can't go back on it once you've made up your mind,' he says.

'I'm positive. It's for the best. It's not as though we've been intimate for a long time now. I just don't see myself as being his wife. I want to be my own person. Make my own decisions. Bring my son up in a loving atmosphere.'

'He wasn't kind to you?' he says, enquiringly.

'He was a wonderful husband and father. I can't fault

him on that. I suppose it began when Ollie was born.'

He leans forwards, showing interest in my continued spark of conversation.

'He changed. Not overnight of course. But he grew increasingly anxious. Wanting to know my whereabouts. Calling me at work. Texting me on his way home. I used to see it as interest in me and Ollie. I used to think of him as my protector. It made me feel safe.'

'And then?' he says, lifting the glass to his mouth and taking a sip of the iced wine, reminding me of my own warming in my hand.

'He accused me of sleeping with somebody else. I'd been ill. I had a virus. It lasted for several weeks. It was like a really bad case of flu that just wouldn't budge, and then when I finally felt fit enough to return to work I found out that he'd enlisted his mother in taking Ollie to school and feeding him without consulting me.'

'Ollie didn't return home for two weeks, and by that time he'd missed me so much that I felt as though he blamed me for not being there. That a wedge had been placed in front of us. It took me several weeks to ram myself through it. Only when I did, Zack didn't seem the same.'

Zack had been working and looking after me. I felt helpless.

'He used to leave work twice a day on his break and for lunch just to check up on me. I thought he was worried about me, but it became increasingly unbearable.'

'When I did feel up to going out to dinner again or able to do the shopping, he told me not to worry about it. He said that he'd continue to do everything for me until I felt ready.'

'But you were ready?' he says.

'Yes. There was nothing wrong with me. It was just a stupid virus that got out of hand. He said I wasn't looking after myself. That I was running myself into the ground. He said that I was taking on too much at work and home, but I think he secretly enjoyed taking care of me.'

'Did he offer to help you, before you fell ill? Take some of the weight off you?' he says.

'No. But then, when I couldn't do it he took care of everything. Suddenly there was no room for me in the kitchen. He moved the kitchen drawers around so that I no longer knew where anything was. It was as if he enjoyed looking after me too much. As though me being ill made it easier somehow for him to love me.'

'They call them caretakers,' he says.

I look up at him from where my eyes had fallen to the stack of fishing magazines laid in a neat pile on the table in front of me.

'Pardon?'

'People who prefer others to remain in a vulnerable or otherwise incapacitated state. They like to take care of people because it gives them purpose. A sense of belonging. Such people tend to feel above others. It's like an extreme version of a superiority complex,' he says.

'Really? How do you know about this?'

'I studied psychology. You should look it up. It's very interesting. I could describe some people with my eyes closed,' he says.

'Did you try to work me out, before I sent you the photograph?'

That was a big deal for me. Something I would never have done before. Not even if I hadn't have been married. It reminds me of those pay-per-view sites where women swap photographs of themselves, half-naked, to strangers for 10p a text.

The line I work for offers that as an extra aside. One which I'm not at all interested in, no matter how desperate for money I become. Hopefully not as desperate as I am to get this over with now that my wine glass in empty.

'I have to use the bathroom. Where is it please?'

'Second door on the right,' he says, appearing to be as nervous as I am.

The house is old. It creaks and has the typical musty smell of a home half lived in. Though for a builder he has absolutely no taste in decor or furniture whatsoever.

A wall hanging bellows in the sudden draft above me as I open the bathroom door, closing it behind me, and turning to where the small cabinet above the radiator sits covering the lime green walls with the mirror image of my heavily made-up face staring back at me.

I used too much eyeliner- I knew I had. I feel the flutter of my eyelashes graze a dirty black mark beneath my eyes, less sunken than they'd been last week. Before Ewan paid my debts off, before he caused me to question who I really am when I replied 'yes' to his invitation for a one-night stand in repayment. Though in all honesty if he was doing this simply to be kind, and do a good deed he wouldn't be asking to be repaid, would he?

I fold two squares of toilet roll in half and dab at the skin beneath my eyes, taking away the extra eyeliner, now smeared in a semi-circle beneath my eyes, causing me to look as if I'm related to a Panda at Bristol zoo.

I push my bra up higher so that my bust is accentuated by the midline royal blue dress I'm wearing, just above the knee.

I rarely wear dresses, it's something Zack used to say made my pear shape figure appear slightly bigger compared with my thighs though I've never weighed more than nine stone, I assumed he meant that it made me look fatter than I actually was. By the size of Ewan, I'd say he prefers a woman who appears curvy. I'm far off from being termed that but, at least he won't notice my thin wrists and elbow bones that jut out at an angle, piercing anything that gets in my way.

I've always been clumsy, but I urge myself to remain calm and collected this evening even if my legs feel wobbly, and the beginnings of another migraine form in the back of my eye sockets, threatening to ruin this night almost as much as my anxious trembling hands are stopping me from rinsing them beneath the tap.

If I take any longer he's going to think there's something wrong. If I think about this any more I'm going to back out.

I can imagine myself running from the house with an on-the-spot apology, that won't sound at all convincing seeing as I've left my mobile phone in the handbag on the coffee table in his living room. I can't very well manufacture an excuse that includes an emergency phone call, can I?

I walk out of the bathroom, brushing down the faux silk of my dress and force myself not to think any more about the deed that I'm about to do as I make my way into the living room.

The room is empty, and all but grabbing my bag from the floor where it now lies and leaving the house through the front door, I can't think of anything else to do.

I return to the seat I was in before I left for the bathroom and secretly hope that he's fallen and had some kind of accident. An injured leg, caused by tripping over a table leg in the kitchen or maybe he's eaten something bad for lunch that makes him spend the rest of the evening in the toilet. But he appears in the doorway, his head crooked to the side, just as Ollie used to do before his diagnosis, and a smile on his face.

'Would you like a tour of the house?' he says.

'Shouldn't we eat . . .'

I want to say 'get this over with as soon as possible,' but find that I can't finish my sentence.

'I want you to feel comfortable. I want you to make yourself at home while you're here. If you're going to feel nervous then I'd rather we didn't . . .'

And now it's his turn to leave the conversation hanging mid flow.

'How about that tour then?' he says, after a few moments. 'It might make you feel more at ease if you know who you're going to be . . . well, you know,' he says.

And, I do know. I know that in that moment I'm not going to be able to fulfill my promise to him. My side of the bargain isn't going to be possible. Because no matter how infectious his smile is or how warm he is making me feel, I am not physically attracted to him in the slightest. And I find it impossible to believe that he won't be offended or worse, that he will be annoyed with me for leading him on.

He hasn't given me any reason to mistrust him or to conjure the images which flash up and force their way into my head from the corners of my brain. I just can't shake the feeling that Ewan wants more from me than I'm prepared to give. And right at this moment, I'm not sure that we are equally weighted in strength.

He's much larger than Zack and I'd find it difficult to defend myself against *him.*

What if Ewan wanted to hurt me?

I haven't seen nor heard a sound from beyond the front window since I got here. No cars have passed and not one neighbour can be spotted from here because the house is set back so far from the road that if someone were to scream, I doubt you'd be heard.

What concerns me more though is that he has gone to all of this trouble to make me feel welcome in his home. To feel reassured that this is a one-time thing that I don't have to do, but what if he didn't mean it?

What if lurking behind that kind smile and that

muscly physique lies the repressed urges of a wounded murderer? What if saying no to this man isn't an option?

HIM

We walk into the dining room where the two walls at either side of the large window overlooking the garden are filled with shelves containing hundreds of books.

'Wow,' she says. 'You like to read.'

'My mother owned several first edition copies which began a slight addiction to buying books to fill some of the empty shelves when she passed away.'

'You loved your mother very much,' she says.

I nod in embarrassed agreement.

'Do you read poetry?'

'Yes. I used to write my own years ago. I haven't the time now,' she says, looking down at the threadbare rug that covers the dark stained polished floorboards beneath.

'I sit in here sometimes and take myself far away to different cities and times. Reading is very good for the soul.'

'Have you ever written anything?' she says.

I pause, slightly taken aback by her question though it isn't as if she could know. I blink several times and walk over to where the leather bound book lies face-down, covered in a thin trail of dust.

I blow the dust from it and it lifts up and swarms the air like tiny particles of stars, glinting in the light of the small lamp I flick on beside the small table where I keep a bottle of rum for when the nights require it. I usually light the fire in here too but it's far too warm for that now.

I offer the leather-bound notebook to Claire and nod my head towards the burgundy leather chair which lies in front of the open fireplace. She sits down, opens the book and begins reading it silently.

I watch as her eyes light up and then fade as she takes in every word that is written on that page with such emotional investment that she appears deeply affected by them. As she closes the book and passes it back to me she closes her eyes and looks away. When she looks up at me, still standing in the same spot half covering the dull light from the lamp, I can see that her eyes have lost their usual sparkle. She looks sad.

All I want in that very moment is to comfort her. I lean forwards and allow her to rest her head beneath my shoulder. I bring my arm back around her and hold her with gentleness.

She doesn't cry, but I know that she wants to. She feels it too. The air begin to change all around us as if something is sucking the light from the room and forcing us into darkness. Only it is not the actual light that is being taken from the room but the warmth, and the stillness that takes over as our bodies refrain from moving.

We both listen out for the sound we know we heard but cannot quite place. There is something moving; something lingering- outside.

I question whether it could be a fox. The one I saw wandering the street the other night, but instantly dismiss this thought when there is a terrible thudding sound coming from the back of the house. And then the all too familiar juddering of the handle on the back door.

'What was that?' she says.

'Just a fox. Stay here while I go and see if I can distract him.'

I leave the room with her watching me. I can feel the hair on the back of my neck standing on end. But it's not fear I can feel. I know who it is. The only person it can be. I know I won't rid her with small talk, but that's all I have at my disposal.

I make my way into the kitchen and hold the door handle firmly, opening it with the key that still sits inside the lock. I pull the door towards me as I open it and a rush of cold Autumn air flings through the space between me and Elise, who stands eagerly awaiting me.

'You can't come in. I have company.'

'I need to speak to you,' she says.

'Not here. Not now. Can't it wait?'

'No. It can't,' she says, forcing her way past me by ducking under my raised arm.

She sits behind me on the dining chair, waiting for me to begin speaking, but I don't know what to say.

'Is everything all right,' says Claire, from the front of the house.

'Everything's fine. I'll be with you soon.'

'Are you going to kidnap her too?' says Elise, crossing her legs and smiling.

'It wasn't like that, and you know it. Why are you here? What do you want?'

'Two thousand should cover it or I'm going to the police,' she says.

'I don't have that kind of money lying around the house. And I don't think you should have it.'

'I'm not using. You made sure of that. I want a fresh start. I want to go somewhere, see things, experience everything I couldn't before. I want to start living again,' she says, this time her eyes fall gracefully down to the scars on the insides of her arms.

'I want to be free,' she says.

In that moment, I believe her. I really think that is what she wants.

'You don't want to blackmail me. You want a clean break.'

'Exactly,' she says. 'You need to help me.'

'Haven't I done enough? You have your life back. I gave you that, didn't I?'

'I need to get out of Bristol. I want to leave tonight,' she says.

I study her features. Her face has rounded and the bags beneath her eyes have gone. So why does she want to leave so soon? Who has she annoyed?

'Why tonight?'

'My landlord let Kieran into my flat. He's taken everything. I have nowhere to stay. He's been asking for me. I can't face another showdown. I don't need the drama in my life right now,' she says.

I'd invite her to stay here for a few days but I very much doubt that she'd take kindly to that idea. A kidnapped woman returning to her kidnapper is not something I believe I've ever heard of before.

'Tomorrow. I can get you the money tomorrow.'

'What money?' says Claire.

I turn and find her staring at me, then she turns to Elise and her mouth grows wide.

I'm waiting for her to scream. To run. But she doesn't. She doesn't move. She's frozen to the spot with the shock visible on her face.

'You're the woman who went missing. You're Elise Fitzgerald,' says Claire.

'I wasn't missing. I-'

'What is she talking about? Money?' says Claire, looking back at me with anger burning behind her eyes.

For one moment I think she might lash out at me. That they both might attack me with one of the kitchen knives that sit inside the block on the worktop behind Elise.

I don't make any sudden movements, wondering if they would kill me right here.

Elise backs away as if she is going to leave us standing here to return through the open back door and out of the garden, but then she stops.

'Is she next?' says Elise.

I can hear the buzzing in the air, like a thousand bluebottle flies swarming through my ears, charging the atmosphere with electrifying energy.

My heart is pounding beneath my chest.

If Elise says any more then Claire will know. She'll think I'm a threat. She won't go through with our arrangement and all this will have been for nothing. I have to think fast. I have to ensure that this doesn't end up looking much worse than it is.

It's obvious in Claire's eyes that to Elise, I'm some kind of monster when she repeats what she'd said moments ago.

'Is she next?'

'What is she talking about Ewan?' says Claire stepping back to the end of the kitchen, looking over her shoulder to where the front door stands.

She can escape. She can leave whenever she wants to. That much is obvious, but she doesn't.

Claire pulls out the only other chair that came with the dining table we were supposed to be eating at together by now, waiting for me to answer.

'I promised I'd lend her some money. She wants to get out of Bristol, make a fresh start. You know how the press can be?'

'No, actually. I don't,' she says. 'Why would I? And what has she done to have to leave tonight?' she says.

Her gaze penetrates my eyes. It's as though she can look right through me.

I cough. A momentary slip that leads to an unforgettable belief that I am vulnerable in their eyes.

'How do you know her anyway?' she says.

'We were neighbours,' says Elise.

'I thought you said you'd lived here your entire life. That this was your mother's house?' Says Claire. 'Or is that not true at all?'

'I have. I've not been dishonest with you. Not once, Claire. It's just that-'

'I'm a drug addict. Ex-drug addict. He helped me. Ewan helped me get clean. I want to borrow some money from him until I can find somewhere to settle down. I want to get out of here. I can see how this might not be possible. I've never been very good with considering others but I'm learning. I just, I'm sorry, I don't understand what this has to do with you?' says Elise, darting Claire a look that suggests she hasn't lost any of her fight.

If anything, now that she's no longer under the influence of illegal substances she appears very much aware and is certainly on top form right now. I admire her tenacity but not at the expense of my evening with Claire.

'I suppose it isn't anything to do with me, but as I'm here . . .'

She says this as if it explains everything.

'I'd prefer to talk to Ewan in private,' says, Elise.

'Well, I find it strange that a woman who was missing for weeks turns up at the house of somebody who I'm sharing a meal with, and more to the point a missing woman who claims that you helped her get clean off drugs,' says Claire, aiming her question at me.

'And why are you demanding money from him?' she says to Elise.

Elise stands there, a thunderous look on her face.

'I'll speak to you in the morning Elise.'

'Fine,' says Elise, bewildered.

'Perhaps we could continue our tour of the house?'

Claire ignores me, watching Elise walk the length of the kitchen and out of the back door, slamming it behind her. I turn around and meet Claire's stone hard glare.

'So,' she says.

'Shall we?'

I offer her my arm to link hers through so that we can pretend we are two residents in an episode of Downton Abbey, but she doesn't take it.

'So, are you going to tell me the truth or am I going to have to leave here right now and never speak to you again,' she says. 'I mean, the money will have to be repaid some other way, I suppose.'

She follows the length of the table with her eyes and then looks up to me and says:

'Oh, I see. Are you paying her to . . . as well, or is she a prostitute or something?'

'No. Not at all. I'm helping her out. She wants to get her life back on track. I'm a friend. We've never been together.'

'So I'm the only one. I'm the only woman who's agreed to prostitute herself for you. Is that it? Is that the only way you can get laid? By paying people off and then making them feel as if they owe you something. Am I compensating you for covering my debts or offering you something you won't otherwise be able to access?' she says.

'Claire, that isn't how this is. I don't even know if-'

'If what?'

'I don't even know if you want to be with me. I don't think you want to do this at all. And I'm not going to stop you if you don't. I'm not going to-'

'No, You're damn right you won't. I'm leaving Ewan.

I'm going home to be with my boy,' she says.

'Wait. Please, wait Claire.'

'I'll get the money back to you. All of it. However I manage it, I will, and then we're done,' she says.

'Claire, please listen to me.'

'What?' she says, stalling at the front door where I've followed her.

'Forget about the money.'

'Oh, no. Don't try that one. Guilt-tripping me isn't going to get me into bed with you either. You'll get your money. If it takes me a few weeks you'll have it. But I don't want to see or speak to you until then. Are we clear?' she says, the ball finally being placed in her court.

She looks pleasing on the eye when she is empowered. Whatever that ex-husband of hers did, it must have been enough to stunt her inner growth. She seems to have increased her confidence and developed a strength from this conversation. Something I didn't see within her when she arrived on the doorstep only a couple of hours ago.

'Crystal clear, Claire.'

'Right,' she says, stepping out into the ice cold night air and walking towards the largest full moon I think I've ever seen. It is so low in the sky that it looks as though it is falling.

I watch her walking away. Knowing that at any moment Elise could reappear from behind the bushes and tell her everything. I can only hope that she doesn't, for if she did I wouldn't know what to say. I wouldn't know where to begin to explain myself out of this strange situation we've all found ourselves within.

I watch her form disappear past the top of the hedgerows and the sound of her wedge-heeled boots walking away from the house and back to her normal everyday life.

I wasn't expecting to hear back from her.

I certainly didn't count on her to continue working for the chatline or indeed answering me when I called at the usual time we'd set aside every other day since she joined. 6:00pm is our time.

I definitely didn't expect her to answer.

'Claire, it's me.'

'I thought so, how are you feeling?' she says.

Though she only sounds remotely interested in my answer because she is working. And this kind of conversation begins typically with 'how are you feeling?' or 'what are you doing?'

'Okay. How are you?'

'Fine. I'm fine. Maybe.'

'Not now. Here, I mean. Perhaps later?'

'Yes, okay,' she says, before I say goodbye and hang up.

If a conversation could be any more awkward then I'd be very surprised.

I look out of the window watching two birds nesting in the trees beyond the window, imagining what it must be like to share complete companionship with somebody. And for the first time in many years I feel genuinely lonely.

While Claire continues rebuilding her life from a cloud of never-ending debt that has hopefully eased in magnitude a little, and Elise begins her new life in Huddersfield with the two thousand pounds I drew out of the bank for her this morning, I sit here in an empty, silent house, watching the skies turn darker by the second, listening to the rustling leaves as they continue to fall from the trees.

Winter is coming. Soon there will be frost on the ground and the house will grow cold and damp.

179

HER

Zack sits with his mobile phone in his palms, moving it from one hand to the other as he speaks. I'm growing increasingly nervous over how to excuse myself from this *date* he has so elaborately arranged for us. How can I get out of it without him coming to the wrong conclusion?

'You're having second thoughts, but why? What's changed since yesterday?' he says.

I want to say not a lot, but then he'll see from the way I avert my gaze that I've done something. He'll never forgive me if he finds out where I was or who I was with.

I try to invent something believable but that goes out of the window when Ollie appears in the doorway, his grandmother standing behind him with a sour faced expression painted onto her walnut textured skin. Too much sun has made her look as though she's been living in Spain, not holidaying in Kent. Who knew that such a place could be warm even at the start of winter?

'I'll take Ollie out to the car,' she says, sheepishly. Leaving us alone to continue our discussion as to why it was so unreasonable of me to apply for a divorce after almost seven months of living apart and being officially separated for eight.

'I just don't understand. I thought you wanted to meet with me to talk about this, not flake out at the last minute and . . . oh, I see. You have somebody coming. Is that it? He's going to be here at any minute isn't he?' he says, pleased with himself.

'Who is going to be here?'

'Whoever you were with last night, when I called five times to confirm our date. Your mobile phone was switched off,' he says. 'See.'

He holds his mobile phone out to me and shows me the five unanswered calls recorded in his call log.

'I was tired. I had an early night.'

'And Ollie. Where was he? Because your mother-'

'My mother? You're checking up on me now?'

'No. But I knew that if I mentioned her you'd fold. So it was her who was looking after him while you went gallivanting?' he says, sitting back in the chair, folding his arms.

'I can go out too you know. I can have friends.'

'So he's a friend. Why have you never told me about him before then? Don't you think I would have known he existed while we were married?' he says.

'I didn't know him then-'

'So it is a man. Look, I don't want to pry. Believe me I don't, but somebody has to be the responsible one here.'

'Responsible. Ha!'

'And what is that supposed to mean?' he says, floundering under his accusations now that I have something to say about responsibility.

'You haven't paid a thing for Ollie since we left. My mother has always had Ollie over for a night or two here and there. What the hell has that got to do with you all of a sudden? We may not be together any more but I don't have to start asking for your permission every single time I want to make a decision.'

He glares at me then. I can see the hatred in his eyes. Something has snapped inside of him. Something irreparable, just like me. We are broken. Neither of us wants to give in to this notion though so we continue to stare each other out for what feels like an eternity until I hear my phone ringing.

I left my mobile on the chair as I went to answer the door. Zack reaches out and grabs for it before I have the chance to do so myself.

'Hello. Who is this?' he says.

'Claire, it's for you,' he says, passing the phone to me. 'It's your lover boy,' he whispers so that Ewan can't hear.

I know it's him. This is the third call he's made since I got home.

'I'm busy. What do you want?'

'How lovely,' says Zack. 'What a charming way to begin a relationship. What do you want?' he says, repeating me.

I ignore him and walk away from the kitchen so that I can speak in the hallway, affording me a little more privacy though obviously whoever built this flat did not intend for such things to be an issue. It being mainly open plan, I can't divert my gaze as easily as I'd like to from Zack, who sits watching my every move

I wonder if he can tell from just my posture how nervous and freaked out I am right now. My husband sits a few feet away from where I stand talking to the man I was convinced to sleep with to pay back three thousand pounds he lent me to pay off my debts.

'I can't talk right now. Please, call back tomorrow.'

I put the phone down on the worktop.

Zack stands up, instantly drawn to the space behind me where he tries to convince me that he is not snooping as he checks the number that is still lit up on the screen before it begins to fade.

'You ended the call,' he says, surprised.

'Bloody PPI. They call day and night.'

I try to laugh it off, but it doesn't wash with him.

He knows. He knows something. Not *that* surely. But he's not stupid.

'He knows your name,' he says.

'They called last week. Same bloke, I think.'

'You can fool yourself, but not me. I'm your husband remember? I know you,' he says.

He takes his coat from the back of the chair and loops it over his arm, twisting the small fabric label until I hear it snap. He's watching me while he does it. Is he threatening me?

He breathes in a deep breath and exhales slowly out of his mouth as though practicing some kind of meditation exercise.

'I thought better of you, Claire,' he says, shaking his head, making his way over to exit the kitchen and hopefully leave through the front door very soon.

He stops dead still in the hallway and waits for me to respond. He can wait all night for all I care.

'I've done nothing wrong.'

The deathly silence of the house fills me with dread. I don't know why I feel scared or why now, but something is shifting in the atmosphere between us. Twisting and churning.

'You're a callous bitch,' he says.

Never has he sworn at me before. He continues with a sudden tirade of vile words until he is left almost speechless. I can visualize the steam pouring from him. Has he finally run out of things to say? He looks depleted. His burst of adrenaline has been shot down. Torn away are the threads that once bound us. We are the people I most despise. Two people out for blood, wanting to win a battle they created the moment they chose to spend their lives together.

'You are not who I thought you were, Claire. You are disgusting. No mother would dare put her son through this. You leave me, taking him with you, and then you find yourself somebody else within weeks,' he says, his exaggerated hand gestures causing him to knock an ornamental picture frame off the shelf. I was hoping to fill the frame with Ollie's school photo next week, but now it's been sent smashing to the ground.

'There is nobody else Zack, and for your information, it's been months. You hate me, but not as much as you hate yourself. You're tired, beaten down and-'

'Only because of you,' he says.

'This has nothing to do with me.'

'Damn right it does. You are fooling around behind my back-'

'Behind your back?'

'So you admit it. There is somebody, isn't there?' he says.

I shake my head in disbelief but it's no good. He either doesn't notice or he doesn't hear me.

He is standing right in front of me now with his face so close to mine that I can smell his anger scorching the blood inside my veins. I want to hit him. I want to lash out and punch him in the face but I convince myself that this is all he'll need to take this conversation one step further and accuse me of being an unfit mother.

'Ollie left his jacket,' says Fiona, Zack's mother returns from the car where Ollie will be strapped in oblivious to our childish rant, waiting for his grandmother to take him back to hers for hot chocolate and homemade cookies. Something good mothers do for their children. Perfect mothers. Right now I'm far from perfect in Zack's eyes.

'How long have you been standing there, mother?' he says. His tone altering to that of somebody caught out when they are about to do something they may later regret.

Was he going to hit me? If his mother hadn't have intervened, would he have hit me? Is that how far this has now gone?'

'Long enough,' she says, turning away to head back out to the car.

'No. Don't go yet. I want you to see this. I want you to see how she gets,' he says.

'She gets?'

I repeat him in the same tone hoping to pick something up from these words I so clearly do not understand.

'What is wrong with you?'

'What is wrong with you?' he says.

He turns to his mother and continues his tirade of false accusations without any need for me to dispute them or convict myself of them, for as he continues his charade I lose it, properly.

'She was about to hit me. If you hadn't have walked through that door she would have hurt me. Can you see it now, mother? Can you see what I've been telling you is true?' he says.

'Oh, what complete and utter crap. Your mother never liked me. And now she has good reason. Her son's wife has made something of herself without him and she can't stand it.'

'She's not to be trusted, mother. Can you see that? You can see it now, right?' he says.

She nods.

'Oh, for fucks sake. I'm not seeing anyone. I'm not interested in anyone. All the crap you've put me through has put me off men for life. I've had enough.'

I leave the room and push past Fiona, not noticing her fall as I make my way out towards the car.

'Ollie, you're not going. Come on out of there.'

185

'But nanna promised me.'

'I don't care. She's changed her mind. Come on.'

'I haven't changed my mind Ollie,' she says, dragging her skin and bones from the crumpled heap she'd fallen into, probably deliberately, in an attempt to make me look like a granny beater now too, only she's much stronger than she likes to have us believe. She once broke the arm of a man trying to mug her with her bare hands.

'Get out of the car, Ollie.'

Fiona calls out then.

'You don't have to. You can come with me. You don't have to stay here and listen to this nonsense. We can-'

'Ollie is staying with my mother until you calm down,' says Zack.

Everyone knows not to tell somebody in the midst of anger to calm down. It makes them worse. It exacerbates their frustration so that it spills out in any way it can.

'That's enough, Zack. I've had enough.'

'So have I,' he says, jumping into the back of the 4x4 his mother owns.

Whatever need she has for such a large vehicle I couldn't tell you.

Ollie turns his back to me and his mother steps into the driver's side, starting the engine and revving it in the same way that he does. I know where he gets his temper from. A short fuse is rarely an inheritable gene, but in this case, well . . .

'Zack, you can't take Ollie without my consent-'

'I'm his father. I have the same rights as you,' he says, winding up the passenger side window and turning his face away from me.

'Don't ignore me. He's my son. He belongs with me. I'm his mother. He lives here, with me.'

'You're in no fit state to look after anyone, Claire. You can't even take care of yourself. Get your affairs in order- literally, and then come and see me,' he says, his voice carried away by the sound of the screeching tyres as his mother shunts off the driveway and floors it around the corner, only slowing as she realises that I'm not in hot pursuit behind her.

Why aren't I?

'You're not taking my son away from me. You're not doing this Zack. I won't let you!'

I can see the curtain twitcher across the road peeping through her nets to see what all the fuss is about. The noise of our raised voices has caused quite a stir in number seven too as they stand in the garden looking up and down the street wearing annoyed expressions on their faces, upset that their Friday evening TV has been disturbed by our domestic dispute. They pretend not to have seen me though I've caught the gentleman's eyes twice.

I run back to the house reasoning that this isn't going to get sorted out any time soon, with me standing on the corner of the road.

I have to do something. He has no right to do this to me. To cause me such distress. Ollie needs stability. Can't he see that? Seeing us fight, tearing apart each other in the road is not going to help my case, I know this, but I have to show Ollie that I care. That I'm the one he needs. I have to make sure that Zack doesn't try to twist Ollie's head to his way of thinking too. He's obviously been working on his mother for some time because she would never, in a million years, defend a man over a mother. Especially the mother of her only grandson.

Not unless . . . no, he wouldn't. He wouldn't be so twisted as to use that to his advantage, would he?

His mother has always taken the side of a woman over any man's accusations. Ever since she began working in a children's centre, supporting contact between parents who otherwise would be estranged from their own children had the courts not decided that it would be better for both parents to be involved in their lives. She has always said that men can be manipulative. To the point that they can turn their own children against the mother they've always known and loved. She wouldn't defend any father, not even her own son, in keeping a child away from their mother. Especially not her own grandchild.

We've never seen eye to eye. We've never held more than a few words any time we've found ourselves in the same room. I always found her overly opinionated. One of the critical parents of a generation who grew up in the post-war 1950's where it was unheard of to suggest to a mother to go out and start working when she had children at home to clothe, feed, wash, and a house to take care of. Beside her backwards, old-fashioned way of living she sees how important a woman is to her family. How much falls apart and breaks down when a mother is ill or has to work. She knows because she's seen it. Volunteering only once a week after her children had left home, got married and started families of their own, the children's centre was her way of giving back. Or should that be continuing to give, even after her husband had died and she had nobody left to take care of at home.

How could such a woman suddenly and drastically change her mind, alter her very core morals and beliefs in one quick swipe of Zack's made up tale of how self-destructive I've become? Even swearing blind that I've become violent, and thus a danger to our own son.

No child should ever have to go through what he is forcing our son into. I cannot imagine what is going through Zack's head right now, where he's found these selfish ideas from, but I can guess. He didn't get them from his mother. She's getting them from him.

Zack's destroying a relationship between me and my son by using her. For whatever wrong he believes I have dealt him. The only problem with this theory is that if I am right then this means only one thing. He's turned her against me in the most cruelest of ways. He has told her. He has told her about his sister and what I said to her the last time I saw her. He has told Fiona everything and turned the entire conversation over to meet his own interpretation.

He said at the time that I should have trusted her. That he'd done the right thing. That she was not trouble or rude or spiteful. He almost had me believing those lies myself. But I know what I saw. I know what I heard. The things she said can never be taken back.

She was telling Ollie about his sister. She was telling him about the crash, and then she pulled him close to her so that his little head had no option but to brush up against her chest and then she turned her head away from me as I trimmed the honeysuckle bush. But I still heard her whisper to him that it wasn't an accident. That I made it happen.

And with this thought the same flash of anger I felt back then, when I ran over to her screaming for her to shut up, fills me once more. I can almost see the scissors in my hand now, my fingers clenched around the silver steel. But I know there's nothing there. The only thing that is the same is the adrenaline that forced me forwards and into her face, shoving her backwards to the ground.

The trouble is she told Zack that I'd tried to stab her. Fiona didn't believe her then, but will she now? Will she, after seeing that angry spat earlier between me and Zack, finally begin to believe him? Will her wonderful, can do-no-wrong son confess all to her? Disclose what he thinks about me? If he does then he'll have something real to use against me. He'll have his mother's support. And we all know how much more that will stand up in a civil court, don't we?

There is nothing stopping Zack, according to the law, from taking his own son to go and live with him. What if he doesn't bring him back?

There is only one thing I can do, but I'm not in the right frame of mind to consider contacting the police, or my solicitor. I will show Zack and his mother how much I will fight for my son. And when they see that I won't back down they will understand just how strong a mother's love for her son is. How far a woman is prepared to go to save her child from the madness that their father is creating.

I grab my keys from the hook inside the front door, noticing for the first time that there are three metal loops but only two keys. Why did the locksmith only give me two keys and three loopholes?

I shrug off the question and run over to the car. Swing the door open and jump inside.

HIM

It has not been easy. For the past couple of days I've been wanting to call Claire to ensure that she is okay, but I've had to force myself not to. It wouldn't be right.

I cannot bolster my way into her life. She needs space. And I respect that. It just doesn't sit right with me when there are people out there in trouble, or in need of a supportive hand of encouragement; me- being able to give it, while they continue to suffer and refuse to accept any help.

Billy sits with his legs folded, stuffing a ham sandwich into his mouth. The sight is grotesque. Why don't people have the manners to close their mouths while they eat any more?

He looks up at me and nods his head in encouragement whilst looking over his shoulder to where he has laid out his lunchbox, open to the dust and paint fumes of this large office space in which we work.

'Take one,' he says, spilling breadcrumbs from his lips as he speaks. Sending them cascading down his trousers and onto the floor.

'Thanks.'

I mumble about having eaten a late breakfast, though I doubt he believes me, considering I've been here since 7:00am and he hasn't seen me eat anything since I got here.

I look out of the foggy windows that have finally been put up, to see that the sky is a fierce grey where I expect rain will fall from at any moment. The clouds have been simmering for some time and I'm grateful that the glazed glass shelters us from the cold outside.

Last week was awful. The winds swept through the open building sending plaster dust and pots of paint flying across the room. The strength of such natural environments reigniting my belief that nobody has any real control over the universe. That it does as it will despite whatever power you try to hold over such things.

I suppose that is when I realised that I should give Claire some time. Allow her to discover her true worth without me. She has a son to take care of and a divorce settlement to contend with. She doesn't need me to involve myself in such things. She'll contact me when she's ready. In the mean time I will get on with my own life. Working, refitting the bathroom, pretending that the emptiness isn't burning into my soul as each day unfolds.

When I can finally get away from work and return home later that evening, there is a postcard waiting for me. It is sitting on top of the pile of bills and nonsense that has accumulated on the mat since I left for work this morning.

I bend down to pick it up and it is then that I see who it is from.

Elise has been staying in Ireland, and is currently residing in a caravan park. She is happy and free. She is actually thanking me for giving her the opportunity to make a fresh start. She wants me to know that she doesn't blame me at all for anything that I did. She doesn't think she would have been able to achieve a successful recovery had I not have locked her up.

The way she says this both annoys me for her use of words on such a public display of writing and relieves any anxieties over whether or not I was doing this for the greater good or if I had, in fact, caused her any emotional harm. The worry that I might have caused her more distress was a constant, overwhelming my every thought during almost every minute of every day.

I'm glad that she took the time to write to me. Glad too that she is living well and appears content in her new life. I only hope that I could say the same for Claire. Just to hear her voice. To know that she had reached a place in her life where she felt that things were getting back on track would cause me immense comfort. But I can't call her yet. I have to allow her to contact me. I don't want to appear possessive over her time.

She is under no obligation to me, however she wishes to believe that she is. I am not expecting her to pay me back. I only wish that Elise didn't arrive the other day to spoil what had otherwise been a pleasant evening.

We didn't get to enjoy the meal I'd been preparing for two hours before she arrived. I ate the sweet alone, raspberry roulade- just like my mother made it.

HER

When I arrive outside the house, it's dark, and there is a bruised blanket of clouds above me. There is no evidence that I've had to pay for a new window to be fitted on the passenger side of the car, as I glance at it. I shiver from the early winter cold as I step out of the car and onto the kerb. The house is unlit and, from what I can gather, does not appear as homely as I'd once felt inside the confines of such immaculately expensive walls.

Zack's car is not parked on the driveway as it should be and neither is Fiona's. I came straight here. They should be arriving at any moment, unless they've got caught up in the rush hour traffic.

I check my watch, but it's almost 7:30pm. The commuters travelling to and from London or Wales, and the constant stream of pedestrian's crossing over the main road should have all but died down by now.

I look over my shoulder feeling the tell-tale pin-pricks of somebody watching me that I've experienced several times since the flat was broken into while we were away, but there isn't a soul nearby. It isn't any

194

easier knowing that I'm standing alone on a deserted street with the feeling of being watched filling the vast open space surrounding me.

I turn around and step back into the car, locking the doors behind me in a futile attempt to feel both safer and warmer. Though with old cars like this it is usual for the winds to still bite your skin even as you enclose yourself within the metal, glass and plastic fibres.

It feels like I've been here for decades. I'm almost losing hope until a single set of headlights filter through my peripheral vision and track their way towards the house.

Whoever it is though, doesn't stop. Preferring to slow down, catching my attention then crawling away, back down the road after completing a three-point turn where the driver narrowly misses taking the front lights and bumper away from a car, parked too far out in the road.

I revert my attention back to my watch and notice that over half an hour has passed since I've been sitting here.

I don't mean to fall asleep.

I lay my head back and allow my heavy eyelids to close for just a few seconds but wake to a loud car horn beeping mere yards from where I lie with my neck to the side, the seat slightly leant backwards to allow me a more comfortable rest. I turn my head to meet the bright glare of headlights and see the man waving at me as he continues to beep his horn. I sit up. Wind down the window and lean out to be met with Zack. No sign of Ollie or Fiona.

'What the hell are you doing out here. It's ice cold. Why aren't you at home?' he says. His voice more a yell of irritation rather than concern.

'I came to talk.'

'What, now?' he says. 'Tomorrow would be more convenient,' he says.

'Ollie has school in the morning. I have his packed lunch bag and his uniform.'

'There's no need. We have all that,' he says.

'Where's Ollie?'

'In the house,' he says.

'No, he's not.'

'Are you calling me a liar?' he says.

'No, of course not. I'm just saying I've been here for what . . .' I look down at my watch and see that it's almost 9:45pm. 'I've been here for a couple of hours and-'

'You don't say,' he says, shaking his head.

'What, you knew? You knew I was here all this time and you didn't wake me?'

'It's not my job to look after you, Claire,' he says.

'I don't need looking after-'

'What are you doing here anyway? It's freezing,' he says.

'I told you. I've come to bring Ollie his things and I thought we should talk.'

'I'm done with talking. It's been a long, tiring day,' he says. 'Ollie has things over at my mother's and you don't need to worry about a packed lunch. I'll sort one out for him, okay?'

'No. It's not okay. I want to see my son.'

'We've gone over this,' he says, looking down at the ground where heavy rain has begun to pelt down leaving traces of dark matter on his beige work boots.

'I just wanted to wish him goodnight.'

'After that rant back at yours I doubt he'd want to hear it,' he says. 'Besides, he was tired. There was a lot of traffic so he's staying at my mother's for the night.'

I'm about to say something but he holds out his hand in a mock gesture for me to stop, and for the first time I do.

I listen intently as he tells me that it was Ollie's

choice to stay with Fiona. That she's going to drop him off to school in the morning with a packed lunch, wearing his uniform. A spare one that Zack bought for him a while ago.

I'm beginning to think that he planned this. The argument, the distress, all of it. But whatever for, I have no idea.

'Go home, Claire. Try to get some sleep. God knows you look like you need it,' he says.

I know I won't sleep at all if my son isn't there, at home with his mum where he belongs, but I don't say anything.

I offer him a nod and he looks relieved to be able to go inside his large house and leave me behind. I wonder when he stopped hating me and began not to care. Now I think that without him missing me, disliking me even, I'm at a loss as to how to react to his demanding and often irritating comments. Though of course, it's probably better that I don't react to his behaviour now. Right at this moment, I know what this looks like. This heated discussion in the middle of the street, late, on a cold, dark night.

I take heed to his goodbye and leave. Driving the car away from the house, I look into the rear-view mirror and see Zack walking up the path towards his lonely miserable evening in front of the TV with a microwave meal, and smile.

I don't want to wish ill upon him but he has a way of making me angry when there really is no need to do so. My annoyance is only reignited when I see Ollie creeping away from the car. Zack aims his automatic key fob towards the vehicle I didn't even see Ollie was inside of, and the hazard lights flash, resetting the alarm as it's locked.

Zack holds out his hand for Ollie to take and both of them walk into the house just as Fiona steps back from the open door, closing it behind them with a quick glance up and down the road where I'm sure she spots me driving around the corner, watching in stunned silence as I exit the road with my knuckles growing white from the tension I place on the steering wheel.

Why would he lie to me? Why would he not allow me another second with my child to say goodnight? What have I done wrong?

I awake the next morning, still fuming from the night before. How dare he keep me from my son with such ridiculous excuses. He doesn't care if Ollie sees us arguing. He wants that. He wants him to see his mother lose control. Then he has more ammunition to throw back at me.

I can almost hear him now: 'You lost it. You were angry. You were frightening our son.' Ludicrous ideas. Thoughts of retaliation swarm through my head as I leave the house and set off to work.

I'm almost reaching the solid footwell of the steep steps that ascend down to my second customer's house when my mobile phone rings in my pocket. I look up at the clear blue sky, almost forgetting that it is October, and that yesterday brought with it a dull lifeless energy, sapping autumn away in an instant.

The caller display flashes blue, telling me to take it. I'm in no hurry, but I accept the call from the school hoping that Ollie hasn't done something awful again.

Thoughts of a stolen packed lunch box or another fight with Jacob cause me to ask Mrs Pritchard to repeat herself when she offers me yet another reason to be angry with Zack.

'What do you mean he isn't there? He stayed at his father's last night.'

'Miss Donoghue-'

'As I've already told you I am soon to be no longer married. That isn't my name any more.'

Miss . . . look, I'm sorry but this really cannot go on,' she says.

I can hear her patience wearing thin, even down the line.

'This is nothing to do with me. You'll have to call Zack.'

'I already have. He's in his office,' she says.

'Where the hell is Ollie then?'

'That's why I am calling you. It's almost 10:00am,' she says.

'I'm working too, you know. I can't just up and leave everything to sort out his mess all the time.'

I stop dead in front of Mrs Farnham's house, twisting my body around and aiming back for the car. I'm sure she heard the sigh escape my lips but she doesn't say anything.

'He must still be with his grandmother, Fiona. I'll bring him in myself. But I can't do this again, all right.'

'But Miss-'

'Next time there's a problem call his father. It's only ever when he's over there or Zack's involved that there is an issue.'

I put the phone down before she can think of anything more to say.

I don't dislike the woman. I feel sorry for her actually. Since Zack's behaviour has grown increasingly annoying I've found that I've become a bit tense.

But no more Miss Nice. This ends today.

If Zack wants to play dirty then so will I.

HIM

I'm not expecting her to answer. She hasn't been logged on to the chatline for almost three days, I was beginning to think that she was avoiding me or at least, feeling too embarrassed to speak with me over what happened the other day.

She sounds sheepish, off guard, and for a few moments, I almost fail to recognise her voice.

'Are you all right?'

'Yes. How are you?' she says, in monotone symbolism.

She really isn't okay, but would rather not discuss it on here. I understand.

'What have you been up to? Any nice outings over the weekend?'

She takes a few seconds to respond. When she does she tries to cover up the fact that she has been crying. The tearful, heavy breaths coming from her end of the line suggest to me that something else is going on here. This is not going to be one of our typical flirtatious conversations. In fact, since our recent face-to-face meeting which ended horribly wrong, I feel an emotional distance between us whilst, at the same time, a spiritual connection of sorts.

I feel her pain. I understand her heavy heart is breaking. I want to hold her in my arms and wipe away those salty tears falling down the pale skin of her cheeks, but I can't. Not if she doesn't let me.

'If there is anything that I can do, you know I will.'

'There's nothing that you can do for me, Ewan.'

'I'm here for you.'

'Not on here, please,' she says. 'I'm okay.'

'Are you sure?'

'Positive. So what do you want?' she says.

I know she doesn't mean it to come out quite like this. She pauses and doesn't speak again until I ask her where she's been for the past three days.

'I've been busy. You know, with work and stuff,' she says.

'You shouldn't be on here, you know. You sound as though you could do with a break.'

'Where do you think I should go?' she says.

'Somewhere hot and exotic.'

She's perking up a bit now. At the mere mention of other climates, of leaving this miserably shaped weather and her problems behind, she slips back into an easy form. Reminding me that this was how it was before she agreed to meet me.

Perhaps it is this, the excitement, the intrigue, the mystery and depth that we seek on this telephone line. The other stuff just seems to get in the way.

'I am sorry about before. That you had to, oh, you know.'

'I do know, and thank you. Thank you for being my friend,' she says.

I am eager to continue our conversation but I get the impression that it won't be long before she dismisses me as always and shows those slight change of hands that she deals me, suggesting she'd like to call it a day. That she wants to be alone. That the conversation is over. And so I decide to be the first to acknowledge this small fraction in the altered air between us.

'I have to go.'

'Oh, really. That's a shame,' she says, lacking in emotion.

'Yes, isn't it. But I'm afraid duty calls. I have a recorded programme to watch on the television that I was hoping to see now, whilst I have the time. Perhaps you would like to speak to me again tomorrow.'

'Sure,' she says, her voice brightening a little.

I detect joy in her voice now. Not so much that she is pleased to be rid of me but glad that she no longer has to feign interest in another boring conversation over the other night. I think she has forgiven me. At least, I hope she has.

I'm surprised to hear from Claire the following morning. Not least of all because she has a business proposition for me.

Not a lucrative, get rich quick, money-making scheme. This is more like the kind of thing you would ask of a lover. And I am anything but that. In fact I am so certain that there are no sparks flying between us that it doesn't take me very long to ask her why she has asked me and not a boyfriend, a brother or her father. That's presuming he is still around though she assures me she can think of nobody else.

The risk is plain to see. But I wonder if she has considered such definite instruments in supporting her case as well as I have.

'What makes you think that I can help you?'

She pauses as though considering her alternatives. It's obvious when time drags on that she feels there is no other option.

'You should really talk to Zack. Let him explain. It's important that he doesn't allow your problems to override his son's education, I understand that. But you should really talk to him. Give him a chance to explain.'

'Worm his way out of it with another poor excuse?' she says. 'No. I've tried that. He won't listen to me. It's like talking to a complete stranger sometimes. I don't know what's got into him, but I'll be damned if I'm going to let him beat me this time,' she says.

'This isn't a game. He has rights. The court will examine this and then you will be questioned as to why you didn't just go to a solicitor to sort this out properly.'

'I'm not asking a lot, am I?' she says.

She doesn't see that this is *exactly* what she is doing. I'm beginning to think that I should have stayed away from this. It's not my business to be warning off fathers from wanting contact with their own children.

'It's my only option right now. I can't afford legal costs at the moment,' she says, slipping from her reserve.

'But I thought you had all that under control now. The finances I mean.'

'Yes, I do. But this on top of everything else is more money. More money than I've got or am likely to have in the next few weeks. Now that I've started paying back some of the other debts it looks like I really will be debt free by December. But not if I take him to court. All that will go out of the window,' she says, depleted.

'Let me help you then.'

'Oh, no. You've done quite enough already. Money isn't going to help this time. I need more than that. I need to get my son back. I have to make Zack see sense,' she says.

I'm beginning to think she's started to lose her own.

'What do you want me to do to put this right?'

'Dress up smart. Wear a suit. Go over to his house.

Explain to him that you are working for child protection. Tell him that you have some concerns. He'll let you in then. He'll think it's something to do with me. Once you're inside you begin recording,' she says.

'What am I going to say?'

'We'll discuss it fully later. I have to go. I've put some food in the oven and I smell burning,' she says, hanging up.

I know it's not my responsibility to ensure her son's safety. I haven't even met him. I don't know what he looks like. For this to appear real I'm going to have to find out a little bit more about her. I'm going to have to follow her to work.

I know the area. She lives in one of those ex-council flats that somebody bought years ago, did up a bit and then decided to rent out to families who have no luck in the council housing application process.

It doesn't look much from the front, but when I get closer to the door and peer inside the window of the living room I can see how lived in her home feels.

It isn't badly decorated. Not anything like Elise's flat. Filton still holds the feel of a community. A small village inside the bustling main roads of North Bristol that house it. A town inside a city. The perfect area for shops, parks, walks, work, and a main gateway to the centre.

I'm daydreaming as I walk back over to the pedestrian crossing, hoping to snatch a quick dart across the road, back to my car, before the heavily laden bus comes charging down the road.

Before I make a run for it I notice something odd about the man walking along the pavement. He steps back as if ensuring that nobody is home before making his way down the path and letting himself into her house. I've never met the man so I can hardly comment on his appearance, but he certainly had a key. And what's more, he seemed no stranger to visiting Claire's property while she is out.

I doubt very much that she's found herself a romance whilst balancing work, taking care of her son, and dealing with a debt the size of Everest. It's much more likely that this man is or was, at least on some level, close to Claire. An ex-husband perhaps? Trying to find another way to convict his wife of insanity. Looking for something to evidence his mistreatment of her over a custody case he has no idea is about to begin. Or perhaps he is there for something else entirely.

Either way, I remain seated in the car opposite the flat for some time, waiting for him to reappear until finally he does with what appears to be a satchel on his back. One of those old ones with faded straps and mismatched patterns woven together within the string harness. It's misshapen and ugly.

But it's not the bag he carries out with him that strikes me as though he planned this little detour on his way to work, but the sheer weight of whatever it is that he is carrying inside it, which causes him to look suspicious.

His back is bent forward and he strains his head upwards trying to contain some semblance of a normal posture whilst obviously dealing with incredible pain. His shoulder is bent slightly to the left and he walks with a new found limp that wasn't there when he arrived. What is he playing at?

When I start the car I creep it along the road until he leaves my view, hoping that nobody will be intimidated by my subtle leering at a man across the street who is so visibly weakened by something, some illness that began only when he broke into the property of his ex-wife, taking with him a bag, filled with something heavy.

I drive away with only one thought on my mind. I must not tell Claire about this. Not yet.

HER

I'm putting the dishes away when I get the call. The call I've been waiting for the past day and a half to receive.

Ewan is on the other end of the phone. He sounds as if he too is taking this morning to tidy up a bit.

'Nothing much to say really,' he says. 'Zack left for work as usual. What exactly are you looking for anyway?'

I consider this for a moment. But I honestly don't know what to say so I don't bother to address the question.

'What did you say to him?'

'I haven't actually said anything yet. I wanted to wait until I was sure that he would be at home, alone,' he says. How's Ollie?'

'I picked him up from Zack's mother, the other day when he hadn't been dropped off at school. I had to take him in myself and haven't heard from Zack since. So at the moment he's okay. He was a bit sulky when I picked him up from school. I think he thought his father would be collecting him, that he'd be staying there again, but he seems fine now. Why'd you ask?'

'I care, that's why,' he says.

I press the phone to my other ear while I wipe the windows with a cloth. The vinegar smell filling my nostrils; sour, making me want to retch.

'So, how's work?'

I say this more to keep up the thread of our conversation, and not because I'm particularly interested. I have enough on my mind without needing to add other's problems to it as well.

'We've almost finished the new build. It's going to be converted into flats. All the internal walls are being put in place at the moment. It looks like it'll be complete by December,' he says, but I'm not really listening.

'Has Zack always had a limp?' he says.

'What?'

'He was walking funny as if he'd hurt his leg. I just wondered, that's all,' he says.

'No. He must have tripped over something.'

'Yes, so work is, well, work, I suppose,' he says, nervously laughing on the other end of the phone.

I find my mind has wandered again. Drifting as it often does when I'm brought to attend to something else during a conversation on the phone. Normally it's Ollie asking me something utterly pointless or doing something he knows he shouldn't, but feels the need to because my attention from him has been diverted elsewhere.

Out of the corner of my eye, I can see the small shadow of a little boy standing at the front door.

'Hold on.'

I place the phone down onto the kitchen worktop and walk through the hallway up to the front door. Knowing who it is standing there before I open the door and see him.

'Ollie, what are you doing here? You're meant to be in school.'

He looks down at his shoes, still soaked from the rain earlier this morning. He doesn't look up to me when he speaks.

'Mrs Pritchard said . . . mummy, you're not going are you?' he says, his midnight blue eyes filling with tears.

'What did she say?'

'She was talking to daddy. I heard her say you were going to be in trouble. You're not going to a prism like Charlie's dad are you?' he says.

'That's prison Ollie, and no. Where did you get this idea from? And why are you here when you should be in school?'

'I ran,' he says.

I take hold of the sleeve of his thick blue jacket and pull him inside out of the cold.

'Ollie, you can't do this. You shouldn't be walking all this way alone at your age. I'll have to take you back. I have work to do and you're meant to be in school. What will they say now?'

He looks up at me with a sad expression, wounded from months of changes that I'm out of my depth in recovering from myself. I can't imagine what must be going on in *his* head.

'I'm sorry, mummy,' he says, turning and running up the stairs.

I pick up my mobile phone.

'Ewan, Ewan, I'm sorry but-'

The dial tone has gone. I reach down and feel the worktop is soaking wet from the cloth lying next to where I'd placed it.

One afternoon away from the prying eyes of teachers who already think me incapable of keeping my son in line won't do any more harm than has been caused already. But I'm annoyed that now my phone is swimming with water that I can't call them to let them know he's here, at home with me- safe.

I open up a bag of rice, pouring half of the contents into the open bin, and sink my mobile phone down into the bag to soak the water up.

The landline was cut off last week again. I haven't had the time to sort it out. I'll pay them Friday. Until then we have no phone.

I stand at the bottom of the stairs and call out to Ollie. When he doesn't respond I shout.

'Ollie, you don't have to go back to school today, but I'd like you to eat something. It's almost lunch time. I'll bring you up an indoor picnic.'

This is something we used to do in the summer when we didn't have enough petrol or I was too tired to take a bag of food up to the park. I'd make him a picnic lunch that he'd gorge on upstairs whilst playing on his X-box. He doesn't seem to care much for going to the park anymore, and sometimes I have to beg him to turn the X-box off, fearing that we'll run out of electric, but today I let him use it. I don't want him thinking I'm against him or that I'm worried for him.

I can't help it though. This is all my fault. If I hadn't have asked Ewan to call on Zack then . . . no, wait. Ewan hasn't spoken to Zack yet. What were him and Mrs Pritchard discussing then?

'Ollie. I know you don't want to go back to school, but I have to get hold of them. My phone isn't working. Can you come downstairs? I need to speak to Mrs Pritchard about something. It won't take long. Then we can come back and have that picnic.'

He stands at the top of the stairs, wiping his eyes with the sleeve of his jumper.

'Come on, Ollie. Let's go. The quicker we get there, the quicker we'll get back.'

He treads slowly down the stairs, taking as long as possible to reach the bottom, then when he does he follows me out to the car.

A burst of sun filters through the thick grey clouds, offering the slightest retreat from the ice cold air. We trundle along the busy streets until we reach the foot of the hill where the school sits divided by trees and a jumble of houses opposite.

When we reach the reception I can see Mrs Pritchard still engrossed in conversation with a pupil over his behaviour in class. At least, it's not Ollie this time. Though I'm sure she thinks this is a more serious offence. I can't help but agree this time.

'Ollie,' she says, exclaiming this in a high pitched tone.

She holds out her hands, but Ollie doesn't want to come closer.

'Miss . . . it doesn't matter. Let's go inside my office. We were so worried. We called the police when we couldn't get hold of you or Mr Donoghue,' she says, ushering us over to where her office is.

I look behind her expecting to see PC Plod now, but whoever they called either hasn't bothered to arrive yet or has already been and gone.

When we step inside her office Mrs Pritchard looks to me for something, anything to explain my son's behaviour. But of course, I can't say much because I don't know. I wasn't there.

'I don't know what happened. He arrived on the doorstep. You shouldn't allow a child to leave the premises. Anything could have happened.'

'I'm so sorry. Please, sit down,' she says.

I take a seat beside her whilst Ollie chooses to remain standing. I'm sure it's because he thinks he is going to be interrogated, but he doesn't seem to realise the seriousness of his absence.

'I called Zack because there was a problem. Ollie has been tearful, quiet, not himself, and I thought-'

'Haven't I told you before to call me? I'm his mother.

He lives with me!'

'Yes, but you see, Ollie said-'

'You listen to a child before speaking to the parents?'

I sit there stunned. Does she not have children of her own? Does she not understand how frustrating this is?

'Mrs Pritchard, I'm working from home and my six-year-old son arrives on the doorstep halfway through a school day. What do you want me to do?'

'His father picked him up,' she says. 'He was here.'

'Oh, really? Is that true, Ollie?'

He turns his head away from me as he speaks. Not wanting to look into my eyes as he regales the conversation he had with his father only an hour ago.

'Daddy was upset. He said something about a man coming to his house, and he said that he was concerned for my safety. That you might have to go to court. I don't want anybody going to prism,' he says.

I can see Mrs Pritchard's face light up. She looks bemused. Now we are officially dysfunctional parents in her eyes.

I look her in the eye. 'It's not like that. No need to get up on your high horse.'

My mouth is working overtime. It won't allow my thoughts to be filtered before I continue to rattle on about Zack, his inability to father Ollie, his recent change in behaviour, him taking Ollie to his mothers, failing to ensure he was dropped off to school, and my 'phone call' to child protection. I don't want to continue this conversation with Ollie in the room so I point out to where one of the resource staff are standing with a new tray of books and ask him to read one quietly with her if she'll let him.

She smiles and sits down, her back against the wall. Her large baby bump accentuated by her dress, as she holds a book open for Ollie to read.

I lean in closer to Mrs Pritchard and continue in

whispered words.

'His father is using Ollie as a tool to discredit my ability to mother him. I won't have him turning my son against me or threatening to take me to court to apply for custody. I have to do this, it's the only way.'

Mrs Pritchard smiles warmly and holds her hand over my wrist.

'I understand how frustrating this is, for all of you, but Ollie needs stability. Zack really shouldn't have just left him on your doorstep or wherever he did. He shouldn't have allowed Ollie to run off like that either, upsetting and worrying us all. If there is anything that I can do to help with your case, then I can support you in any way you wish,' she says.

And with that, I smile and thank her.

'Ollie, would you like to stay?'

He doesn't even look up as he nods.

I leave the office and kiss goodbye to Ollie who is still engrossed in his book as I leave the school, heading back to the car.

I may have found an ally in Mrs Pritchard. Who'd have thought it?

It isn't until I reach the space where my car was that everything zooms into focus. I've lost my car. It hasn't gone missing or been stolen. No. A single flyer is taped to the lamp post beside the now-empty space where I'd left it, notifying me that the car has been seized for lack of insurance.

I catch the bus back to the flat. It takes no longer than if I'd walked, but the bus stopped just as I reached the bend in the road and I didn't want to miss the opportunity to get out of the biting wind, even for just a couple of minutes. It was worth a pound.

I step off the bus and follow the side streets along past the old police station and through the narrow cul-de-sac. When I turn the corner, the flat in front of me, I am met with a huge transport truck that takes over the entire narrow road with its heavy bulk.

Zack is standing in front of the house shouting to the driver who ignores him and continues to spout orders to the two men who are recovering items from my home-again.

I run as quickly as I can, right up to the driver. Not realising what has taken over me. Mere insanity or pride over my belongings I'm not sure. They are not going to take any more from me. I've had enough loss to last me a lifetime in this past year. It's time to stand up for myself.

I ignore Zack as he attempts to prise my arms away from the box that one of the men is carrying as he leaves the path, making his way towards the back of the truck where several boxes packed with my household goods sit amongst the sofa and TV.

I kick up with my foot, hard, so that the sudden jolt sparks a series of hand gestures from the driver, who now steps out of the vehicle hoping to save his colleague from injury and the abuse I hurl at him as I grab the box from his pain-stricken arm and run into the house with it. I dump it down in the hall and run back out to take another. I manage to successfully steal back three boxes before the back doors of the truck are locked shut, my furniture and clothes held tight. I'm unable to get them back.

Zack looks pitifully at me, expressing a feigned look of sorrow at my predicament whilst averting my gaze.

'You let them in, didn't you?'

He doesn't answer me so I raise my voice an octave.

'How did you let them in without a key? Or did you use the one you secretly kept when you had my locks changed?

He doesn't reply. I'm not expecting him to apologise, but admitting it would be nice.

The truck pulls away, taking with it almost

everything I own. Even the laptop I use for work.

'Give me the key. You aren't to have a key to my home.'

'He sifts his hand through the inside pocket of his jeans and pulls out a key with the same distinctive cut as the two I have on my keyring.

'Good job I did. They were about to break in through your bathroom window,' he says, looking unashamed.

'The bathroom window wasn't open. You have no right to be letting yourself, or anyone else for that matter, into my home. You got it? You have no right.'

'I'm still your husband. Who do you think they were going to ask to pay back the money, despite not living with you for the past seven months, Claire?' he says.

No matter how he tries to get himself out of this one I'm not giving him the satisfaction of thinking he's won this one out. Not this time. It's payback. And he *is* going to pay dearly for this.

'You left our son to run home alone.'

Not a faint hint of embarrassment covers his face.

'He ran away. What was I supposed to do, chase after him? It was only a few yards. It's not like I was miles away. Anyway, I knew you were in,' he says.

'Chase after him? Yes, that is exactly what you are supposed to do. You're his father. Father of the year, apparently. So act like it. And, how did you know I was home? Are you following me, because-'

'Of course not. Don't be paranoid. I'm a good father. Don't ever try to say that I'm not or that I'm incapable of looking after our son. Just don't,' he says, raising his hand out towards me.

His brings his hand back down to rest against the trouser leg of his suit. When did he start wearing suits?

He's begging for a fight. I can see it in the way he challenges me. It seems as if nothing is out of discussion in this conversation and so I go for the killer. The one thing that's been playing on my mind since me and Ollie returned from Paris. I have to know, however, I don't want to know what the answer will be. I have to do this for Ollie.

'I called the police. They have no record of you reporting a break-in. Why didn't you call them as I asked you too?'

Is it me or does he hesitate just a fraction?

He looks me in the eyes as he speaks, but I'm not convinced that he is being truthful.

'There was no evidence of a burglary, Claire,' he says.

'How did you know there was one? If we were away, what were you doing here anyway?'

I can't prove it. I can't give anyone a reason why my ex-husband would want to lie over something like that. It doesn't make any sense.

His gaze is steady, never leaving my face.

'I was checking up on the place. That's when I saw the front door ajar. I thought at first that you'd left it open. But then, when I found the letters I assumed you'd done it for an insurance job,' he says.

'You thought I'd leave the front door of my home open on purpose?'

'If the flat was broken into while you were away, no matter how they'd entered or what they'd taken it would be classed as a burglary. The problem is, the place was only mildly untidy when I got here-'

Then something hits me.

'Hang-on. What letters? You said you found some letters?'

'I found them when I was clearing up the living room. Dozens of them. Bills mostly, some of them were from debt collection agencies.'

'You were snooping around my home, your child's home?'

'I was worried for you. How could I call the police if

you'd done this yourself? Faking a crime is wasting police time. It's a criminal offence,' he says.

'I didn't fake anything. I didn't plan this. None of it.'

He nods once, but he doesn't seem at all satisfied with my answer.

'It's hard on your own. Taking care of a child on minimum wage, paying rent on a flat you don't even want o be living in, but I'd never do that.'

'I'm thinking of selling the house. We won't get much for it, but it'll be enough for us to both find somewhere cheap to live. The divorce settlement will enable us to both move on,' he says.

I stand there stunned. Is he really suggesting selling the house to pay me off? Is this the same man who refused me a divorce only last week?

'So what do you think? That's what you wanted isn't it?' he says.

He sounds so persuasive that I have to do a double take.

'Do you mean it?'

'I'll head down to the estate agents first thing in the morning. If that's what you want. You're the mother of my son. I'll sign the divorce papers too and send them off tomorrow on my way. How does that sound?' he says, shrugging his arms in a gesture of 'can we be friends again?'

'Great. That's great. The sooner we get on with this the better, for Ollie's sake as much as ours.'

I detect a slight scowl from Zack at the mention of Ollie's name, but dismiss it as the cold afternoon air causing him to clench his teeth.

'Sure, he says, not sounding very convincing any more.

'What are you going to do about your stuff? You can't sleep here tonight without a bed. And Ollie, he'll need his things. They've taken everything. He hasn't even got soap to shower with, has he?' he says, shrugging his shoulders again as if he's picked up this new annoying habit since we've been apart.

A coping mechanism or a forced pretence of friendliness? I can't tell which it is but he seems okay now. Less irritable. As if he's finally got what he wants. Whatever it is though I'm not sure.

'I'll let you know.'

'Well, you'd better hurry up and decide. You have to collect Ollie from school in an hour and you can't cook dinner without an oven, can you?' he says, a nervous laugh escaping his lips.

'Like I said. I'll let you know.'

His shoulders tense as he walks away and I suddenly feel as though he came prepared. Did he know this was going to happen? Had he somehow planned it?

I notice too, how his gait isn't bent over as Ewan said it was when he saw him the other day. Zack doesn't appear to have injured his leg at all.

HIM

Zack stands with his hands on his hips, a look of sheer annoyance etched onto his face. I don't have the heart to tell Claire that Ollie gets his looks from his father.

I can see the photograph behind him in the white pearlescent frame on the shelving unit behind the door.

The paintwork is pristine. New shiny laminate floor gleams in the little light that filters through the open doorway, reflecting the contours of his sharp facial features.

'Come in,' he says, obviously not wanting the neighbours to hear what I'm about to say.

I follow him into the living room, that appears to have been cleaned in preparation. Of course, he couldn't possibly know to be expecting me. But it's odd that for a single man his home is so well kept.

I take a seat on the cream sofa, folding my hands in non-confrontational exhibition on my lap. Something I learnt during my clinical training is that things being said to somebody unwilling to hear them come better from open posture.

'What are you saying?' he says.

'We are concerned for your son, Ollie. He is missing a lot of school, he has recently been reported to the police for running away from school, and he seems to be unsettled. Is there any reason for this recent behaviour that you can think of, Mr Donoghue?'

'I haven't got a son,' he says, unflinchingly.

I think I've misheard him so I repeat the question.

'I don't have a son. I've no idea who Ollie is,' he says.

I look around the room and notice that there doesn't seem to be any evidence that Ollie comes to stay with him once a week. Aside from the photograph in the hallway you wouldn't know that he existed at all.

'I'm sorry, I don't understand what you're saying. Ollie, the boy you fathered with his mother, Claire. You're saying that he isn't yours?'

I lean forwards slightly without meaning to, but this doesn't instigate further annoyance from Zack as I hoped it would.

Challenging somebody over their beliefs is possible by mimicking an individual's behaviour- mirroring, they call it. Except with aggressive or violent clients that is, who will grow increasingly agitated at this boundary breaking close proximity.

'I don't have a son. What part of that are you not clear about?' he says.

'The photograph in the hallway, is that not Ollie?'

'What photograph?' he says.

He motions for me to take a look. I leave the comfort of the chair and stepping into the hallway I freeze when I see that there is a blank space where the frame stood only moments before. Why would somebody go to such lengths to hide a photograph of their only son?

'I'm sorry, I must be mistaken. I'll see myself out.'

'What were you concerned about anyway. That this boy you are talking about doesn't appear to enjoy school very much or what exactly?' he says.

'That it may be better for him to remain in his mother's care for the time being. His father seems to be quite unstable. I can't really speak any more on the topic to you as it's confidential. But it would be a good idea if I spoke with my colleagues at social services about this address.'

I watch his eyes widen at this.

'My address, what for?' he says.

'His mother seems to think that his father, Zack Donoghue lives here. We'll have to investigate this further.'

'You didn't say anything about an investigation,' he says, more interested now that the conversation has tipped slightly over towards procedures and action rather than conversation and concern.

'I really think that I should be heading back now, I-'

I don't get to finish my sentence as a sharp pain spreads through the back of my head jarring me mid-sentence.

It takes me a few minutes to reorient myself. I sit on the floor, staring at the slightly fraying end on one of his shoe laces.

'I'm sorry, I don't know why I did that. Please forgive me,' he says.

I run my fingers over the back of my head, feeling the slow trickle of blood begin to surface through my closely shaved hair.

I look down to his hand still holding the frame that contains the photograph of his son. Ollie's little three-year-old face beaming for the camera that no doubt is being held by his mother.

Mothers are the silent ones in a picture. A hand or blurred image of hair. They collect these moments like memories in their minds, but rarely find themselves in the framed pictures themselves.

The glass covering the photograph is cracked on one

side and the frame is smeared with my blood. Zack looks frightened.

He steps back into the living room, slamming the door behind him, afraid that I will rush through there and attack him. I stand with my hand on the back of my head, bewildered. Not sure if I should leave the house or find out why he did it.

Was it a moment of madness? A reaction to the fear of losing any rights to his son? Or a typical reaction?

Something is telling me to leave the house and return to Claire. Tell her what a psycho husband she has, refusing to acknowledge his own child, then cracking me on the back of the head with a photograph of him, one he denied even existed.

Another part of me wants desperately to find out some answers for her. If I leave him like this what will he do next?

'Zack, may I come in?'

I wait for him to open the door.

'I just want to talk to you. Will you open the door?'

When he eventually opens the door just a fraction he looks away as though ashamed of his behaviour; sudden and violent.

He looks genuinely sorry. He doesn't look up to meet my eyes. Instead, he steps back allowing me to enter the living room. I return to the seat I had been sat in only a few minutes ago, and wait for him to begin.

'I'm sorry. I don't know what came over me. I was angry. My wife, she's taken everything. I'm lost without her. I go about my days hopeful that she'll change her mind and come back. I miss her. I miss them both,' he says, stopping to take a deep breath.

'I know you must be upset, hurt, angry even. But you can't blame me. I've done nothing wrong. I'm here for Claire, for both of you. But most importantly, I'm here for Ollie.'

He detects something different in my voice. I didn't mean it to come out the way it has. He looks at me as if I hold all the answers and then he smiles.

'You don't scare me you know,' he says, his jaw clenched together, forcing his misshapen teeth to join in higgledy-piggledy fashion.

'You can't have her,' he says.

'I'm sorry?'

'Claire. You can't have her. She's my wife, she will never be yours,' he says.

I shake my head and raise my eyes, but this only infuriates him further, fuelling the fire I myself set the moment I entered his property pretending to be a social worker.

'Claire is a client, a-'

'I thought the school contacted you? I thought you came here to check that I wasn't mistreating Ollie? You said-'

'I responded to a telephone call from my manager. I have no interest in your wife Mr Donoghue.'

'She can't abandon me and my son, not after everything we've been through.'

I'm no longer sure where this is going. He's clearly fragile. More so than Claire seems to be aware of.

'Everything? What is it Mr Donoghue? Can you tell me?'

'We've been through a lot in the past year. Things you will only understand if you have children. Do you have children Mr-'

'No. No, I don't.'

'With such responsibilities comes stress, tiredness. And then there was the accident.'

'Accident?'

'It was a car accident. She was pregnant with our daughter. She lost the baby. And that's when the problems started. She met someone. I know it, but I can't prove it.'

'Whatever you think your wife may or may not have been doing is irrelevant in this case.'

'So we're a case now?' he says.

'Not exactly, no. If we can ensure that no more conflict . . . no more problems arise that will affect Ollie, we can leave you to get on with your lives. It's really that simple.'

'What makes you think I want to get on with my life now that my wife has left me and taken my son away from me?' he says, the anguish in his eyes.

I don't know how to answer him.

I leave Zack's house and hurry to the car. I'm looking forward to cocooning myself inside a bubble, the fragranced interior of the car, and going over every single word until I hit on the right note.

He doesn't seem the type to be suicidal. But his words ring in my ears like a warning bell. An alarm of something to come. But I cannot for the life of me figure out what it is. He made reference to not wanting to continue his life without Claire. He sounds as though he's given up. But if he has then why all this runaround? Why the pretence of being happy, getting on with things, enjoying his once weekly fatherly role? And what happened to his leg? He doesn't seem to be in any pain. Why was he limping when he left Claire's flat?

Could he really be one of those men who at the slightest hint that things aren't going to go his way takes sudden drastic action without considering the consequences? Would he abduct Ollie? Would he harm him? Or Claire, for that matter? Is he really so unhinged?

I pull away from the house and see that the living room curtain is open just a fraction. I get a quick glimpse of Zack stood at the window, holding the edge of the curtain up to watch me leave. He's smiling. That same sickly smile he gave me when I arrived.

I notice the unease sweep over me like a rush of cold wind though the heaters are on and it's almost twenty-eight degrees in here now.

HER

I awake to the sound of the dawn chorus. Birds sweep to and fro before resting in the tree beyond the window.

I lift the covers from my face and look around the room. It's different now. The bed is pressed back against the internal wall offering a neat view of the tall trees that stand side by side, rustling in the wind. Chimney topped roofs at the end of the garden float as if unattached in the orange flecked light of the sun as it rises up into the sky. I watch the sun lift higher and higher until the clouds consume it before I decide it's time to get up.

By the time I've dressed and walked down into the kitchen Ollie is bounding up and down the stairs collecting bits and pieces of uniform from the pile on the landing, shoes from beside the front door and is now sitting at the table swigging orange juice from a glass, spilling half of it down his clean jumper.

'Oh, Ollie.' I shake my head and he puts the glass down onto the pinewood table and begins stuffing toast layered thick with jam in his mouth as though he's been starved.

Zack appears in the kitchen doorway. He wears

aftershave so strong I have to fight to breathe against it. He fills a cup with coffee and passes it to me without a word. He knows I can't begin the day without a strong cup of the caramel liquid.

'Sleep well?' he says.

'Yes. Thanks.'

'I'm not expected in until 9:30am. Shall I take Ollie to school for you?' he says.

'That would be great.' I yawn.

'Why don't you catch up on some sleep? Go back to bed and I'll bring you up some breakfast,' he says.

'Thanks, but I'd really better get going myself.'

He lets out a deep sigh. 'I only want to help you, Claire,' he says.

I force a smile.

'Thanks, but I have to get to work.'

'You can take the day off you know. Sort something out about your stuff. I don't mind you both staying here for a few days more.'

'We won't be in your way for long.'

'That's not what I meant,' he says.

'This is a short-term blip. We'll be out of your hair by the end of the day.'

He goes to say something but Ollie cuts him off.

'Where's my lunchbox?' he says.

I look to Zack but he turns away with a fixed stare.

'You can have a school dinner today, Ollie.'

'And how are you going to afford that?' says Zack, his back still turned away from me in contemplative thought.

'I have enough money for a school meal.'

'But not to furnish your house,' he says, a short laugh escaping his lips afterwards.

'Not in front of Ollie.'

'Are we going to live here again?' says Ollie.

'No, love. We'll be home tonight.'

'And where are you going to sleep?' says Zack.

'I said I don't want to talk about it in front of Ollie.'

'You don't want to talk about it full stop. That's the problem. You can't just hope this will all disappear. You have to actually do something about it, Claire,' he says, straightening his tie.

'Can't we stay with daddy?' says Ollie, looking up to us both with the same expression he gives us when he's in Toys R Us.

I bend down to plant a kiss on his forehead. He stands up straighter mimicking his dad's posture.

'No, love. We have to go home tonight.'

'You can stay as long as you want, Ollie, but your mother seems to think that she can produce miracles, so we'll have to wait and see,' he says, smiling.

'Zack that's enough. I said I'd sort it.'

'Like you did before, you mean?' he says, winking.

'What the hell is that supposed to mean?'

'Not in front of Ollie. Remember?' he says, taking Ollie's hand and stepping out of the back door.

'I'll pick him up. I'll call you tonight.'

'Sure,' he says, turning back, smiling and opening up the car door.

'Fine.'

I slam the back door on him then guiltily watch as Ollie gets into the car, looking back over his shoulder towards me as he does. Even as Zack pulls away from the house Ollie stares back at the door hoping for his mother to wave him goodbye. But I can't. My feet are rooted to the linoleum floor.

I want to shout, scream, tear my hair out and kick the stupid table but I don't. For Ollie's sake I mustn't lose it. I have to lock my feelings inside. As if tightening my dressing gown and crossing my arms across my waist will hold them in, I stand at the kitchen window, fighting the urge to call Zack to come back and have it out with

227

him, as I watch the car reverse out of the rear driveway and into the lane.

Ollie looks up at me and stares at me through the window with hollow eyes as Zack tells him something then he looks away as Zack peers up at me and shakes his head, turning to smile at Ollie as he shares a private joke with him.

That familiar feeling begins to stir within me, low down in the pit of my stomach. My chest tightening. My body grows tense and I want to hold onto this feeling for as long as possible. Teaching myself not to explode while allowing the darkness to consume me is an effort, but another way of regaining control over him. No matter what I do or where I go he will always be there. Lurking in the shadows.

I go upstairs, get changed back into yesterday's clothes, rub my teeth with toothpaste and head back down to make the long journey to Filton on foot to collect the catalogues.

I'll have to use the carrier bag I paid 5p for the privilege of using, that's still stuffed inside the pocket of my coat, having no bag to collect the catalogues with. The journey is going to take me several trips without a car or the money for a bus and I don't know what I'm going to do for money until the orders arrive on Wednesday.

I huff and puff up the hill, taking the short-cut through West Broadway onto the common. It'll be quicker to follow the main road onto Gloucester Road North and over to where I've left almost two hundred catalogues to be collected this morning.

Pride and irritation stop me from accepting Zack's offer of staying at the house for a few weeks while I get the money together to refurnish the flat. Paying rent on somewhere we're not even sleeping in is out of the question, defying my morals. And the thought of

228

spending another night in that house with Zack peering over my shoulder stirs me on up the road.

Aggressive walking is something I used to do that seemed to wear away my inner struggles, today though it just tires me out quicker.

I find myself leaning against the wall of somebody's house. Watching an elderly man polishing his car across the street, a woman walking a few paces back from where I stand, hurrying along down the hill with a small poodle. Everybody is getting on with their day to day lives while mine is falling apart at the seams.

I register a man and woman stepping out of a car on the opposite side of the road then walking towards me, before cutting in through the open gate and pulling out a set of keys for the front door of the house. I move away from the wall, mumble an apology, mention a bad back and before I have the time to catch the sympathetic glances that the couple offer me, I walk away from the house to continue on up the road.

It seems inevitable really when I think about it, that I would end up in such a situation as this. Zack's right- to some extent I have been denying my reality, hoping for a reprieve. Pretending no problems exist just to survive, and now I can't even do that because no matter what I'd like him to think, I am not coping very well living on my own. At least not right now.

Perhaps I ought to reconsider an alternative that doesn't involve moving back in with him. Maybe I should call my parents and tell them the truth, ask for a place to stay just until I can accumulate enough household objects to class the flat as a home once more.

I pull my mobile phone from the pocket of my jeans and send a quick text.

Mum, What time do you finish work today?
Need somewhere to stay for a bit. Will

explain everything when I see you. Claire. X

Fifteen minutes later, I've almost made it to the first row of houses to begin working when My phone *beeps* inside my pocket with a text alert.

I pull it out and read the message back twice. Nod my head and almost skip down to my first customers path to collect the catalogue that sits wedged between a large brick and a plant pot beside the wide doorframe.

See you at 7:00pm. Mum. X

It begins to rain just as I finish my second load and open the door to my bare flat- empty of feeling and love.

I stand in the kitchen and follow the patterns Ollie drew on the pictures I sellotaped to the walls. Faint outlines of dust and moisture stains frame where the cooker and fridge were.

I get to work on the mildew around the window sills and scrub the walls with a cloth and some washing up liquid that sit alone on the draining board. By the time I've made it into the living room to check my phone, I notice the time and head off to pick Ollie up from school. Only realising as my head begins to spin that I haven't eaten anything all day.

Ollie stands at the gate waiting for me with a solemn face.

'Are we going to daddy's?' he says.

'No. We're staying with nanny and grandad for a few days until I figure something out.'

'Why?' he says, oblivious to the fact that our flat sits empty with only the light scent of lemon washing up liquid bursting through the rooms.

'Daddy said we could live with him now. Like before,' he says.

'Sometimes, Ollie, things have to change. And it's about time they did. I'm going to make everything all right again, but first we need to get out of this rain and the flat isn't ready yet so we're going to have to get a move on.'

'Are you desiccating?' he says.

'No Ollie. We're not decorating. But I have been cleaning the place up all afternoon. I just have to buy some new things and then we can go home.'

'Will I get a new bed like Jacob?' he says. 'His dad bought him a car bed.'

'I'll try.'

'But you said-'

'Perhaps not a new bed but certainly a new desk.'

He lets go of my hand for a split second, but that's all it takes. He falls backwards into a puddle, soaking his only clean uniform and sending wet mud up the front of my jeans.

'Ollie!'

He pulls himself up with tears welling in his eyes and backs away from me.

'Ollie. Look at the state of you. Look what you've done.'

He doesn't look down at his brown stained trousers but instead turns and runs away from me and past the school gates. I chase after him but lose sight of him as I turn the corner.

'Ollie. Where are you? Come back here?'

I run up and down the pavement on both sides, frantically. Calling out his name and promising I'm not angry with him until my throat hurts.

Eventually, I see somebody getting into a car.

'Excuse me, my son, he ran off. Have you seen a little boy?'

'Sorry,' he says, continuing to bring out boxes from the back of his car, taking them one by one into his

231

house.

Has he got him? Has somebody taken my son? Why isn't he answering me?

'Ollie, for God's sake!'

Just as I'm about to pull the phone from my pocket to call the police, it rings.

'Claire, the school just called me. Ollie ran back. He seems upset. I'm on my way over there now. What the hell is going on?' says Zack.

'Oh, thank God he's all right. I was really worried. I thought-'

'What is happening, Claire? This isn't okay at all. It's the second time he's ran off in two weeks. What is the school going to think?' he says, his tone sharp.

'Zack, he's fine. You just said so yourself.'

'I'm on my way now. You should get your act together. I don't want Ollie witnessing you crack up,' he says, putting the phone down on me before I have the chance to explain.

I run back to the school, my chest heavy and my breath ragged as I force myself to hurry. I must get there before Zack does.

'It all happened so fast. He just ran off. I was running up and down the road calling his name but-'

'He's here. He's safe, Miss Donoghue. There's no need to panic,' says Mrs Pritchard.

'I'm not panicking I'm just-'

'You look frazzled. Why don't you stay for a cup of tea. You can leave when the rain begins to clear. It's awful out there,' she says, with a wistful expression as she gazes out of the window.

I hadn't noticed it had started to rain again. Just like I hadn't noticed Ollie run right past me as I paced the pavements on either side of the road, searching for him.

Mrs Pritchard blinks then runs her hand over Ollie's head, bending down to smile at him.

'What a lovely picture, Ollie,' she says.

His face is buried in the paper he is bending over with fierce concentration. The pencil moving quickly along the page at each flick of the pencil. The picture he is drawing growing more evident at each line and wisp of shading until the small dog is almost an exact carbon copy of the terrier I didn't see on a lead as his owner passed me until it was too late and I'd stumbled over, tripping on the lead, landing with my hands in a muddied puddle as I hurried to the school to fetch Ollie. When did I stop noticing things? When did I become so self-centred?

'You will make a fine artist,' says Mrs Pritchard, running her hand along his hair once more.

To witness, such a considered expression of kindness brings a lump to my throat. Seeing this, Mrs Pritchard feels obliged to explain.

'I have a fondness for your son, Miss Donoghue. He is a fine young man with a talent for art, music and literature. All the things I was never very good at,' she says.

I value her honesty.

'I loved art and English in school. But I was never very good at science or maths.'

She nods her head in approval and pulls out a seat for me to take.

'We should really go.'

I make my way over to Ollie, who flinches as I reach down to take his hand.

If Mrs Pritchard sees it she doesn't say anything, but when she does speak I feel that I at least, have somebody on my side.

'What shall I tell his father?' she says.

'What do you mean?'

'You won't want to be here when he arrives. No doubt he will, so why don't you leave through the top gate and

233

I'll stall him here for a bit of chit-chat. That'll give you plenty of time to get home before he wishes to speak to you,' she says.

I nod, grab Ollie's hand and take off as if we're being chased. Because in a way we are.

When we reach my parents house, set back off Keys Avenue, I remember that they won't be home for another three hours.

'Let's go to the library.'

Ollie looks bemused.

'Come on. It'll be fun. You can borrow some books to read and we can stay dry and warm until nanny gets home.'

'I don't want to stay with nanny. I want to live with daddy,' he says.

He has no idea how deep those words cut me. How painful it is to watch my own world spiralling out of orbit while Zack's neat, ordered life continues. Despite the rage that burns inside me for what he's done, to my relationship with my son and for all the destruction he's caused me to create for myself, I want nothing more than to scoop Ollie up into my arms and to never let him go. And so that is exactly what I do.

'Urgh, mum, get off,' he says, pushing me away.

I stroke his hair back from his eyes and smile back at him.

'You need a haircut little man.'

'So do you?' he says, a cheeky smile emanating from his lips.

'Very well. I know just the place. Once we've gone to the library.'

We leave the library with several books each. The rain has stopped now and the early dark night draws in close. I can see Ollie's breath in the air as we huddle up tight

234

against each other as we walk down the hill and up towards my parents house.

Their house is a slightly misshapen version of Ewan's.

It's been several days since I last spoke to Ewan. I wouldn't know what to say now if I did. Though I can't put it off forever. I still have to pay him back, though when is another bleak idea on the horizon now that my income has been slashed by half since being unable to use the chatline, and now I have no idea how I'm supposed to pay him back before Christmas as I'd hoped.

I can't bear thinking about the holiday season now that there'll be nowhere to hang the decorations. No shelf to sit the Christmas cards on. Nowhere to cook a Christmas dinner. Nobody to cook it for. We'll probably end up with two microwave meals with a small pudding each from the reduced aisle in Tesco.

As we reach the corner of the road where lanterns burn and a pumpkin peeps out from behind a skeleton hanging in a bush, I notice Zack's car parked opposite my parents house.

Inside, the large half-curtained window I can see my mother pouring tea from a pot into Zack's cup. Her movements are careless and quick, meaning she's just received some bad news. Something has upset her. My father will be at her side, with his palm faced down on her shoulder as she pours him a cup of tea, wearing a worried expression to match hers.

I can't let them think that I'm not coping. He can't win. I paint a cheerful smile onto my face and press the bell. When Zack's shadow falls in front of the windowed door that familiar sensation of unease creeps over me. I back away from the door just as he opens it.

HIM

I leave the house just after 7:00pm. The wind is fierce and the cold air bites at the exposed skin of my face and hands. I tug my coat up tighter around my neck.

The image of Zack stood smiling at the window haunts me as I step into the car and drive away from Henleaze, following the main road up towards Filton.

I know I have to tell Claire. Warn her that Zack is planning something though I'm unsure what it is, I know it has something to do with Ollie.

My thoughts are still on Zack as I'm crossing the verge which meets Kellaway Avenue when I hear the screeching of tyres. It feels as though time has slowed, but in reality, it must be mere seconds. One quick look in the side mirror and I can see the cause is a van turning into the road behind me. It's going too fast and appears to have swung out from the wrong side of the road and chances the roundabout. It's coming towards me with such speed that my actions can't catch up. I brake, but it's not enough. The car swings out, running the roundabout at such an angle that the driver hits into the side of the car. There's a crunch as the metal is bent inwards, and a heavy dragging sound as the car is being shunted across the road, forcing it onto the pavement and into a wall on the far side of the street.

They say that your life flashes in front of your eyes but it doesn't happen to me. There is a brief moment where I think I pray, though not aloud, and then everything is still. There doesn't appear to be anyone else on the road. For several seconds, it is just us- me and the other driver. Even the howling wind seems to draw a breath.

The heaters continue to blow hot air out into the car but it's silent. I wonder if I've gone deaf. After a few minutes the sound of the engine, its whirring noise, takes over from the sound of my panicked breaths, alerting me to the fact that it is still running.

I look over my right shoulder and see that the driver of the other vehicle is clambering out of the car trying to make a run for it. Whether it is luck or just coincidence Southmead Road police station sits on the corner, just a few yards ahead. Though most of the police stations in Bristol have closed down, this one is still manned.

I wonder how much time has passed. The world seems to be running in slow motion. As I'm thinking this, a car appears to stop on the opposite side of the road. The driver leaves her car, the hazard lights flashing to warn others that she knows not to park on double yellow lines but is prepared to do so to assist me and the other driver, the man who is now attempting to run from the scene.

He's visibly shaken but appears to be lacking injuries. Perhaps he's been drinking. Perhaps he's a disqualified driver. He doesn't stop to check that I'm all right. I face the windscreen and try not to move. Though I'm not in any pain I'm unable to shift my right leg. The entire drivers side of the car has been crushed. The metal forced towards me. Bent. If I look at it I might not be able to contain my hammering heart so I continue to stare straight ahead.

From the corner of my eye, I can see that the woman has made it safely across the road. She stands for a few moments staring at me. When I move she steps back, visibly shaken. I assume she thought I was dead. She is now tugging on the door, her mobile phone pressed to her ear, pointing to the engine which has now begun to smoke. She can see that I can't move so opens the right rear passenger door and climbs into the car.

'Can you get out?'

I shake my head.

'Are you in any pain?' she says.

'No.'

'I'm going to try and bring your chair back. The engine is on fire. I have to get you out of here as quickly and as safely as possible,' she says.

'Are you a doctor?'

'No. I don't have any medical training. I won't do anything that the lady on the phone doesn't tell me to,' she says.

'Okay.'

With a few shunts of the seat, it glides back and my leg is freed. It's sore now that the blood is able to return to it, but I can move.

I follow her out through the back of the car where a police officer is now standing, two officers in high visibility jackets are behind him, running up towards the car. The police car I didn't see or hear has been parked sideways to stop anyone from attempting to continue driving up the road. They move towards me but I can see from their relieved expressions that they thought this might have been a fatality.

I lift my hand up and wave.

'The driver left. He ran that way.'

I point across the road to where the man was heading

only a minute or two before. I follow the officers over to the side of the road whilst one of them takes a look at both of our vehicles, writing down number plates and taking notes of the point of impact and the direction in which the other car came from.

The officer who walks up to me doesn't appear as deeply affected by this situation as his colleagues.

'An ambulance is on its way. Are you hurt?' he says.

'No. There's no need. I'm fine.'

'We'll need a breath test. Standard procedure,' he says, pausing when he sees me inspect the damage caused by the driver's carelessness.

'We'll get this cleared away as soon as possible. The station's only up the road. We'll take your statement inside. I'm sure you wouldn't say no to a cup of tea?' he says, offering me his hand.

'DI Blake,' he says. 'DC Flint will follow us shortly.'

I follow him along the pavement and through the single glass door of the station. He keeps looking me over as we walk side by side into the station past a small reception area and through a set of doors. We're met by a dimly lit corridor which leads through to two interview rooms. I follow him into the little room at the far end. He pulls out a plastic chair for me to take the seat opposite him.

This is the first time I've seen the inside of a police station, except on TV. It's much smaller than I'd assumed it would be. There aren't nearly as many officers in charge as I'd expected and the lighting is just as bad as it is back at home. The energy saving light bulbs giving off only enough light to enable me to see DI Blake's features, ignoring the rest of the room which is perhaps the idea. If the only thing worth looking at in perfect light are the eyes of the officer I'm speaking to then maybe they think I won't be able to hide my honesty from them. Though I've no intention of lying.

'So what happened?' he says, flipping over a sheet of paper attached to a folder I hadn't seen him walk in with until now.

'The van shot out over the roundabout. He left the vehicle. He didn't even check to see if I was injured.'

'We're classing this as a hit and run so it's important that we get as many facts as possible written down while it's still fresh. Can you start from the beginning?' he says.

We leave the station just after 8:00pm. DI Blake is sitting beside me while I look out of the window and see the debris from my car being cleared away. This side of the road has been cordoned off so that a thin strip of it can still be used for oncoming vehicles.

'I knew someone who lived around by you some years ago. It's a nice area,' says DI Blake, trying to make polite conversation.

DC Flint sits beside him, inspecting something on the dashboard. My mind is on Claire. How I'm going to tell her. How I'm going to get to her. I don't want DI Blake knowing where I'm thinking of heading. I accepted the lift to make a quicker route to the bus stop.

I get the impression this isn't routine, especially when most road traffic collisions result in at least one driver being taken to hospital, I politely refused to go with the paramedic they called, arriving at the station ten minutes in to taking my statement, though the hospital is only a few yards up the road from the police station.

'Thanks for the lift.'

I say this as I leave the car walking over to the house. DI Blake sits and watches me enter, waiting until I switch on the living room and hallway lights before he pulls away, careening down the road in pursuit of another accident or emergency. The blue lights flashing in the distance. No sound can be heard from inside the well-insulated walls of the house.

I stumble over the rug covering the kitchen floor and grab some change from a tin hidden behind the cereal box before leaving to catch the next bus up to Filton. It takes me far longer to reach the end of Gloucester Road North without a car. I have to walk for five minutes, down past the Dolphin swimming baths and the large open playing field, the newly painted play equipment of the park gleaming in the lights from the shopping outlet across the road.

By the time I reach Claire's flat my feet ache and my breath is sharp against the cold night air. There are no lights on. I suspect that she's just put Ollie to bed and has decided to retire early herself but as I near the front door I can see that her car is not parked on the driveway. I walk around to the living room window and push my face up to the glass. With my head bent and my hand resting against my forehead, I can see through into the living room. There is nothing inside. All of her furniture is gone.

I doubt that she's moved. She would have told me. It's even more unlikely that she's been evicted, considering she didn't owe any rent. At least not that I know of. The bailiffs must have returned, taking everything away to clear the last of her debts. Whatever has happened though makes it unlikely that she's at home at all.

I consider calling her but I've left my mobile phone at home and it's getting late. Wherever she is I'm sure she's tucked up safe and warm with Ollie beside her. There's no reason to think that she isn't.

Not unless Zack has already got to her. Not unless he's taken Ollie or lured her somewhere. I can imagine her now in a dark room, bleeding from a head wound. Has he hit her on the head as he did me? What if she isn't safe? What if Claire and Ollie are in danger? What if they are with him?

I run from the street and back out onto the main road. I consider waiting for another bus but think that it will be quicker if I run to the next stop. I manage to run past three of them, all the way down towards Monks Park when I see a bus coming. I jump onto it as soon as it arrives and stay standing until the bus stops outside of the Co-Op at the bottom of Gloucester Road. I run up towards Henleaze, knowing this is my quickest option, but knowing too that without a car this journey is going to take me just as long as if I'd walked.

I slow my pace and try to take in a lungful of the thick ice air while I continue on my route towards Zack's. I don't dare to consider that he might not be there. That he too might have disappeared into the night.

By the time I reach the house, I realise what a mistake I've made getting involved in somebody else's drama. He too it seems, is not at home. There are no lights on in the house, his car is no longer parked outside, and I haven't a clue as to where they could all be. Although I'm positive they are together, and that something is going to happen tonight.

I raise my head a little higher and send a silent thought up to the sky, hoping that Claire can hear it.

'Be safe. I'm going to find you.'

I tread back the way I came, through the lane and up onto Kellaway Avenue. All the while I am considering where they might be. What could be happening right now? I only hope that I am not too late.

Zack was planning something earlier. I could see it in his eyes. I only wish I knew what it was.

HER

'What are you doing standing outside in the cold?' says mum. 'Come on in.'

'Why is Zack here?'

'Oh, he was just passing,' she says, coming closer to whisper in my ear. 'I think he's worried about you.'

'He's just passing at 7:30pm?'

She ignores me. Raising her hand up to my cheek as she did when I was a child, testing the heat of my skin against the back of her cold bony hand.

'You do look under the weather lately, Claire,' she says. 'Is everything all right?'

'Can we talk in the kitchen?'

She nods her head and plants her arm around me, showing Ollie into the living room. Her body feels stiff against my own. Something isn't right but I can't put my finger on what it is.

'Shall I make us some tea first?' she says, not waiting for my answer as she flicks on the switch of the kettle and takes a seat on one of the diner stools she bought in Gardners, the last shopping trip we took together before the separation- before Zack became even more of a stranger to me.

'What's wrong love?' she says. Her voice is warm but her posture steely.

'The debts were almost paid off then I came home and found bailiffs at the door. Zack let them in.' I say this hoping to gauge a reaction similar to mine when I saw them in the midst of taking away everything I own, but she remains unmoved.

'They took everything except Ollie's bed and clothes, and what few toys he owns, even his books.'

'What did you expect, Claire?' she says.

'A phone call would've been nice. Some notice. Ollie was with me.'

'That's awful. Shouldn't they have at least told you. Well, I suppose . . .'

'Suppose what?'

'How did they get in?' she says, without finishing what she had begun to say.

'That's the best part. Zack let them in. With a key he'd had made without telling me.'

'I'm sure he was just worried' she says. 'Maybe he had it made in case of an emergency.'

Her face is still unmoved as I continue.

'He lied about the burglary too.'

She turns away from me to pour the water from the kettle, stirring the teabag around just as I do; to savour every last particle of it.

'I can't prove it, but I know it was him.'

'Why would he lie about something like that?' she says. For the first time throughout this conversation, I can see that she doesn't appear surprised, by any of it.

She brings the cup up to her mouth, taking a sip of the hot tea.

'Were you expecting me?'

'Of course, you sent me a text message, remember?' she says.

244

'No, I mean, did you know what I was going to say? How long has Zack been here?'

'Don't be silly Claire. He arrived not long before you. What are you implying?' she says.

Though she doesn't appear to be lying I don't believe her. I'm sure he's been here longer. Long enough for Zack to prepare mum for what I'm going to say, to twist my words so that they sound paranoid, delusional. I'm even beginning to think they do myself until I see a momentary shudder. My mum doesn't get nervous. Something is making her uncomfortable.

'Where is he?'

'Zack is upstairs with your dad. I think he wanted to give Ollie a goodnight kiss,' she says.

I know in that instant that we can't stay here. I have to get as far away from this house as possible, but Ollie is already being tucked up in bed by my father and being read a bedtime story about dinosaurs and will no doubt already be drifting towards sleep.

'You haven't drunk your tea,' says mum.

I didn't notice that she'd made me one.

'I said I didn't want one.'

She frowns and goes to shake her head but thinks better of it.

'What is he doing here?'

'He just wanted to talk,' she says.

'About what? Me?'

'Don't be ridiculous.'

'Am I? You're my mum. He's my ex-husband. I think you should be taking my side not his.'

'I'm taking nobody's side. Don't be so childish. And you're not divorced. Not yet anyway. You really need to start talking. I think he felt lonely that's all,' she says, dropping her voice slightly as footsteps run along the ceiling above us.

Noticing my eyes wander up to the spiral ceiling rose

she says: 'Ollie will be asleep now. Just have something to eat and drink. You'll feel better for it. And please, try to relax. You look so tense.'

Relax? How can I while he's here?

I can't wake Ollie up, not if he's so tired. And I've nowhere else to go. I can't expect Ewan to put us up- not this late. Not that I could let him meet Ollie. Zack would be furious if Ollie told him that not only had I woken him up but I'd then taken him to another man's house to sleep instead of staying at my parent's. And not just any man. But a man I barely know. A man I met on the chatline I work for. Zack would go insane if he knew I did such a job with Ollie under the same roof. Even if he is always asleep when I'm working or at school. I'd never hear the end of it. I don't even really know Ewan all that well. I don't have any friends who have the space to put us up. Not that I could call them this late and ask. That would be an awkward conversation, especially since the break-up. I haven't exactly been the easiest of people to get hold of. I haven't kept in contact with anyone really. It's looking more and more likely that I'll just have to ride this one out. We'll leave first thing in the morning.

I'm shaken from my internal monologue by my mum's voice.

'Are you sure you're all right Claire? You don't seem yourself at the moment. You look worried,' she says, taking another sip of the strong sweet tea she lives off.

'It's not me you should be worried about.'

I don't mean to be so blunt. She looks up at me with wide rimmed eyes. Her facial features settle for just a moment.

'I know things have been difficult recently, what with Ollie, school and oh, don't look so shocked. Zack told me all about it. You should've said. Still, there's no harm done now, is there love? Now that it's all out in the open,' she says, a curved smile appearing in one corner of her mouth.

'I'm not sure what you mean, mum.'

'It can't be easy on your own. Being a mother is one of the most timely, stressful jobs in the world. There's no sick pay, no holidays. Just a daily job with no rewards.'

I'm only half listening. This is always the way with mum, she likes to think of motherhood as something you must sacrifice a career and a life for. What she doesn't seem to understand is that you *can* have it all- if you have the support of your partner. If he shoots you down at every opportunity or becomes jealous of your success over his own, like Zack did towards the end, then you run into a problem. Time and again she has deliberated over whether or not she should have returned to work after I was born. Every time she mentions it the same anger rears its horns out and prepares me for battle.

I can hear footsteps again. This time, they're heading towards the stairs.

'Mum, I want Ollie to have a normal happy childhood. Enough money to keep a roof over our head and food on the table. I have to work.'

'You should be with your husband. You should be trying to make it work with him. It's not always easy, but running away isn't the answer.'

'I'm not running away. It was an amicable decision.'

'Really? It doesn't seem that way. Not to me anyway,' she says.

'It was impossible. We weren't happy. That's not good for Ollie, for any child. Surely you can see that?'

She hesitates as Zack appears in the doorway.

'He's fast asleep,' he says. 'Shall I warm you up some food?'

'No thank you. I'm not hungry.'

I didn't hear him coming down the stairs.

'You should eat love. It's not good dealing with anything on an empty stomach,' says mum, placing a hand on my arm.

'I'm going to bed.'

'I've made the spare bedroom up for Ollie so you can have the study. There's a sofa bed in there. The pillows are in the-'

'I know, mum. Thanks.'

'I suppose you'd better get going.' I aim my words at Zack, hoping for some space to think.

'Me and your dad are watching a fight at 11:00pm. They said I could have the sofa in the living room,' he says. 'I hope you don't mind?'

I want to say 'actually I do' but what good would it be? Besides, I don't live here.

'It's not my house.'

I hope that my mum can hear what I'm implying. That I wouldn't sleep in the same space as him if it was up to me, but she doesn't seem to be listening.

My dad walks into the living room holding up a stack of paper. I can see even from here, on the other side of the spacious living room, that whatever they contain must be important. As he steps closer I can see that they're ripped.

'That little sod has been in my study. He's ruined all of the paperwork for my conference speech tomorrow. What am I supposed to do now?' he says.

'Ollie?'

'Who else?' he says.

'But haven't you just put him to bed?'

'I said there was something going on. I told you there was something not right about that lad, but you won't listen,' he says, his words directed to mum.

She stands there with her arms open in resignation.

'He's only a boy Roger. He can't have known. It must have been an accident,' she says.

'Zack, weren't you up there? Didn't you see anything?'

'No. Not a thing,' he says.

I narrow my eyes at him but he doesn't get the hint. What if it wasn't Ollie? What if Zack did it?

'I think you can still use them. They don't look so bad.'

'Unprofessional,' says dad, scowling and leaving the room in a fluster.

Zack turns to me. 'We need to talk about this. Ollie's behaviour since you left has been on the decline. You can't tell me that this isn't some kind of vendetta against us.'

'What me? Is that what you were going to say, Zack?'

'All children cope differently with divorce,' says mum.

'No child copes very well with divorce you mean?' he says.

She drops her gaze down, following the swirling pattern on the carpet with her eyes.

'Perhaps he needs to see someone. A school counsellor?' she says.

'You're not seriously suggesting that my son has psychological problems?'

'Our son, Claire. He's our son,' says Zack.

I look from Zack to mum and back again.

'I suppose you agree with her. I expect you've been plotting this from the minute I came through the door.'

'Really, Claire that is-'

'Ridiculous? No. I don't think so. I think Zack is afraid of losing me. Afraid of his tidy ordered life crumbling down around him, just as mine is. He can't see that *this*, all of it, is his fault.'

'Anything that has happened has been caused by you. None of it has anything to do with me. You walked out on me. You want to divorce me. You took Ollie from me. Anything that your actions have caused you've brought on yourself,' he says.

'You really believe that don't you?'

He doesn't answer.

'Why are you still here? Hanging around my parents house. Pretending everything is fine. When it's not, is it?'

Mum turns around and follows the grumbling sounds my dad is making as he attempts to sellotape the paperwork together in the dining room. She leaves the kitchen. I can hear her trying to placate him in hushed tones. 'He didn't mean it. He's just a lad.'

Mum leaves dad in the dining room, heading for the stairs. Zack steps past me, lowers his voice and whispers in my ear: 'This isn't over Claire. You won't get away with treating me as if I'm the bad guy. Not anymore.'

I can hear mum's footsteps treading up the staircase. She pauses half way up and I'm convinced she's heard him, but she doesn't halt for long, continuing on up to the bathroom, while Zack shifts past me, brushing his shoulder against my ear as he makes his way into the living room where my dad is now sat ready for the game.

Boxing has always been one of his favorite pastimes. Now it seems Zack is taking an interest in it too. What I don't understand is why. He's never liked the sport. Often commenting that delinquent men with too much testosterone use it as an excuse to punch twelve bells out of each other.

It feels as if I no longer know him. He's changed. Zack has become somebody I only thought I knew. The thought of sleeping in the same house as this stranger is far from uncomfortable.

I'm lying on the fold-out sofa bed with my arm dangling off the side. I can feel the cold from the laminate floor sinking deep into the bones of my hand.

I can't sleep knowing *he's* just across the hall. Why can't he just leave me alone? Let me get on with my life?

For Ollie's sake as much as mine. I'm thinking this when I move my hand up and catch something beneath the bed. My finger grazes against something that feels like a screwed up ball of paper.

I leave the bed to inspect it, lifting the quilt that's slipped down from where I lie and onto the floor. In the moonlight that's flooding through the slatted blinds, I can see that there is a pile of screwed up balls of paper beneath the sofa bed.

I bend down and run my hand along the floor forcing them all out of their hiding place. Taking the first, I open it up and see the finely slanted letters of my dad's handwriting. Each one penned to the same effect. My dad's conference papers scattered beneath the sofa bed. The words *final version* written neatly at the top of the first page. Each numbered beneath in the same pen.

My dad doesn't use a computer to write notes. He prefers pen and paper. An old fashioned man at heart. None of the pages are ripped or sellotaped together. Meaning only one thing.

I stare in the darkness at the mess in front of me. No obvious explanation comes to me. There is no reason why my dad would lie about something like that. What could he possibly gain from making out that Ollie is some kind of psychopathic child, deliberately damaging property?

Like the lying and stealing. There is no evidence that it is him who has done this. Only their word against his. A child. And why didn't they question him? If they truly believe that he has done this then why didn't somebody wake him up and ask him about it? Like I would have done. This isn't right.

Some parents will defend their children until the end of the Earth. They are the parents who believe that their child can do no wrong. That little Joshua didn't mean to kill his father or put the cat in the microwave. That he didn't understand what he was doing feeding vitamins to his baby sister. I'm not one of those mum's who takes their child's side despite the evidence to refute all other possible claims.

I gather the balls of paper up, spreading them back out until they are almost all readable. Except for one that bears the stain of a coffee cup at the corner, they are all usable. I stack the paper in a pile on the desk, leaving it in a position so that my dad will find them easily in the morning when he creeps into the room searching for his laptop and suit that is hanging up on the back of the closed door.

I return to bed, unable to sleep more so now than before and lie there facing the window. I watch through the slats of the blind as the sky grows lighter. The clouds dispersing, giving way to another mild morning.

I awake a couple of hours later to the sound of shuffling feet. Keys jangling in the wind of the open front door. My dad's suit still hangs from the back of the door. The pile of notes still sit on the desk where I left them. Zack must be leaving for work early this morning.

I stretch my arms up in the air and shift the duvet that kept falling to the floor all night from my bare legs. I must have undressed. Too hot from the heat of the wide radiator that sits below the window on one wall. I leave the bed, dress quickly and creep downstairs to the kitchen where Ollie is up and ready, eating a bowl of cereal. The patio doors are open.

Zack stands a few feet away on the stone steps which lead down on to the patio. I can see the smoke through the voile that billows in and out of the open glass doors by the wind.

'You're smoking? But you haven't smoked in years?'

'Twelve. There didn't seem to be any point worrying about that, not now,' he says.

I'm about to ask what he means by that but when he

turns around I freeze.

'What happened to your face?'

'It's nothing. Don't worry about it,' he says.

'You've got a black eye. It isn't nothing.'

'Ollie, go and fetch your lunchbox from the table and fill out your food diary for school,' he says.

Ollie looks up from his now empty bowl, senses the tension in the air and leaves the room without a second glance.

'Food diary?'

'I have time for our son. I help him with his homework,' he says.

'Zack, don't start. Not here.'

'You don't get it do you?' he says. His expression is accusatory.

'What don't I get?'

'Don't pretend you can't remember,' he says.

He's playing mind games now.

'I'm not doing this any more.'

I turn to leave but his arm swings out, his palm landing heavily on the worktop.

'Zack, move your arm.'

'Answer me one thing before I do,' he says.

'I don't have time for this. I've got things to do.'

'Like what? You haven't got a job any more,' he says.

'How do you know-'

'It's obvious, Claire. Maybe not to you, but it is to me. You've lost all of your belongings. How will you work without your laptop? A car? I saw all this coming, but you don't seem to be aware of anything until it hits you right in the face,' he says, drawing in a breath as if he is as exasperated as I am.

'I'm tired of arguing.'

'You weren't last night,' he says, pointing to his swollen, bruised eye. 'You were raring to go.'

'You can't blame me for that!'

'What if I were to tell my solicitor?'

'You've got one now have you?'

'What if I showed him just what you are capable of, what kind of a woman you really are?' he says.

I grab a cup from the counter hoping to distract Zack from his deluded thoughts long enough for him to see that I'm not buying into this whole victim-husband fantasy.

He clenches his left hand into a fist. Then he pulls his arm back and swings. I duck, assuming he is going to hit me but am more shocked at the sound of glass breaking and his own cry of pain.

'You mental cow. What are you doing?' he says, loud enough for my mum to hear.

'Zack? Claire?' she says, running down the stairs.

'What did you do that for?'

'Me? Are you so deluded you can't see what you're doing?' he says.

'Oh, my. What happened Zack? Are you okay?' says mum, stepping over the shattered pieces of mums favourite vase that had been sitting on the shelf above the kettle.

'I'm fine. I'll be fine,' he says.

She turns her attention to me, holding my gaze with that steely glare she used when I'd broken something valuable as a child whilst playing.

'What have you done?' she says.

'Nothing. I haven't done anything. It was him.'

She takes one look at Zack holding the heel of his hand over his already swollen eye, blinking several times to force tears to well up in his one good eye that he uses to force my gaze to remain on him.

'She's mad. She's fucking mad,' he says.

My mum looks down at the cup in my hand. I follow her cold hard stare. It's only then that I can see it. The cup has a thin lined crack down the side of it. A blot of blood is smeared over the rim.

When Zack pulls his hand away from his face a small cut, still fresh, sits just below the bridge of his nose where the bruising around his eye begins.

'I know what it looks like, but it's not . . . that's not. For God's sake it wasn't me!'

'Then who the bloody hell was it, Claire?' she says, looking to me for confirmation over what she thinks she knows just happened.

'He did it to himself. He wants to make me look bad. He wants you to think that I did it.'

'Why would he do that, to himself?' she says, unable to disguise the small laugh that slips from her mouth as she speaks.

'Don't listen to her,' he says.

'Don't worry, I won't. I want you to leave. Both of you. Get your stuff together and go. I won't have this. Not in my house,' she says, turning to leave the kitchen, hoping we'll follow.

'You've lost it, Claire,' he says, slipping in a smile for effect.

'I'm mad? Losing my mind? Well if I have it's only because of you.'

He lowers his voice so that only I can hear him. 'You've gone mad, Claire. Everybody knows it, but you.'

'Mad? I'm not mad. I'm furious.'

I throw the cup at him but he ducks just in time.

The cup hits the wall. The small drop of blood that was coating the rim flecks off and lands like tiny pin-prick dots on the wall where just a moment before Zack had been standing.

'Get out of my house. Get out!' says mum.

She's had enough. I can see spittle landing from her mouth onto the neckline of her chiffon blouse. Ollie appears in the doorway after hearing the commotion.

'Ollie, baby. Come here.'

'What happened to dad?' he says, shock and concern emanating from his face.

'Your mum.'

'Mum? You hurt dad?' he says.

'No, of course not, Ollie. He just wants everyone to think that I did.'

'Yes, Ollie. But it's okay. It's all going to be all right. Because I'm going to get you to school and I'm going to help your mother-'

'Help? That'll be a first.'

'Enough, Claire. Both of you. I want you to leave now or your dad-'

'Where is dad anyway?'

He comes down the stairs in no hurry. His feet barely leaving each step as he shifts on one foot, then the other in anticipation of whatever he believes he's going to be affronted with.

'I found these in my office,' he says, handing the pile of papers I'd left on the desk for him to collect this morning.

'I found them under the sofa bed last night. I put them on your desk-'

'That's your writing isn't it?' he says, pointing at the blue ink that has been scribbled across each page he flicks over in front of my face. The words 'not good enough' written over his own in large letters so that his own writing is almost illegible.

'I didn't do that.'

'Your mum is right. I think you should leave. Both of you. Ollie too. I'm sorry, but whatever problems you're having, you're not bringing them to our doorstep, is that clear?' he says.

'I didn't do that.'

'I don't want to hear another word from either of you-'

'Have you any idea how long it took your father to rewrite all that last night? He did it during the boxing

256

fight on the TV. Zack wasn't able to sellotape it all together so he started again. Sixteen pages,' says mum.

'I found them under the-'

'The sofa. So you keep saying. But you were the only person in there last night,' she says.

I don't like where this is going.

'Are you trying to say that *I* did this? That I deliberately ruined your notes? What would I possibly achieve from doing that?'

'It's not just that though is it. My suit was hanging up on the back of the door.'

'Yes, I know. I saw it.'

'Let me finish,' he says, sounding more and more irate by the second.

I force my lips closed to hear him out. Only when he's finished I want to scream.

'It's been torn. Ripped,' he says.

'Where is it? Let me see.'

He leaves the room. Just less than a minute later returning with the jacket. The sleeve of which appears to have been cut with a pair of scissors.

'Just yesterday you were prepared to blame Ollie for your conference papers being shredded up and now this. It's not Ollie. It's him.' I point to Zack who winces and pulls his hand up to his face.

'Your mum is right. You should both leave now,' says dad.

'Where are we supposed to stay? I have no appliances, no bed. Nothing.'

'I don't care,' says dad. 'Just get out.'

I grab my coat from the hook in the hallway.

'Come on Ollie. I'm taking you to school.'

'Where are we going when you pick me up?' he says.

'To a friends.'

AFTER

4. I had recently separated from my husband Zack Donoghue. I had no concerns over his ability to provide for or take care of our son, Ollie until our trip to Disneyland when it became evident that Zack was struggling with money. I had recently been trying to pay some debts off myself and we both agreed that we would try to continue with our contact arrangement despite this fact. Zack had Ollie over to his house every weekend. Though I was able to afford the rent and council tax it was a struggle to cover food as well as pay the utility bills and cover my debts. These were mostly credit cards, catalogues and loan repayments.

Whilst on holiday with Ollie in Disneyland my flat was broken into. Nothing was taken but the place was trashed. Zack called me and told me that he'd deal with everything. When we got back he said he'd given a statement to the police and tidied up the place for me.

However, during a conversation about the burglary, I began to suspect that Zack may have been hiding something from me. His behaviour was erratic and I felt I could no longer trust him. I'd been thinking about a divorce for some time, so to me, seeking a solicitor to file for a decree absolute felt like the next step. I wanted to move on. That's when the problems began.

Zack was convinced that I'd left him because of an affair. There was also one moment during a conversation that I questioned whether the burglary had even occurred at all. Though I put these thoughts down to feeling unsettled and insecure. Ollie had mentioned twice that he had seen a man following me, and I had felt as if I was being watched several times. This was both before and after I'd met Ewan. I became paranoid that somebody, especially Zack would find out about us meeting up that day. I tried to convince myself that I was being foolish, but I couldn't help feeling distracted. In hindsight, I believe that my intuition was trying to tell me something and I was choosing not to listen to it through fear.

Although Ewan had paid off my debts without my knowledge I still felt as if I owed him. I didn't find out until the debt collection company called me (Amira and Sons) to tell me that he'd paid them. They were calling to confirm collection of my belongings that afternoon. He later told me when I called him that he'd asked for the name of the company who had come to my house with a court-ordered repossession of goods notice in order to pay them. I'd promised to pay him back as soon as I could.

Zack and I had always vowed to keep any disagreements between us or conversations regarding Ollie's welfare away from Ollie. But on occasion over the weeks following my date with Ewan, Zack began to exhibit odd behaviour, even when Ollie was around.

At one point, Zack entered my home uninvited with a third key he'd had made when changing the locks on my flat after the break-in. He said he'd seen my debt collection notices but the letters weren't kept anywhere visible. He gave me the key but I felt anxious that he'd been in my property without asking my permission, and that he'd kept the key hidden from me.

I did not disclose my concerns to Ewan until later. Ollie had been having some problems in school. He's been accused of stealing, and then lying about it. He'd also been hanging around with a friend who I believed was dishonest. His school work seemed to be suffering and after several visits to the school, one of which when he had left his father and came home alone, and another time when he had run off back to the school while we were discussing his behaviour with his head teacher Mrs Pritchard. I thought that I had done everything that I possibly could and was at rather a loss as to where to go from there so I asked Ewan to visit Zack, pretending to be from child protection. I understand that impersonating a social worker is wrong but at the time, I felt as though I had no choice. Zack didn't seem to be taking Ollie's behaviour very seriously and he had only ever ran off or disappeared when his father had been with him or was involved somehow. I hoped that it would frighten Zack - the thought that social services were involved - into ensuring that Ollie's schooling was made a priority and that he'd see how his own behaviour was affecting him.

I trusted Ewan to a certain degree. Since our date, he became a very good friend. Somebody, I felt I could trust. He appeared rational and intelligent. He did not ask for anything in return. He even tried to talk me out of visiting Zack, but he went anyway.

HER

I'm sitting in a small room away from the court. The cornflower blue paint-work is fresh. My victim support worker sits behind me in the corner beside a faux bamboo plant in an orange vase. A single plastic beaker of tepid tap water was placed in front of me and a box of tissues sit to my left though I can't remember now who put them there.

Through the screen perched on the desk in front of me I can see nobody in the courtroom except his defence barrister though I can hear them, their voices murmur in the background. One of the jury is shuffling in their seat. Everyone except the barrister are mere shadows of my consciousness, waiting, listening, making notes, watching me, looking for a sign of guilt or omission of some kind. They are waiting for Karyn Aston to catch me out.

I can picture their faces now, eyes on the screen, listening intently, their neurons firing beneath their skulls, trying to pinpoint something, anything; a reason why the knife didn't penetrate far enough through my skin to end my life as it did his.

Karyn, his barrister focuses on my eyes. I can feel them piercing the screen even though we are over thirty feet away from each other. She turns around to address the judge, who returns her question with 'you may.'

My own barrister Paul Leighton QC sits on the opposite side of the court. His strange white wig the only thing of him that I can see. Though I have been told that it is him, I can only picture his face in my mind.

Karyn Aston can be heard reciting my statement. A copy of it sits in front of me. As she reads from it I follow each word, each sentence. My life has now been narrowed down into a set of paragraphs. Of course, I understand that this is not *my life* but a mere chapter of it, though right now it is the only important piece of it. The one and only chapter of my life that I wish to never think about again contains the only event related to my narrative that the court is interested in hearing.

I am a case. My story is numbered as such. I am a witness to a part of my life that I have no intention of reliving. Yet I am forced to. Made to repeat and rehearse each part of that night with detailed honesty and clear instruction from his barrister and to do so without omitting any detail whatsoever.

My eyes hover over the words as Ms Aston finishes reading it aloud to the court. When her voice stops I clear my throat and prepare to begin.

She looks up into my eyes. Through the screen, she appears young as though every crease and wrinkle, any imperfection that she will later develop is yet to begin to trace itself along the contours of her face. She has a slightly upturned nose but a perfectly symmetrical set of eyes that glisten deep jade in the light, though now she stands slightly away from the screen, stepping back to focus on my entire portrait, her eyes darken slightly as if she is being taken on by a visceral entity.

She addresses me politely and gives me her full

attention as she speaks.

'Miss Donoghue, can you confirm that this statement is an accurate portrayal of what occurred on the night of 11th November 2014 when you agreed to meet Mr Ewan Carter face-to-face at his home address in Redland Park?' she says.

'Yes, it is.'

'May I ask that when you answer my questions you answer them specifically,' she says.

I wonder if she is acting like a headteacher on purpose. Does she speak to everyone like this or just me? The hints of something unsettling begin to resurface, starting in my chest. I brush it away and focus on the task in hand, knowing that this is my only chance to be heard.

'You say in your statement that you could see light emanating from the basement, something which drew you down the steps, which is where my client was when you entered the property. As we know the basement itself is well insulated and therefore, no sounds or indeed light can penetrate outside of it. How were you able to see the light from where you were standing if that is so?' she says.

Already they think I've lied.

'I could see light through the open door.'

'Of the basement?' she says.

'Yes.'

'Something you failed to mention in your original police statement is that the door was ajar,' she says. 'Witness fallibility is considered, may I add. It is just that one has to ask why you decided to enter the property if you were sure my client was not inside in the first place and then go down into the basement instead of remaining in the house.'

'It's a good job I did.'

'The basement was found to be well insulated but

with an open door that would make your assumptions correct,' she says.

'They are not assumptions. That is what happened.'

What purpose does she have to deny my statement as truth and then conclude that it was just that- the truth? This woman is an idiot- or indeed very clever.

'What were your thoughts when you found my client?' she says.

'I wasn't thinking anything.'

'Weren't you frightened?' she says.

'Of course, I was. But that's a feeling. I couldn't think. My mind was blank.'

'As Dr Cramer suggested in his preliminary report, trauma can cause individuals to run on autopilot. Acting without thought,' she says, turning away from me to deliver this piece of information to the jury.

Turning back to me, she stops. Her eyes focused intently on mine as if willing me to break. But I won't. I can't. Not now. 'Is that why you didn't call the police straight away?' she says.

The psychological assessment of the offender is an important part of the trial according to the Crown Prosecution Service's investigative process. Both of us underwent evaluation of our mental health before today. I read the report, my copy only given to me by my barrister this morning. I know what she knows so she shouldn't be making me feel anxious like this. I already know what to say and how to act. I've been coached in what to expect in yet this question is still hovering over me, in the air. Karyn is growing impatient.

'Let's look at this another way shall we?' she says. 'I put it to you that you knew what to expect when you entered the basement that night and that you planned revenge. That you wanted to cause him harm. That you were so afraid and angry over your incarceration that you planned to kill him,' she says.

Jumping straight to the gun just as Mr Leighton warned me she would. I bite my tongue and consider my words carefully.

'That isn't true. I cared about him once. I could never do that to someone I had once felt comfortable with.'

'But you didn't feel comfortable then, did you?' she says. 'In that moment you felt afraid and hurt.'

'I didn't feel safe, no. I was frightened.'

'But you don't deny planning something?' she says.

'I wasn't planning to kill him, no.'

'You were planning something else?' she says.

'I thought that if I tried to reach him on a human level that he'd let me go. That I could find a way out of there.'

'That's not what you said a few moments ago though is it Miss Donoghue? You told me in front of the court that you weren't planning anything. And now you are telling me that you were,' she says.

My resolve diminishes. I don't mean to but I can't stop the words from spilling out. Can't she see what she is doing or is it intentional? Weaken her spirit, make her feel trapped, then she'll say anything for this to be over with.

'I wasn't planning what you are insinuating. I wasn't planning on hurting him. I wanted to get out. I thought that if I could get him to release me from the handcuffs I could buy my way out of there.'

'Just like you did when you agreed to sleep with Ewan? Buying your way out of situations seems to be something you do regularly, isn't it?' she says.

'No. That's not true at all.'

'I put it to you that you intended to kill Zack. That you deliberately made him angry enough to attack you so that he would then feel guilty; remorseful over his actions towards you, so that he would let you go. When he did you planned to kill him,' she says.

'No. That's not what happened. That isn't how it was.'

I feel like screaming but I'm brought back down to Earth by one subtle cough behind me. It's my victim support worker; the woman who has been coaching me through the process and will continue to do so throughout the trial. For the past twelve weeks, she has been my rock- my confidant, the closest person I have to a friend, though once upon a time I used to feel that way about Ewan.

Her presence reminds me that I'm not alone. I'm no longer fighting a battle. I don't have to lose it to be noticed. Not here. Not in the safety of the court. I am not alone in this small room where they told me I wouldn't have to leave, not even for sentencing. I do not have to go through this on my own.

I hear his voice in the background as his barrister begins to address the jury, his words a lingering note of apology. 'I'm sorry your honour. I shall remain seated.' And I know instantly that it is him.

Ewan Carter sits somewhere in the court in a suit. Probably the first he's ever worn. He will remain stoic. His broad shoulders hugged tightly by brushed cotton. Inexpensive aftershave will have been dabbed on to his exposed skin. His face, wearing a concentrated expression coated in stubble from having spent several weeks held captive inside an almost bare prison cell.

I wonder what he is thinking. If he regrets his actions on that night. The night my world was shattered and my son torn from my arms. The night I left the safety of my parents house to be trapped like an animal in a basement with only the iron smell of blood for company. My son's face the only thing I could see. His smell the only scent I wanted near. His skin the only thing I wanted touching mine.

I press my hands to my temples in an attempt to push these thoughts from my mind as I continue to answer as honestly as I can the questions his barrister is throwing at me. But I can't ignore the feeling of being watched.

Even here my skin prickles as if he has followed me to the court. I can picture him sitting there, smiling. Basking in the knowledge that at any moment I will be spun out of orbit and thrown in a heap just like I had been that night as he tossed me to the concrete floor as though I was nothing.

An animal wouldn't be treated in such a way. But to him, I suppose it was normal. The cuffs were already there. The scarf was left, pulled taught around my mouth. The chains rattled behind me as I was secured to the wall.

The only sound was his heavy breath in the darkness. His voice when it came sounded gruff as if he had been exhausted from something. He'd been doing something before I came to the house. Something strenuous. Something physical that caused him to become so tired it took him a few moments to catch his breath once he'd stepped away from where I was, half sat, half lying down on the ground, bound to the wall.

'You should have listened to me, Claire. You should have thought about what you were doing. I was following you and you didn't even know,' he said.

I wanted to say 'yes I did. Ollie told me.' But my voice was silenced by the silk fabric of the scarf tied tightly against my lips. All I could muster was a croak. I sounded like a toad in a brook. A small creature that could so easily be trodden on and nobody would notice I was gone until it was too late.

My mind ceases to race and spin, settling back to the square cavernous court. My skin still prickles in anticipation. I can feel him here in the room with me even though I know he's not.

HIM

I don't mean to be so obvious in my movements. I certainly do not want to disrupt the court but I cannot help the anxiety which rises up from the soles of my feet and spreads upwards towards my throat, constricting it. I feel as though I'm being suffocated. I cannot breathe. My mouth is dry and I'm finding it increasingly difficult to swallow.

I can see her face on the screen. She appears to be taking this well considering her statement is being ripped apart in front of twelve strangers who sit taking notes, a jury consisting of almost equal sexes.

She can only see Karyn, my defence barrister but we can all see her.

She is not hiding behind a screen through fear or guilt, it is because only she knows what really happened that night. It isn't yet my time to speak; besides I wasn't conscious when it happened, I'd been knocked out by that point. The memory of that shattering pain jolting through my head causes me to reach behind me and touch the scar that runs in a diagonal point behind my ear and right across to my temple.

I didn't know who hit me. I didn't see them. How could I? It was dark and there is no window in the basement. No moonlight penetrating through a small piece of glass. No sounds of traffic, horns or tyres crunching the only gravel driveway nearby. No trees rustling in the wind. It was dark and silent where I lay, pinned to the radiator with a single handcuff.

I was beyond helpless. I was unconscious for most of it. The only fragments I can bring forth from the back of my mind are the piercing white lights flashing in columns above me as I was taken on a trolley down the hospital corridor. Then again when I awoke, some time later, with a police officer standing in the doorway and a nurse staring vacantly at the ECG monitor attached to me with octopus-like tentacles. Circular stickers with wire attachments recording every breath I took. The bleeping sound of it coming back to haunt me in the dead of night as I twist and turn on the thin mattress of the bed, covered only with one sheet in my prison cell.

'Miss Donoghue, you were stabbed seven times. You had injuries which suggested that this was aimed at ending your life. You were supposed to die. We do not dispute the fact that he wanted to kill you, I merely suggest that you wanted to kill him too. That is all,' she says.

'I would never, could never, kill anyone,' she says, her fierce spirit suddenly torn in that one single comment.

'You must have thought about it though. During the long, cold night in that dark basement, you must have at least once thought about killing him,' she says.

'No. Not once,' she says. 'But I considered ending my own life.'

There is a pause and then Karyn speaks again. This time lowering her voice and painting a less accusatory expression on her face.

'Miss Donoghue, I put it to you that on November

11th 2014 you went to that house not knowing who would be there. That you quickly realised that you were in danger and that you intended to talk your way out of it and escape by any means possible. That you had decided that once you were freed you would kill Zack and that you would buy your way out of the consequences as you have previously stated you would,' she says, turning to the judge. 'I have no further questions, your honour.'

'But that's not true,' says Claire.

The court is hushed and Karyn Aston addresses the court.

'I conclude that Miss Donoghue knew exactly what she was doing on that night when a gentleman's life was so cruelly taken from him,' she says.

The judge nods towards the screen and a female clerk, wearing a crisp white blouse and a slimline skirt that ends just below her knees leans forwards to switch off the TV screen so that Claire cannot see anyone within the court as she turns it away from my defence barrister.

The monitor is switched off but the microphone still enables us to hear her reach for a tissue and press it against her face. Burrowing her eyes, sore from crying into the soft cotton to muffle her tears.

The court begins to murmur in whispered voices. Everyone seems to instantly begin to swap notes and shuffle in their seat. Having been sat here for almost three hours myself I can feel the cramp begin to dissipate from my foot as I raise my leg slightly, stamping down and grinding my foot into the polished wooden floor, attempting to make as little sound as possible to rid the pain, whilst everyone else quiets themselves.

'I have no further witnesses to call to the stand your honour.' says Karyn.

Judge Robertson draws his eyes across the court and presses on.

'I would like to end this hearing for today and continue tomorrow when we will hear from Mr Ewan Carter, our second witness in this horrific case,' he says.

'I thank you all for being here today. May I remind you that we begin at 9:00am sharp. If any of the jury are going to be late again, please inform the lead juror beforehand otherwise, you shall be dismissed from the case.'

I watch through the paned glass cubicle I am standing in, whilst everyone else is being led out of the court by one of the three ushers who appear at each level of the spacious, brightly lit room. I look up to the glass skylight in the centre of the ceiling and stare up at the grey/blue sky as the two prison officers step forward to escort me out of the court and back inside the prison van waiting for me at the front of the building.

I'm glad to be able to see the top of the bus station as we exit. I can watch the usual hustle and bustle of Broadmead pass us by, pretending I am still a part of it, though I'm hidden behind blacked out windows made from thickened shatterproof glass, only feet from the pavement and the people, but anchored inside a vehicle meant for taking me back to that cramped cell with the barred windows.

Claire has given her side of the story. Tomorrow it is my turn to be vilified, to be taunted and questioned. Now though I shall be returned to Horfield prison where I shall reside until this is over. But it will never be over will it?

It will forever haunt me, and not just as I lay back, with my hands behind my head, supporting my aching neck on that hard bed, but for the next fifteen or twenty years. Until my dying day I shall not ever be able to forget that night. The night Claire stepped into my life.

One more night, some months later and everything I'd built up was taken from me. My home still taped up as a crime scene. A knife taken from my kitchen that intended to kill has been kept inside a see-through plastic bag as evidence. So too have the handcuffs and rope I had purchased months before. My entire life has been displayed to the public as being fractured. Causing me to display psychotic symptoms, ranging from a need to imprison women for my own deviant sexual perversions to the portrayal of me as some kind of wounded child- a frightened boy who wanted to save everyone from their own destruction. But nobody can explain the reason why I am not being charged with false imprisonment or abduction. The police, the court, even the jury agree that I did not intentionally lock anyone up against their will, because neither Elise nor the others will give evidence against me. None of them will admit to the police or the courts, the public or the prosecution that I did anything but help them. I made them better. I supported them to get clean from drugs and alcohol. I did for them what no other person could do. I secretly think they are grateful.

I am instead being charged for something I feel that I had no control over. Something that I do not remember. I am seen as a hero to some, and a cold-blooded killer to others. My charge is murder. However they say it. Whatever words they use. And tomorrow I will deny that charge. I have to present myself as the innocent party. I have to offer the jury and Claire's barrister enough evidence to create an element of doubt. Then it is up to them to see past the veil or not.

If I hadn't have returned to the house when I did then who knows what would have happened. Zack might be here. I might not be awaiting a lengthy prison sentence. Claire would still be none the wiser as to who Elise really was, and the family and friends of us both would have been spared this ordeal, the media portrayals and courtroom drama of this entire situation. A scenario I could not have predicted, yet on some deeper level, possibly hidden from my subconscious, I must have known would happen. For if I did not then why had I gone down into the basement and not straight into the living room with a strong cup of tea?

But I suppose more important than any of that is the one question I cannot answer. Why was Zack there? And how did he know that Claire would be too?

HER

It's the second day of the trial. I've been told that Ewan is standing in the witness box. I cannot hear what is being said in the court and the screen isn't being used today. I've asked to attend but my presence today isn't needed.

I'm sitting in the same room I was in yesterday, only today there is no water and the vase has been moved to the centre of the table. The beechwood desk sits in front of me, and Kerry, my victim support worker, is seated by my side, though today she doesn't need to be here either. It's merely a waiting game.

Elise has refrained to comment on any of the stories provided by the press. She has refused to attend all of the hearings so far. She will not be giving evidence by live link as I have done. She was found in Ireland and she is not pressing charges.

They found the body of Amy Sitcombe buried in the back garden of Ewan's property. I've been told that he is pleading not guilty to murder. Though I won't know until later what he is guilty of. Whether he really did not mean to kill her as he told me. The preliminary post-mortem suggests that Amy was an alcoholic. Her brain suffered a symptomatic seizure as a result of delirium tremens though they cannot identify whether or not this was the cause of her fatality. They are presuming that Ewan is at least, guilty of manslaughter by keeping her prisoner in his dungeon - as the media have said - causing her to lapse into a coma. If she hadn't have been there she would not have died. That's the prosecutions verdict. Though Ewan's defence barrister, Karyn Aston, is trying to convince the jury that it was an act of impulse that lead Ewan to dispose of her body, burying her just a few yards from his house.

Paul Leighton QC, my barrister has asked me not to attend today's hearing. During our coaching sessions before the trial began, Kerry said the same thing. But I can't sit back and watch an innocent man be sent to prison. I know he did wrong. An act of guilt prevented him from calling the police and telling them about Amy. But he didn't kill her. Not deliberately anyway.

The door opens and Mr Leighton walks into the room carrying a tray with two small Styrofoam cups of tea and four biscuits wrapped tightly together from the vending machine, in clear plastic. He registers the sleepless face I've been wearing for several days now and takes the seat beside me. I lean back and notice that his eyebrows are furrowed. He wants to say something but is trying to think of the right way to tell me.

'His defence team are considering altering his plea to guilty,' she says.

'What for? He didn't do anything.'

'If he pleads guilty to perverting the course of justice and involuntary manslaughter he will most likely be given a reduced sentence of ten years,' he says.

'Ten years?'

He nods his head and hands me one of the Styrofoam cups of watery tea.

'Concealing the death of somebody is a criminal

offence which obstructs the coroner from his duty and prevents the burial of a body. It's a much lighter sentence than he may have got for false imprisonment. And certainly much less than murder,' he says.

He continues to talk but I'm not really listening. All I can think about is Ollie. What would he have been doing right now if none of this had happened? How much of this is my fault? After all, if I hadn't have gone there that day Zack would he here, Ollie too. And Ewan wouldn't be facing the next ten years of his life in a prison cell.

'You did the right thing, coming here today. You might not realise it yet but the media is actually on your side. You are being portrayed as a loyal mother who made one mistake and has paid for it in the most awful of ways. You may not see it, but in time, when the trial is over, you will be able to move on with your life,' he says. 'It will be hard. I don't doubt that, but it will get better with time.'

'How can I move on? Without my son, I have nothing.'

I long to hold Ollie in my arms. I long to hear him laugh. To feel his fingers clasping mine as we run together along the wide open grass as we did that day not so long ago. Back in the summer when the trees were heavily laden with thick green leaves. Their branches almost scooping down to the ground as if wanting to pick us up. The sun bright, filling the sky. The heat on the backs of my shoulders as we stood overlooking the river in Snuff Mills. An ice-cream balanced in Ollie's hand, dripping down his small fat fingers as he attempted to lick it all off.

But it wasn't like that was it? Sammy the Squirrel was buried in the same way as Amy. It rained that day. He ran off, away from me, up into the brush, where the trees are crushed together. Pine needles and bracken covering the ground below them. The damp soil beneath him lifted as we buried a squirrel together in the rain. The mossy earth mixed with the smell of wet leaves and the dead body of the animal he watched me cover over with soil after dropping him into the sludgy mud.

There was no sun that day. There was no ice-cream. We ate a McDonalds in the car then drove home in silence. His intent eyes beaming down on me as I buried that rodent are the same that I see now. Vacant. Lifeless. Those eyes will never leave my head.

Had I spent more time with Ollie, listened to him more, tried to understand what he was trying to tell me when he stole and acted out, running away and giving me the silent treatment, I might have been able to foresee what would happen. I might have been able to stop it.

'Ollie should be here with me.'

But he's not. And I miss him.

HIM

'My mother was a heroin addict. She died of a drugs overdose five years after my father left her. Marie was found by her boyfriend with a needle in her arm, off the coast of Kilkerry where she'd moved back in 2000. I didn't think I'd ever get over it.'

'Is that why you saw yourself as some kind of saviour, able to reduce the suffering of Amy, Elise and then Kylie?' says Mr Leighton, the barrister for the prosecution.

His questions are thoughtfully considered and just as I expected them to be: aimed at suggesting that I wanted to hurt these women. That I was going to trap Claire in the basement and use her as some kind of sex slave. Because of course, without the evidence to prove otherwise; neither Elise nor Kylie making a statement and the charges of false imprisonment thrown out at the first hearing, nobody knows any different, do they?

'I suppose what I'm trying to say is that my mother was my motivation. Her death was preventable. Her life was meaningless.'

'But she was a mother and a wife. She meant

something to the lives of the people she loved,' he says.

'She meant the world to me.'

'And your father,' he says, racing quickly to finish the reasons behind my *madness*.

'That's true. Yes. I thought that if I could help Amy to get sober and stay away from the drink that she would be able to live her life free of that dependency.'

'You thought that you could save her,' he says.

'I suppose so, yes.'

'But you couldn't. She died in that basement from a severe symptomatic seizure, caused by your negligence and then you hid her body so that she could not have the burial she rightly deserved. The rights of her family and friends to say goodbye at the appropriate time was stolen from them. You are at least guilty of that, wouldn't you say? He says. 'Ethically and morally of course.'

I sigh. Run my clammy hands across my eyes, sore from sleeplessness, and down my forehead. Blinking back the tears that threaten to well in the corners of my eyes.

'I loved her.'

'Of course, you did,' he says, brushing my feelings off just as Dr Cramer did during her psychological assessment on my ability to stand trial.

'You snatched away Amy's life. And then you took away any decent chance of a memorial for her, didn't you?' he says, offering me a glint of repressed rage when he looks into my eyes. The second time I've seen that look from him in two days.

'Should it have been Elise or Kylie you would have done the same,' he says.

Would I?

'No.'

'You'd have done the right thing? You would have called an ambulance? You would have allowed her family to lay her to rest?' he says, turning to address the jury.

'I put it to you that Mr Carter would have kept their deaths to himself too if he'd have found himself in similar circumstances. I am not saying that Mr Carter deliberately set out to kill Amy, I merely suggest that as an involuntary act what he did was wrong, and more than that, against the law.'

'Objection, your honour, council disagree with the prosecution using subjective questioning,' says Karyn.

'Objection agreed,' says the judge. 'Please continue your questions objectively.'

A nod of the head and Mr Leighton continues.

'The post-mortem evidence suggests that Amy did indeed die from the condition of which she was a known sufferer, however, should she have been at home, continuing to use alcohol in an addictive way or not, she would have had access to the vital medicine which would have saved her life. Medicine that you did not provide her with despite the fact that you had clearly made provisions for pharmaceutical medication to be included within the forced rehabilitation that you provided for these women, do you agree?' he says.

'To a certain degree, yes.'

A noticeable sigh can be heard throughout the court as if each and every person present, until now, has been holding their breath.

Beyond reasonable doubt. The prosecutor's job is to prove that beyond reasonable doubt I killed Amy, unwillingly, unknowingly, accidentally. She died because of me. My defence barrister has to defend my actions by agreeing with Mr Leighton's verdict and affirming that I did so unintentionally, involuntarily, unequivocally.

'I put it to you that you did not intend to kill Amy, but that your actions did assist with her death. You agree with this statement . . .' he says, directing his words to the jury once more, ' . . . that Mr Carter acted alone. That he had no intention of killing Amy but that he did not consider the consequences sufficiently before conducting this monstrosity of a rehabilitation programme within the confines of his own home. That is inside a secure, soundproof basement, without light. And without the proper provisions.'

He turns his attention back to me then and says: 'Mr Carter on the night of 11th November 2014, you and Miss Donoghue had a disagreement. Isn't that right?'

'No.'

'An argument ensued whereby you intentionally stabbed her, seven times, and then when Zack Donoghue arrived you attacked him with the aim of killing him. Isn't that right?' he says.

'No. That's not true. Why would you say this? Why would Claire say this. That isn't what happened at all?'

'Claire has declined to attend any further hearings related to this case. The debacle that was yesterday's hearing shall not be discussed here today. What I am asking you Mr Carter is if you intentionally stabbed Miss Donoghue and attempted to murder her husband-'

'They were getting a divorce. And no I did not stab anyone. You know I didn't. It was him. Zack stabbed Claire and then himself. He wanted to kill himself. He wanted to die.'

'And why do you think he wanted to die Mr Carter?' he says.

'Because he thought he'd killed her. He thought Claire was dead.'

'An act of guilt?' he says.

'I believe so, yes.'

'You believe so. But what is the truth, Mr Carter? What really happened on that night is only known to the three people who were there, isn't it?' he says.

I don't answer him. Instead, I look up to the freshly

painted ceiling and beg for mercy to whatever may be above.

'You, Mr Carter, and Mr and Miss Donoghue are the only ones who really know what happened that night. Claire refuses to be here and Zack . . . well, he cannot be here either can he?' he says.

Of course not. We all know why of course. But it seems nobody in the court wants to say it aloud. Zack can't be here because after he collapsed on the floor, covered in his own and Claire's blood he was taken by ambulance to Southmead Hospital, where he was given two blood transfusions and surgery to stem the bleeding from his left lung, where he'd perforated several blood vessels and caused his own lung to collapse. At least that's what we told them before he was transferred to Bethlem Royal hospital- where he will remain for some time.

Do I feel guilty for lying to the police, telling them that it was a desperate act of suicide, that he wanted to kill them both in some Romeo and Juliette suicide pact that he'd imagined would lead to his own and her solace? I'm still unsure as to the answer to that question though I do believe we did the right thing. Both of us. Agreeing that this would be the best way forward. Better for all of us. Everyone can see how twisted he became once the divorce papers arrived in the post. Nobody doubts that he was mentally unstable. The only sad thing is that he never got to sign them. They are still legally married.

HER

I am walking down from the court, past the empty building that used to house an Australian bar and a lap dancing club. There are two police vans and a car parked adjacent to the court. An ITV van is set up with a reporter on her mobile phone across the road in the centre, where the remembrance monument sits. It's been coated in wooden crosses and wreaths. The same monument where the remembrance Sunday celebration was being held on the day our lives changed forever. Only that wasn't really when my life began to spin out of orbit, was it?

Everything happened so quickly, I didn't see any of it coming. Now when I look back I can see little snippets; signs that something awful was about to occur. I denied it. Nothing bad would happen to me, right? Wrong. I was very mistaken, something terrible happened. I lost my ex-husband, friend and almost my son in the same night. Just one night in that basement and my entire world was tipped upside down.

If only I could turn back the clock. If only I was able to foresee the future that lay ahead of me. I would never have let him go. I might not have had to watch as my son tried to intervene to save me, his mum, from Ewan's knife. Or from his dads delusional state. His obsession with me and with Ollie taking over every sane bone within his body.

I have cried tears of sadness and of pain. Of anger and regret. But today I cry with relief. That Ewan and I got away with it. Nobody suspects a thing.

HIM

It is day four of the trial, and already we are nearing the end of this bitter journey. A journey that began the day I asked a single mother who I knew nothing of to accept my gift of a large sum of money from my hand in order to bring her back from the brink and continue on with her life. Claire and Ollie's lives were in my hands, and I let them go.

'In light of the charges brought against you, the fact that you have altered your plea and the fact that you have, throughout this trial been most cooperative, we consider your admonition and I now ask the jury to confirm that they have made their final decision in relation to this case,' says Judge Robertson, casting his eyes across the jury.

Leaving his eyes on the head juror, he says: 'Can you confirm to me that you have agreed on a collaborative decision for the defendant in this case?'

'I confirm that we have made our decision and that our decision is final,' says the man.

For the past two days the man has worn the same tailored suit. As if he has suddenly developed a feel for courtroom drama and has decided on wearing the correct attire. Now that it is almost over I cannot help but wonder why he bothered. Especially since he wore smart jeans for the first two days.

'Very well,' says Judge Robertson.

It is only now that I can feel my pulse begin to quicken.

'Please can you answer each of the following questions one at a time,' he says.

'Yes your honour,' says the head juror.

'For the crime of failing to notify the appropriate authorities of a death and then concealing the body, a crime against the coroner, what is your verdict?' he says, addressing the jury.

'Guilty, your honour,' says the head juror.

'For the crime of perverting the course of justice, what is your verdict?' says Judge Robertson.

'Guilty, your honour,' he says.

'And for the crime of involuntary manslaughter, what is your verdict?' says Judge Robertson.

'Guilty,' he says.

The court is hushed. The murmuring filling the space between us all. The public gallery empty but for two reporters tapping the tips of their pens away, taking notes, no doubt twisting words to create their own interpretation of our stories. The tales they wish to weave and will display to the public in tomorrow's Post.

I glance around the pew-like seating area where the jury are no longer deliberating but wearing relieved faces, now that for them it is over. Judge Robertson interrupts the silence to deliver the final wound to my already sore heart.

'I ask that we take a ten-minute break whilst I decide upon the appropriate sentence for the defendant,' he says, eager to make us wait a while longer. My patience wearing its thinnest than ever before.

For ten agonising minutes I sit beside Karyn, who leans across her dockside seat to offer me a consolatory word of advice.

'Just sit tight. It's almost over, she says, a slight downturn on her otherwise smiling face.

The two prison officers, a man and a woman this time stand on either side of me, breathing heavily. Limbs aching from standing too long. Mouths dry and stomachs grumbling for something to eat. They offer me no small-talk. No smile.

I look back over to Karyn, who is now tapping the end of a biro pen against the backdrop of my life. A file of paperwork containing every grim detail of my life.

Karyn looks defeated. I fear this is the one case that she has most recently lost and it doesn't sit very well with her. She notices me looking longingly at her bottle of Evian and intrudes upon the silent atmosphere; heavy and warm within the glass box I still sit inside of. She offers to fetch me a small bottle of water from the vending machine but the two prison officers standing either side of me shake their heads as the judge returns to the court room.

'It's time,' says one of the court ushers.

I've barely been seated for five minutes. This isn't how I'd expected to spend my final moments before being sent back to prison, this time without the thought of leaving keeping me contained in a bubble of delusion I so anxiously relied upon to get me through the last twelve months.

Back inside the courtroom everyone, including me, are on tenterhooks. Nobody knows what this means for me. Nobody cares. All they can see is a killer. Whatever my reason for doing what I did, they want justice for the man who took an innocent woman's life and tried to take that of his friend and her husband.

Judge Robertson clears his throat, takes a sip of water

from his freshly made glass and begins.

'For the charge of perverting the course of justice, I sentence you to one year in custody. For the charge of failing to report a death and of concealing the body, I sentence you to three years in custody. For the charge of involuntary manslaughter, I sentence you to six years in custody. All sentences shall run concurrently and so you are hereby sentenced to a minimum of ten years in custody without parole,' says the judge.

Gasps, hoots, the shaking of heads and sighs of relief can be heard and seen all around me until the judge declares that the court must be quieted.

As I'm marched away from the stand that appears no larger than a signal box on an old railway and feels much smaller inside, I begin to feel unsteady on my feet. As we leave the court room my entire body begins to shake and my head spins. Thoughts of my impending future deter me from continuing to walk. The murmurs and relieved speech behind me cause my head to reel. And then before I reach the exit, where the large locked door separating me from the cool afternoon air outside is hidden from view, my knees give way.

As I hit the ground I wonder if this is what a heart attack feels like. A tightening knot inside my chest. A thudding pain in my neck and shoulder. My arm tingling with numbness. And then I close my eyes and feel myself drift away.

I am floating on a sea of agonising pain and not one person considers bending down and ensuring that I'm not going to die. Except Claire.

I see her brush past people, almost knocking them to the ground. A crowd has gathered around my fallen carcas and it is she, only her, the woman who's life I have so elaborately destroyed who stands before me, tugging the mobile phone from her pocket and unflinchingly gives the call operator every detail she can, telling them to hurry.

Everybody stands around her, looking, voicing her bravery and stupidity, all in equal measure. Although nobody wants to say it, I can see it in their eyes as I black out for possibly the first time in my life, not being one to drink much, I've often wondered what the term *blackout* actually means.

I can hear people talking all around me. 'What is she doing? Why would she care? Not unless . . .? Not if . . .? Have they got it wrong? Have they sent down the wrong person?'

The ambulance arrives. It wouldn't do to have the murderer die before he leaves the court to begin his lengthy sentence for the murder of his so called girlfriend would it?

Then come the strobe lights. The flickering in and out of blackness. The sounds carried away by the wind as I'm air-lifted to hospital in a helicopter. And then the silence. The deathly silence. Like a foggy night alone at home, with no television on. Only here, there is no light. Just empty darkness. And still silence, as if I am dead. Perhaps I am.

Then perhaps not. I find my hearing forced back to the sounds of life. Noise. Whispers. People; the sounds of living all around me. I am being propelled back to life.

BEFORE

5. When I came home one day to find Zack outside of the flat while bailiffs were taking my belongings I tried to reason that he'd done the right thing, letting them in, but I was angry and afraid. Annoyed at him for seemingly not caring about what happened to me and Ollie and afraid of where we would sleep. Though Ollie's things weren't taken I had no bed and all of our appliances were taken.

I decided to stay at my parents, only when I got there Zack was there. I felt betrayed by my parents. It was as if my concerns weren't being listened to. Not even by them. My dad's conference papers were destroyed-twice. His suit was cut with scissors. My mum blamed Ollie. My dad blamed me. Then Zack appeared with a black eye. I took a cup from the worktop and it was cracked. There was blood on it. That's when I knew Zack had done it to himself. Then he started an argument, punched himself in the face. Mum asked us all to leave and dad was upset. I thought it would be better to take Ollie to school first.

I didn't want to ask Ewan if we could stay but I couldn't think of anywhere else to go. So after I'd dropped Ollie off I called him. When he didn't answer I went around to his house. He wasn't there when I arrived but the front door was open. I went inside. I didn't think I was doing anything wrong. But in a way, I'm glad I did because when I entered the kitchen I could hear shuffling from the basement. When I went down there I couldn't believe what I was seeing.

There was a bed and a small metal box on the floor beside it. That's where I found Ewan. He'd been chained to the bed with handcuffs. I thought he was dead. I panicked and ran up the stairs, only when I got there Zack was stood at the top of them.

He told me that Ewan had abducted Elise and that

when he got there another woman, Kylie was locked in the basement. I didn't want to believe him but the evidence was clear. There was the bed and handcuffs that Zack had used to tie him in the basement with. He told me that I was lucky that he hadn't held me captive.

I thought back to the evening we'd met when Elise had arrived and I told him. I told Zack that I might have been next if she hadn't have turned up, but then I remembered that she'd said something about money. I guessed she was blackmailing him. Though at the time it made sense, I still questioned whether a woman who'd been held prisoner by a man would go back there, even to scare him. I was confused and scared.

Zack told me that I shouldn't call the police. Not yet. And that we should discuss what to do. All the time I was worried about Ewan. He was chained up in the basement and the thought of him escaping and coming after us frightened me.

HER

Me and Ollie arrive at Ewan's around 7:00pm. It's dark and cold. There are no lights on in the front of the house and I'm in two minds whether to stay here and wait for him to return home from wherever he's gone or to find a B&B for the night, whilst it's still not too late, when I notice through the living room window a shadow strike past the large bookcase and out of the room. It stops for a moment before shooting off down the hallway towards the back of the house.

'Come on Ollie,' I whisper. 'Follow me.'

I creep down the side of the house, past the dustbin and jump when I'm alerted to a sudden loud crash behind me.

I turn and see that Ollie has fallen down. The small recycling bin is upturned on the ground beside him, its contents lying across his shoulder. A waft of rotting food and sour milk bottles flood my nostrils.

'Sorry mum,' he says.

'Can you get up?'

He pulls himself up and brushes himself down. Facing his palms up towards me to show me the muck that he's collected between the creases of his fingers.

'It's okay. We'll get you cleaned up in a minute.'

I head towards the back of the house, with Ollie following along behind me.

When we reach the back door I know instantly that there is something wrong. The door is unlocked. Ewan isn't the type of man to just leave his home accessible to intruders. I step towards the door, about to grab the handle and step inside. I hear the sharp sound of something splintering beneath my feet. I look down and notice several small shards of glass covering the floor.

I pull the door towards me and see in the streetlight reflected from across a house down the road that the door has been forced open from the outside. They must have used a brick or some other heavy object to break the glass in the door, running their hand through the gap to pull the handle inside and enter.

'Hello? Ewan?'

I wait several seconds for a response but something propels me forwards and I find myself standing inside the narrow hallway. The kitchen door to my right is closed.

I'm not sure what stops me from calling out again. Perhaps I think the intruder, whoever it is, might still be inside. Perhaps I'm not as frightened as I am curious. Accelerated by adrenaline and stupidity, I walk through the hallway and towards the front of the house. The living room door is open wide and I can see from here that a slit of dim amber light flecks the living room to one side, allowing me a concave view of the entire room. Nothing appears to have been moved or taken.

I think of the bookshelves, the rare titles that fit snugly against one another on the top shelf and of how delighted Ewan was as I took interest looking through them that day. The day I came here to do the unthinkable with a strange man, who for some reason is still causing me to do the most ridiculous of things. This time with my son in tow.

I turn to Ollie to tell him to stay back, leave the house, wait for me outside in the back garden or to call the police or any one of these things but when I look behind me I catch the back of his coat as he disappears behind the half-closed basement door. The light is coming from inside the basement. Not the streetlight outside as I thought it was.

'Ollie, come back.'

He either doesn't hear me or doesn't want to listen to me. He's of that discoverable age. Where boys want to explore their surroundings, go on adventures and be mischievous. I call out to him once more but see that there is really no other option but to follow him down the steps and into the basement.

I open the door wider and take the first step, noticing instantly that there is a heavy breathing sound, much like an injured animal or a fully grown man sleeping. Snoring away, oblivious to the fact that he is being watched by a very small six-year-old boy who stands at his side staring at him. His face bearing the look of shock horror and puzzlement.

I'm repulsed by the sight before me. There is a mattress on the basement floor. No windows and a tin metal box lies on the ground beside the man who is handcuffed to the radiator.

His body is slumped in a way that suggests he has suffered some kind of injury. I'm not sure what I am witnessing. Has Ewan been taking part in some kind of odd sex game whereby he's accidentally locked himself to the radiator with his own handcuffs or has somebody done this to him? Somebody mad enough to want him to pay for trapping them in this sparse, damp space.

A pair of women's shoes are on the floor beside where Ollie stands. He hasn't noticed them or the bra

296

hanging on the edge of the bedpost where whoever it was that did this to him had once been.

'Let's go, Ollie. We shouldn't be here.'

I'm about to take Ollie's hand and take him up to the top of the stairs so that I can come back down and check on Ewan to make sure that he is alive. That this is just as it appears- a sex game. Nothing more. Not a sex game gone wrong or a hostage situation.

I take Ollie's hand in mine and he looks up instantly, dismissing my fierce gaze that suggests 'let's get the hell out of here' and looking back at something behind me. Over my shoulder and to the right.

I turn and see Zack standing in the doorway. Gone is the frustrated, aggressive stance he showed to me earlier. In fact, I'd go so far as to say that his face is devoid of emotion. Then he smiles. He raises his arm slightly and something glints, hidden behind the sleeve of his dark coat, the waterproof one I bought him for his birthday last year. Whatever it is shines from the light of the single bare lightbulb above us.

His smile seems to grow as he flexes his hand out, the knife in his hand, but I can't tell if it's just the way the low energy bulb forces what little light it can on every object within the room or if he really does look as menacing as he appears from this angle.

Our shadows seem to grow, extending upwards and lengthening across the floor, split along the walls and ceiling. Ollie's shadow darts up the stairs.

Zack steps towards me. The black handle of the knife gripped tight by white knuckles. I step back, tripping over Ewan's leg that looks too pale for somebody who has just been tied up and left there. Is he dead? I think, as Zack springs forward. The blade aimed towards my chest. I twist my body, trying to turn away from the knife but still I feel the chilling sting of metal as it pierces my skin. And then I scream.

HIM

Zack pulls the knife away from her stomach and holds it up to her throat. Blood seeps through her tight fitted top, turning the lilac fabric crimson.

'Over there,' he says, ordering her to sit down on the floor against the wall behind the bed where he's attached the handcuffs to the chains in the wall.

He looks strained as he applies the cuffs to her wrists.

'Don't move. It will be all right. Everything will be better now. You'll see,' he says.

He's deranged. He's gone completely insane.

'What are you doing?' she says, wincing.

'You're going to do what I tell you to,' he says, grazing the blade of the knife into the thin skin around her throat.

I know then that no matter what I say or do it isn't going to be enough to stop him. I am fastened to the radiator, unable to break free before he kills her. There is nothing that I can do whilst handcuffed and incapacitated with a head injury. If I try to break free now there won't be enough time to save her. But if I pretend to be unconscious he'll grow bored, go to find

Ollie, though I'm sure he's left the house by now as I asked him to when I whispered in his ear to run for help. That a bad man had hurt me and would hurt him too. I didn't mean to scare the child. I just didn't want him to get hurt. He's a good lad. Strange but good.

Kylie will have heard the noise by now. Ran off with my wallet no doubt to score heroin. I haven't seen her since Zack broke through the back door and found me in here with a tray of food for her to eat. The bottle of pills balanced beside a bowl of homemade tomato soup and a plate of freshly baked bread slices, thick butter smeared on each of them. Just the way she likes it.

I'm not sure what made me take the sharp knife down into the basement with me. I couldn't find the butter knife. I thought it would do.

I'd only been inside here for a couple of minutes when I heard the sound of glass breaking. I undid Kylie's handcuff and told her to run. She bolted out of the door in the throes of withdrawal. I knew it wouldn't be long before she succumbed to her addiction. Out there on the streets is so much different than in here, with your every whim catered for you become institutionalised rather quickly.

I read up on these things before offering my services to these women. They refer themselves to me for detox. Agreeing to be confined to the basement until they are completely clean from drugs or alcohol.

Amy was the first woman who asked me to lock her up and not to let her out no matter how much she begged, pleaded or screamed. Her death was accidental. I buried her because I couldn't see how anybody would understand how she came to be in such circumstances. Why would anyone think that a woman had asked me to imprison her for three months to help her do what every other agency she'd involved had been unable to? No state detox, NHS addiction service or social care organisation had been able to support her past the first week of detox and into some semblance of a normal life through a rehabilitation programme that actually worked - except I had. Or at least, I would have if she had told me she was an epilepsy sufferer. If she hadn't have left her medication at home.

I force my thoughts back to the present, back to the sound of tearful crying coming from the other side of the room where Claire is chained to the wall. I don't dare to open my eyes until Zack leaves the room. It is almost an hour since he slammed the metal box down on the back of my head, handcuffing me to the radiator before I had the chance to realise what was happening to me.

I hear the door slam. The bolt on the other side being flung across, holding it secure from escape. This time, it is not Amy's, Elise's or Kylie's freedom at stake but mine and Claire's.

Once I'm sure he's walked away from the basement and up into the house where I only pray Zack is alone, Ollie safe somewhere with Kylie, getting help, in a police station somewhere- I open my eyes.

Claire is sat up with her head in between her knees, crying pitifully.

'Claire.'

She stops, looks up and gasps with shock.

'What the hell is going on? How are we going to get out of here?' she says.

'It's okay. I've got a plan. Listen carefully.'

'A plan,' she says, laughing. 'What the fuck is all this anyway, some kind of dungeon? I knew there was something wrong with you. I knew I should never have trusted you. I suppose this was your idea all along wasn't it. You and Zack are in on this together.'

'That's not-'

'Oh, it looks perfectly planned to me Ewan. You're a pervert. A twisted, vile-'

'Claire, will you just be quiet for one minute and let me explain? You've got this all wrong-'

'I don't think I have.'

'Claire, he'll be coming back down soon to check that I'm still unconscious. He thinks he knocked me out-'

'You mean you've been lying there all this time while he ties me up, banging on about-'

'Claire, please, listen to me!'

She stops talking and notions to the locked door.

'How the hell are we going to get out of here?' And where's my son?' she says.

Twisting away from me, she strains against the heavy metal grazing the skin on her wrists.

'Claire you're hurting yourself, please don't move. You're in shock. You've been stabbed. Let me help you.'

She ignores my request and begins shouting 'Ollie? Ollie, please come to the door. Open it for mummy, Ollie please.'

'He can't hear you. The walls are sound-proofed, double insulation. I think he's gone to get help. We still have to get out of here, though.'

'But how?' she says.

'The key for these handcuffs is in my pocket.'

'Why didn't you say so before? What is all this for anyway? Why do you have all this stuff?' she says.

'Claire, I need you to focus. Undo my handcuffs.'

I shimmy as far forward as I can get before my wrist is tugged back.

'If I break the pipe it'll burst. There's no way out for the water. The basement will fill up pretty quickly. You have to untie me first. Then I can help you.'

She hesitates for a moment.

'I'm not going to hurt you. It's not me you should be afraid of, it's him. He's obsessed with you, Claire. He attacked me, handcuffed me to this radiator and then said that he was going to make you pay.'

'For what? I haven't done anything,' she says.

'He thinks you've taken his son away from him. That you're blaming him for the stealing and lying. Ollie ran away because he was frightened of Zack.'

'He told you this?' she says.

'Not in as many words, no. It's just a feeling. A gut feeling. I'm almost never wrong. You have to believe me, Claire. I would never hurt you or your son, but that day-'

'When you went to Zack's?' she says.

'Yes. I never got the chance to tell you, but he said something about Ollie, well, not exactly-'

'Just spit it out,' she says.

'He told me he didn't have a son. He denied Ollie even existed, and then when I told him about the photograph I'd seen in the hallway as I was coming in he told me to go and get it. When I went back out there the photograph was gone. I knew it was there. He was adamant that I was imagining things. He was trying to convince me that he didn't even know you and then he smashed it over my head. I can't remember what we were talking about now, or even if we were, I was on my way out. He hit me over the head then sat down on the sofa, crying like a baby. Telling me how sorry he was, how frightened he was of losing you both, that he would do anything for you, and then he said something like it didn't matter anymore anyway. I assumed he meant that he wouldn't be around any more. That he was contemplating suicide. I was frightened he might take Ollie, abduct him or something-'

'You're a fine one to talk about kidnapping. You know all about that by the looks of it,' she says, casting her eyes across the room at the evidence for her suspicions.

'It isn't like that, I swear. I would never hurt anyone. Please, you have to believe me. Just untie me and I can get you out of those cuffs.'

'If you don't let me go I'll make sure Zack hurts you,'

she says.

I don't think there's much need. He seems intent on hurting us both.

'Fine. Just hurry. I don't think it will be long before he returns and we need to stick to the plan.'

'Tell me what it is first and then I'll undo the handcuffs.'

She doesn't concern herself with why I have the key for them in my pocket. She's intent on letting me go so that I'll release her. This place is weighing her down. She's growing tired and letting her barriers down. One at a time she's loosening up. Trusting me. I only hope she doesn't grow so exhausted and consumed with escape, that she forgets why we're here in the first place.

It is not the fault of her own actions nor mine that brought us here, but that ex-husband of hers. Zack is set on bringing her down. Punishing her for leaving him and taking his only child, their son away from him. He is also angry at us both for our arrangement.

'You slept together,' he said. 'I know because I followed her. I've been following her for months. She came here, stayed for over an hour and left, smiling. I'd know that smile anywhere. It's a smile of satisfaction. I expect you paid her debts off too. No doubt made some kind of prostitution pact.'

I couldn't deny it. I've never been a very good liar.

She shimmies forward and slips her hand inside the pocket of my jeans, tugging the key out and straining against the single handcuff applied to her sore arm as she squirms and pants until the key is wriggled through the lock and the sharp snap sounds. Alerting us both to the fact that I am now free and she is not.

'Help me then,' she says.

'Promise me one thing first. You will stick to the plan.'

'You haven't told me what it is yet,' she says.

There isn't time.

'Follow my lead. Pretend I'm dead. Keep your wrist inside the loose cuff so that it looks like it's still on you then he won't know what's hit him.'

I jump up and lunge for the handcuff, trying to wriggle it free, but it won't budge. That's when the door opens.

I jump back quickly and pray that the click I heard means that the handcuff has come undone, before landing back down on the floor and placing the handcuff over my wrist to make it look as though it's still attached; that I'm still unconscious.

The sound of the bolt being flung back over the door as the handle is lifted up and Zack steps inside causes Claire to gasp. I open one eye, knowing that where he stands, Zack cannot see that I am awake, not until he comes closer will he be able to tell that I've moved. And then it will be too late.

Zack lunges towards Claire, stopping short as I jump up from the floor and grab his leg, distracting him from duty. He turns around and stabs me twice in the thigh, too quickly for me to retaliate.

I fall to the floor. Behind me Claire screams. I cannot stand. When I look back she is cowering in the corner. Her arms and legs wear thin trails of blood. She is holding her shoulder where the liquid oozes out across her chest and down the front of her top.

As I force myself to stand hoping to shove Zack away from her he belts me across the face and I fall backwards, hitting my head on the wall. It's not his weight or strength that enables him to win me out. It's his temper. He's gaining power from the adrenaline and sense of control.

Claire cries. Her palm facing him, trying to protect herself from one more wound of the knife. The one that might kill her.

I try to move but my head is swirling. My limbs won't follow my brain's instruction. Then I look up and see Ollie standing in the doorway.

'Dad, no. Don't!' He says.

Zack twists his body around. He seems to contort. I can no longer tell what are bodies or shadows any more.

'Son,' he says, releasing his grip on the knife.

The blade falls to the floor as he turns to Claire and then back to Ollie.

'Don't hurt my mum. Leave her alone,' says Ollie.

Zack is standing in front of Claire, his head bowed. I don't know if he is looking at her with horror for what he has done or smiling with satisfaction because my head swarms with another shot of pain as something heavy lands on the side of my head, above my ear. And then again across my temple.

I can feel the blood trickling down my face. I open my eyes long enough to see Ollie bend down behind his father and take the knife from the concrete floor. He raises it up high above his head, the blade pointed towards his father's chest and I pass out.

AFTER

6. He was standing over me. His expression blank. He didn't look angry or scared. He was just standing there staring at me. He didn't seem to notice that I was bleeding. After around five minutes, I pulled myself up and sat there not sure what to do. Then he pulled out a knife and held it to my throat.

I was scared. I didn't know what he was going to do. He dragged me over to the corner of the room and pulled out a metal chain, clamping a handcuff to it and snapping it over my wrist.

He told me not to move or do anything stupid then he left the room, locking the door behind him. I was too distracted with thoughts of Ollie and how I would be able to escape if I couldn't free myself. Ewan was still unconscious. Lying on the floor across from me. I began to scream. It didn't rouse him and if Ollie was somewhere in the house he didn't hear me. I thought that the only way I could get out would be to make such a noise that the neighbours would hear and come running over to see what was going on. I was scared that nobody would find us. I began to cry. I wanted Zack to come back even though I was afraid of what he might do when he did. I just wanted to know that Ollie was all right. I had to know that he was safe. That he wasn't hurt.

When Zack did come back he was angry. He ran straight up to me and began stabbing me. I must have passed out because I don't remember what happened next. I was in so much pain. I thought I was going to die. I remember nothing until the paramedics arrived. They told me that Ollie had called them and that he had been very brave. They told me that he was safe and that he'd saved our lives.

Zack had been taken by ambulance to Southmead hospital. I had no idea that he'd stabbed himself. Or that he had been planning a suicide pact for us both. I'm still shocked at this information now.

I believe that the facts stated in this witness statement are true.

Signed: C. Donoghue
Dated: 12th November 2014

HER

Today is like a reunion of sorts. I visited Zack this morning. I took the train to London. Inside, the hospital contains the usual scent of disinfectant and alcohol hand gel, but it's much cleaner and gentler than I expected. Bethlam Royal is no longer termed Bedlam as it was once known by.

The suicide note that DI Blake and DC Flint found where Zack had left it on the dining table in the morning suggested that he wanted to kill us both. He worded it as though we'd planned the entire thing together, ending our lives as though we could forever belong to one another. It was used as evidence during the trial.

On my way out of the hospital, I told the nurse that he was convinced I was the devil incarnate and that he didn't appear much improved from last month. She said that his medication had already been increased and that they should be able to see some difference in his behaviour soon.

The depot injections make his speech slurred and his eyes vacant. It is like watching the undead rise from their graves in an old 1970's zombie film.

I spoke to Elise this morning. She wanted to thank me for standing by Ewan throughout the trial and for calling the ambulance when I did. I saved his life, she said. He had a heart attack, but he's doing all right.

I leave the prison with an hour or so spare so I decide to sit in the new coffee house across the road from HMP Horfield. I look across the road imagining him in there, wondering how he always manages to smile even though he's facing a decade-long stretch.

He says that he has found peace within himself. Something that I am still working on.

A mother's love is a bond that cannot be broken. It is unconditional. I'd do anything for my son. Ask any mum and she will tell you the same. Like I've said before I should have noticed the signs. I should have known something was wrong. Children don't become violent for no reason.

Due to the fact that Zack is mentally incapacitated, I have decided to wait until he is well enough to sign the papers before re-applying for a divorce. Not only does this mean that me and Ollie can stay in the house for as long as Zack remains in the psychiatric hospital, but if I wanted to, I could sell the house and move away as it is still in both of our names. I am also Zack's next of kin and so I have to agree to anything relating to his psychological or physical health. Legally, there is nothing that he can do about it, not since his mother has decided not to have any more to do with any of us.

I know who is to blame, of course. Sophie. His sister. It seems it wasn't only Zack playing mind games with his mother but Sophie too.

My mobile phone is blasting through the pocket of my jeans.

'Dad, is everything okay?'

'Me and your mum were wondering if you'd like some *me* time. We'd like to take Ollie up to the mall in

310

Cribbs Causeway to watch the Christmas lights being switched on,' he says.

'Sure.'

'You know we still feel awful for everything. Zack just seemed so convincing.'

'Don't dad. Just don't.'

He does this every time. He especially blames himself for not seeing it coming. For believing Zack's lies.

'We'll collect Ollie from school and drop him home later,' he says.

'Okay. I'll see you later. I love you.'

'Love you too,' he says. 'Goodbye.'

'Bye, dad.'

I slide the phone back inside my pocket and look up and down the street watching the people and the traffic rush by. Life doesn't seem so bad any more.

I return to work tomorrow, having managed to secure enough money from criminal injury compensation to buy a small white van with the company logo printed on both sides. I have big plans for my trading business now that things have settled.

When Ollie returns home that evening he is giggling and his speech is loud and excited. Just as it should be. The court case and the past twelve months don't seem to have affected him too much. Children are resilient.

It is only as I'm tucking him up in bed that night does he mention what happened that night, for the first time since the trial.

'Does anybody know what I did?' he says.

'No, Ollie. They never will. It is our little secret and we must not speak about it any more okay.'

'Okay, mummy,' he says.

I will do anything for my son. I would even lie for him. Just as Ewan said, nobody has any idea who really stabbed Zack. That is between me and Ollie.

AUTHORS NOTE

Baxter's theory of opposition is briefly mentioned on page forty-two, in relation to her studies based on dialectical approaches of the interplay between opposites. Opposition in this context is regarded as a positively unified experience between persons. The actual quote used is not cited from Baxter herself but has been fictionalised in order to simply define the meaning of 'opposites attract' within the sentence. The comment bears no similarity to anything Baxter herself has ever stated or written but is simply added in by the author in order to explain the phenomenon she wishes to convey.

Leslie Baxter's (1993) work is aimed at bringing together the commonalities that tension within relations can provide, and explaining such individual factors as combining to create a whole system of familial relationship.

Barbara Montgomery (1993) describes opposition theory as being able to describe three identifying oppositions. Namely: openness/non-openness; connection/autonomy; dominance/submissiveness.

The idea for adding such a theory into the text of this book was to highlight the commonly held belief that we work well together within partnerships, groups, and teams if we are standing alongside individuals with different personalities, traits, states, or of differing abilities to ourselves. Both desire and the common bond are what unites individuals within sexual relationships in particular.

For more information relating to Baxter's theory of opposition you may refer to this referenced link:

http://family.jrank.org/pages/390/Dialectical-Theory-Relating-Process-Contradiction.html

[accessed: 28th September 2015]

For my research on court procedure, legal terminology, sentencing for the charges mentioned in this book and coroner's reports relating to involuntary manslaughter I used the following website: www.cps.gov.uk.

ACKNOWLEDGEMENTS

Firstly I must thank my editor, Sue Mason who has done an incredible job in polishing this novel up from a rough diamond to a sparkling gemstone. Secondly, I must thank my beta readers for their invaluable comments whilst this novel was in the proofing stages. Especially: Lynn Mercer and Tracy Crouch whose feedback was invaluable. Thirdly I must thank my husband for putting up with my endless need to write, and for listening to me drone on about the characters who live inside my head. And finally, I offer a huge thank you to my readers on Goodreads, Amazon, and everywhere else. It is only because of you that I have made it this far.

ABOUT THE AUTHOR

Louise Mullins is the Amazon best selling author of *Scream Quietly, Damaged,* and *Why She Left. One Night Only* is her fifth psychological crime thriller.

Louise Mullins is a qualified Psychological Therapist and writer, currently training to become a Clinical Forensic Psychologist. She lives in Bristol with her husband and three children.

KEEP IN TOUCH

Website:
https://louisemullins2010.wix.com/author

Goodreads:
https://www.goodreads.com/LouiseMullinsAuthor

Facebook:
https://www.Facebook.com/LouiseMullinsAuthor

Twitter:
https://twitter.com/MullinsAuthor

LinkedIn:
https://uk.linkedin.com/in/louisemullinsauthor

Wordpress:
https://louisemullinsauthor.wordpress.com

16345935R00176

Printed in Great Britain
by Amazon